THE HOUSE ON THE POINT

THE HOUSE
ON
THE POINT

A TRIBUTE TO
Franklin W. Dixon
AND
The Hardy Boys

BENJAMIN HOFF

St. Martin's Minotaur ⚘ New York

The author wishes to thank Simon & Schuster Inc.—in particular Brenda Bowen, Vice President and Publisher of Children's Publishing, and Felice Javitz, Corporate Counsel— for generously granting him and St. Martin's Press permission to make use of the Hardy Boys characters, and for their understanding and support.

The Hardy Boys® and The Hardy Boys Mystery Stories® are registered trademarks of Simon & Schuster Inc.

Selections from the writings of Sir Arthur Conan Doyle are reprinted with the permission of the Sir Arthur Conan Doyle Literary Estate.

Selections from the writings of E. C. Bentley are reprinted with the permission of Curtis Brown Group Ltd., London on behalf of the estate of E. C. Bentley. Copyright E. C. Bentley.

"Abandoned Farmhouse" is from *Sure Signs: New and Selected Poems*, by Ted Kooser, © 1980. Used by permission of the University of Pittsburgh Press.

www.minotaurbooks.com

Jacket and frontispiece illustrations by Paul Bachem

ISBN 0-312-30108-1

First Edition: October 2002

10 9 8 7 6 5 4 3 2 1

For Frank, Joe, Chet, Biff, Tony, Callie, and Iola

CONTENTS

"The Child is father of the Man." So states a poem I read in grammar school. I didn't understand the statement at the time. But nothing could seem clearer to me now.

In childhood I contracted an illness that, because it was misdiagnosed and improperly treated, lingered for years. Turning itself on and off, it changed me at intervals from an outdoor child into an indoor child. Outdoors, my favorite activities were nature exploration, baseball, and wheel sports. Indoors, the illness encouraged me to pursue an occupation that otherwise would probably not have taken up much of my time.

Lying ill in bed, I would open a book and start reading. After a few pages, pain and fatigue would fade into the background as I journeyed to faraway places, became acquainted with fascinating people—many of whom had never existed in the physical world, but seemed as real as if they had—and traveled back and forth in time. Books became for me (to quote from another poem I encountered)"magic casements, opening on the foam / Of perilous seas, in faery lands forlorn."

If I had not learned to love reading, I would never have become a writer. And, in all probability, I would never have gotten acquainted with the Hardy Boys.

Three powerful motorcycles sped along the shore road that leads from the city of Bayport, skirting Barmet Bay, on the Atlantic coast.

It was a bright Saturday morning in June, and although the city sweltered in the heat, cool breezes blew in from the bay.

When I was ten, I read *The House on the Cliff,* the second in a series of mystery-and-adventure stories written for young adolescents by Franklin W. Dixon. The Hardy Boys Mystery Stories featured as heroes Frank and Joe Hardy, teenage sons of private investigator Fenton Hardy. The characters and plots were fictional. So, as I learned years later, was the author.

"Franklin W. Dixon" was one of many pseudonyms used by writers employed by literary empire builder Edward Stratemeyer, founder of the Stratemeyer Literary Syndicate and creator of the Rover Boys, Tom Swift, and other characters in 101 series of books. The first "Franklin W. Dixon" was Canadian writer Leslie McFarlane, who wrote Hardy Boys stories from 1927 to 1946. A later one of note was Edward Stratemeyer's daughter, Harriet Stratemeyer Adams, who conducted a condense-and-rewrite updating program from 1959 to 1973.

Edward Stratemeyer would give his writers the names and descriptions of characters for each series and outlines for the individual stories, and have them work out the page-by-page construction, action, and dialogue. He gave the claimed author of each series a pen name, which he copyrighted. He paid the actual author, who was sworn to secrecy, a small fee per manuscript—which, in the case of the original "Franklin W. Dixon," would be completed in three weeks. He kept all the rights. At the Stratemeyer Literary Syndicate, fairness to factory writers was nothing to be concerned about. Neither was literary quality. Edward Stratemeyer, like many other men of his era, was in business to build a rigidly controlled enterprise and amass a fortune as quickly as laws would allow.

Today most of the characters he originated are gone and forgotten. They did all they were intended to do—earn their creator an enormous amount of money—and then faded away. But like the other Stratemeyer-engendered sleuth, Nancy Drew, Frank and Joe Hardy didn't fade. Since their appearance in 1927, the perennially youthful American mystery solvers and adventurers have remained in the public consciousness, living on through the original tales, the revised editions, various television adaptations, and the stories that began in the 1980s when Simon & Schuster acquired the rights to the Stratemeyer Syndicate and started creating fresh adventures, giving the boys from Bayport a new life. During the seventy-five years of the series' existence, approximately 90 million Hardy Boys books have been sold.

Why do the Hardy Boys Mystery Stories continue to appeal to young readers? Several theories have been advanced over the years, all of which, I believe, have merit. But it seems to me that the primary reason for the popularity of the stories is that they address an ambition deep in the human psyche: the desire to solve the puzzles that life gives us.

Whatever one may choose to call it, that desire motivates the engineer, the archaeologist, the criminal investigator, the social reformer, the seeker of wisdom, and those of many other callings. Individuals learn, grow, and enrich their lives through finding solutions to internal and external mysteries. Civilizations advance in a similar manner. It could be said that without the investigating and solving of mysteries, personal and societal progress would be impossible.

As a boy, I didn't think much about that sort of thing; I just liked the Hardy Boys stories—despite what my parents, my teachers, and other adults had to say about their lack of literary merit. They provided relief from my illness and an escape from the drudgery of school. And they gave me inspiration. If Frank and Joe Hardy could solve mysteries, I reasoned, so could I. That inspiration has been with me ever since.

I read *The House on the Cliff* in the summer of 1957, while vacationing at the small Oregon coastal city of Cannon Beach, on the opposite side of the continent from the Hardy Boys' mythical city of Bayport (which, I imagined from its description, was located somewhere on the coast of Maine). Although the book's dust jacket had been updated, the story itself was as it had been published thirty years before, with late-1920s roadsters, motorcycles, and powerboats. It was the first book I read of the series, as well as my first encounter with what would eventually become my favorite category of literary entertainment, Vintage Mystery. It told about strange events centering on a derelict stone house overlooking the waters of fictional Barmet Bay.

Walking the sand at the far end of North Beach at night, I would look up at the long, dark shape of rocky Chapman Point, which stretched from a forested hillside out into the sea. Light would be shining down through the trees from a hidden, mysterious house far back on the crest of the point—a house, I imagined, like the one I was reading about. Someday, I thought, I would find out what I could about that house. Maybe there would be a mystery associated with it.

Fourteen years later, as a young investigative reporter, I followed a winding driveway through a thick stand of evergreens to the house on Chapman Point—a historic residence that, though built of wood and in excellent condition, was indeed very much like the one on the cover of the book—to interview its owner about some suspicious bulldozing she'd reported seeing in the forest across the adjacent road. Over the ever-present whisper of waves breaking on the rocks below, we exchanged information we'd obtained separately about the development company that owned the land in question—a company headed, so I'd already determined, by a man with two names, two signature styles, two questionable corporations, and a tendency to make claims that couldn't be substantiated.

A few weeks later, thanks to the dedicated work of my informant and a friend of hers and to the publicity generated by a series of newspaper articles I wrote that incorporated all our findings, a fraudulent land developer was out of business, a number of people were spared the loss of their money, and a beautiful natural area was saved from obliteration.

After a year of investigative work for two newspapers, I returned to college and—I thought—left the solving of mysteries behind. But habits established in childhood run deep.

A few years after graduation, making use of my Eastern art–and–philosophy upbringing, Asian studies education, Taoist training, and puzzle-solving inclinations, I wrote a book intended to demystify the often garbled and misunderstood Chinese philosophy of Taoism.

It was followed, after three years of investigations in America and England, by a book that cleared up long-standing mysteries concerning a 1920s naturalist and best-selling author whose life and reputation had been ruined by a series of what I found to be false accusations.

A few years later, wanting to say more about Taoism, I wrote a second demystifying book on the subject.

Shortly after its release, I was signing copies in a bookstore when I noticed a recently published reprint of the original edition of *The House on the Cliff.* For a few moments as I thumbed through it, I was ten years old. I seemed to hear the surf breaking on the rocks off Chapman Point.

Thinking that the book would be a good present for my fiancée's son (not admitting to myself that I'd like to read it, too), I bought it and took it home. And read it. Which didn't take long.

Disappointed by the factory-book writing, I bought the 1959 revised edition, which I'd never encountered, hoping to see some substantial improvements. I didn't get very far in reading it. The first two or three chapters, which I'd remembered from childhood as being the best part of the book, had been altered beyond recognition.

Someone ought to rewrite the story, I thought, by thoroughly reworking the original—but without abandoning the beginning. Someone with feeling for it. Someone who can craft a plot and put life into it. Someone, preferably, with crime-solving experience. Someone—but I didn't know who. I gave the books to my stepson-to-be and soon forgot about them.

Coming across the two editions on a family library shelf recently, I paused and reflected on how indebted I was to Franklin W. Dixon. I asked myself how I could repay that debt. Maybe, I thought with a laugh, I could attempt to repay it by rewriting his story.

Suddenly the idea didn't seem funny. Maybe I *could* rewrite it. But if I were to do so, I told myself, I would need to cut almost everything in it down to my estimate of what Edward Stratemeyer's outline might have been and build from that. No, I decided—remembering the plot that came unraveled as it went along—I would need to change most of the outline, too. I might, I considered, want to change an occasional name or character, as well.

What, I wondered, could such a book be titled? If I were granted permission to write a new version of the story, it couldn't be released as *The House on the Cliff*. Besides, I thought, I wouldn't put the house on a cliff; I'd put it on a point of land. Yes, I mused—*The House on the Point*.

How would it start? I could base the beginning, perhaps, on that of the original story, in which Frank and Joe Hardy and friends appear on motorcycles, trying to escape the heat of a summer day in Bayport . . .

> *The two remaining motorcycles came to a stop and the drivers mopped their brows while the two other boys dismounted, glad of the chance to stretch their legs. One of the cyclists, a boy . . . with light, curly hair, was Joe Hardy, a brother of Frank's, and the other lad was Chet Morton, a chum of the Hardy boys. The other youths were Jerry Gilroy and "Biff" Hooper, typical, healthy American lads of high school age.*

I hoped that any character descriptions I might give would communicate more about appearance, if not personality. But, I considered, I wouldn't want to intrude any more than necessary with a narrator's descriptions of the Hardys and their companions. As much as possible, I thought, I'd like to have them describe each other and themselves through their conversations and actions. I would want *them* to tell the story—the participants themselves, my old friends. I would watch and listen to them in my mind and then write down what they did and said. As much as possible, it would need to be *their* story—not mine or anyone else's.

Suddenly images and dialogue started coming to me, as if someone were running parts of a movie in my mind—one that seemed to bear no resemblance to anything I'd remembered reading in *The House on the Cliff*. I saw and heard Chet Morton running to his car, the police chief talking to Frank and Joe, Callie Shaw and Iola Morton sitting in a soda fountain booth, telling the brothers their plan was too dangerous, unless *they* were there to . . . When, I wondered, were these events supposed to be taking place? The clothing, hair styles, and furniture looked like those of the 1950s. No, earlier than that—the 1940s, maybe.

I closed the book and put it back on the shelf. It was a pleasant dream, I thought, but I needed to return to reality. I had a writing project to complete. I imagined someone saying "You're writing *what*—a Hardy Boys story? What's the matter—don't you want to grow up?"

I knew that if I were to write a book such as I was imagining, I would encounter such a response. I'd been through that sort of thing with a couple of previous books. Well, I decided, I wasn't going to go through it again. And I went back to what I'd been working on.

But Frank and Joe Hardy and their friends kept coming into my mind, day and night—doing, questioning, discovering . . . I was haunted by scene after scene of a story that, whatever I tried to do, wouldn't leave me alone.

Finally I became aware of what the Hardy Boys movie-in-my-mind was trying to communicate to me: The characters I had been familiar with in childhood had a story to tell, and I needed to let them tell it. At the very least, I thought, the story could be entertaining—and perhaps not only to myself. After all, millions of people had read Hardy Boys books in childhood. Maybe some of them, in adulthood, could benefit from being reminded of what I was being reminded of—that what we are today is due, to one degree or another, to the influences of our early years. And maybe young readers could benefit from the life lessons that Frank and Joe and crew have always been willing and able to teach.

Besides, I reflected: For better or for worse, we human beings shape the world around us—driven to do so, it would seem, by what is within us. If we have a less-than-healthy amount of childlike happiness and fun in our lives, what sort of world are we going to make?

And so I set out for Bayport, to visit—and learn from—some old friends of mine. I knew I'd be welcome.

Books can have magical power. They can create, or cause to be created, what did not exist before. The influence of *The House on the Cliff* on my mind long ago—the life-shaping inspiration of a story read in childhood—is important, I suppose, only to me. But it's had an effect on this world, just the same. Now the cycle is complete—years ago, the story shaped me; now I'm shaping it.

Thanks, Mr. Dixon, for everything you've done for me. I hope you'll like the book.

NOTE

In the 1930s and 1940s, big-band music was America's major source of entertainment and recreation. Young Americans went to ballrooms and clubs to dance or listen to the bands, got together at soda fountains and ice cream parlors to hear their songs on the jukebox, played their records at home on the phonograph, or tuned in to their live broadcasts and recorded music on the radio. The big-band culture generated most of the nation's slang, including the terms used in the following story, such as: clock puncher (musician playing for money, not enjoyment); kick out (improvise a hot solo, "swing," "jump"); long underwear gang (dull band); ride man (solo artist who kicks out); solid sender (hot musician); and zeal girl (female hot music—and musicians—enthusiast).

THE HOUSE ON THE POINT

North Shore Excursion

It was Sunday, the twenty-ninth of June 1947. Ordinarily, summer would come late to the small northeastern coastal city of Bayport. And even on the hottest days, breezes from Barmet Bay and the Atlantic Ocean would cool the streets and houses. But there was no breeze in the city today to lessen the severity of the record-breaking heat. And by the early afternoon, the humidity was stifling.

It was cooler, however, on North Shore Road, which skirted the bay.

North Shore Road, originally part of Highway 1, had been forsaken by the regular coastal traffic years ago, when the highway was widened and rerouted inland to provide more direct access to Bayport and beyond. The old, narrow road left the highway several miles north of the city, meandered down along the rugged coastline, then followed the graceful curve of Barmet Bay into Bayport, where, at the outskirts of town, it became Main Street.

This afternoon, the usual quiet of North Shore Road was disturbed by the noise of three motorcycles speeding away from the city, each carrying two teenage boys.

On wooded Whittier Head, where the road curved north away from the mouth of the bay to overlook the ocean, the lead motorcyclist—a handsome, serious-looking young man with wavy brown hair—pulled off at the viewpoint turnout and stopped. The second motorcycle, and then the third, came up alongside him.

The second driver, a tall, athletic-looking youth with short-cropped brown hair, frowned and pointed back to the road.

"Let's make mileage!" he shouted over the noise of the engines. "We can look at the view some other time!"

"Yeah!" agreed his stocky, strawberry-blond passenger. "We've got a good breeze, as long as we keep moving!"

The lead motorcyclist switched off his engine.

After some hesitation, the others did the same.

"Why stop now, Frank?" asked the driver of the third motorcycle, a teenager with straight, razor-cut blond hair and features resembling those of his slightly older-looking leader.

"I've been thinking it might be nice to go someplace in particular."

"Why?" asked the blond. "What's wrong with just riding?"

His chubby, red-haired passenger laughed. "Frank Hardy always has to have a plan," he observed. "Joe Hardy never thinks he needs one." He paused, then added: "But then, he's a junior."

Joe smiled and looked back at the redhead. "I sure don't need any *Chet Morton* plans," he retorted. "Every one you've made has landed someone in trouble!"

"We *have* a plan," said Frank's tall, swarthy passenger. He stood, swung a long leg back, free of the seat, and stepped away from the motorcycle.

"We wanted to get out of town. And that's what we're doing, in case everyone's forgotten."

"What an astounding memory!" Chet exclaimed.

Frank smiled at him. "As Mr. Weldon told the entire chemistry class—"

" '*Phil Cohen concentrates on reaching his goal.*' "

Joe nodded. "That's why he was a leader in the Boy Scouts."

"Speaking of Boy Scouts," said Phil, stretching, "where do *you* recommend we go, Jerry?"

"I'm the last one to ask," replied the strawberry blond. "Considering that we only moved to Bayport a few weeks ago."

"Long enough for an old Scout like you to get his bearings. So what's your vote?"

Jerry pointed dramatically up the coast. "Old Scout say just

2

keep go north," he growled. "By side of big sea water. Old Scout say that plenty good." He grunted. "End of trail no matter."

He poked his chauffeur in the ribs. "What say Biff Hooper?"

The latter turned in his seat. "Biff Hooper say if Jerry Gilroy do that one more time, Jerry Gilroy find out why Biff Hooper state high school boxing champ."

"Boys, boys," Chet said cheerfully. "There's no need for violence. We need to get away from the heat, not add to it."

"The heat's not all we'll need to get away from," said Phil, looking out to sea. The others followed his gaze.

On the horizon huge, dark, anvil-shaped clouds were gathering. *"Cumulonimbus capillatus,"* Phil recited.

"Never a dull moment," Chet remarked with amusement. "First heat, then rain."

"*Lots* of rain," muttered Phil, his eyes on the horizon.

"No jackets," said Joe, looking around for shelter. "No hats . . ." He turned to his companions. "So what do we do now—go back?"

"Not me!"

"Never!"

"Gloom peddler!"

"*I* know," said Chet. "Let's go hide out in old man Polucca's house!" He glanced from one uncertain face to another. "*That'll* keep us dry." He laughed. "Paralyzed by fear, maybe, but dry."

"What do you mean, *paralyzed by fear?*" Jerry asked. "And who's old man Polucca?"

"Who *was* old man Polucca," corrected Frank. "He's dead."

"His house isn't, though," Biff added. "Unfortunately."

"What's all this about?" asked Jerry.

"Come over here, son," said Chet, climbing off the motorcycle.

He led Jerry far out on the viewpoint, then stopped and pointed up the coast. "See that long hunk of rock sticking out into the ocean? That's—"

"Walton Point."

"Very good. Now look landward along the top of it, to where the tall trees begin. The Polucca house is just back from there. It's the only house on the ocean side of the road for a long ways."

"How can you see anything in those trees, at this distance?"

"Here," said Frank, walking over to them. "Take a look through these." He handed Jerry a pair of binoculars he'd taken from his saddlebag.

As Jerry turned the focusing knob, the rocky promontory came into closer view.

Massive Walton Point rose high above the ocean, its blunt tip obscured by a huge rock, the beginning of a jumbled cluster that reached far out into the water. At the crest of the point, almost hidden by tall, windswept evergreens, part of the roof and upper story of a large stone house could be seen.

Crouching among the trees—so it seemed to Jerry—the house looked sinister, threatening, predatory. Its one visible window, like a watching eye, heightened its look of lurking malevolence—an appearance intensified by the ominous light in the sky and the dark, gathering clouds moving in from the sea.

"What a spooky place!" exclaimed Jerry, lowering the binoculars. The others had joined him. "No wonder Biff said the house is alive!"

"That's not the only reason," Phil assured him.

"Some people have seen lights there, late at night," said Biff. "And heard strange noises."

"One stormy afternoon not long after Polucca died," said Frank, "a passing car broke down near the driveway. The driver walked to the house, looking for help. He got a big scare, instead."

"What happened?"

"He saw someone at an upstairs window, looking down at him as he approached. So he pushed the front doorbell button, hoping for some assistance. He waited a while, but no one came to the door. Thinking the bell wasn't working, he knocked and called out. But no one responded. So he looked in a couple of windows and saw that the house was empty—no furniture, nothing. He didn't waste any time getting out of there."

Jerry shuddered. "And who was Polucca?"

"Leo Polucca," replied Frank, "was a strange old man with a lot of money. Nobody seemed to know how he got so much of it. He kept to himself—he didn't have any friends. Not in Bayport, anyway. He died a little over a year ago."

"In the house," Joe contributed.

Phil groaned. *"Oy vey.* I didn't know about that."

"Everybody avoids the place," said Frank. "And I mean *everybody.* Whoever goes near gets scared away."

"Well?" Chet rubbed his hands together. "How about it?"

A Chance of a Ghost

Approaching thunder rumbled in the rapidly darkening sky as the motorcyclists turned right from North Shore Road onto an unpaved driveway leading into a dense, largely evergreen forest.

They proceeded slowly and cautiously along the winding drive, turning out occasionally to avoid clumps of vegetation.

As they advanced, the forest closed in behind them. The rustling of the rising wind in the treetops and the whispering of the nearby waves accentuated the loneliness of the place.

The driveway made a final bend to the left, then widened gradually into a turnaround.

As the trees pulled back, a large gray stone house with worn gray trim came into view on the right.

The motorcyclists drew alongside each other and switched off their engines. Subdued by the gloomy surroundings, the six adventurers looked in silence at the scene before them.

Much of the turnaround had been invaded by grass and weeds. On the ocean side of it, the dark house lay as if waiting for someone, its empty windows staring across the open space before it to the trees beyond. A loose upstairs shutter banged in the wind.

"Creepy old place," said Phil at last.

"It doesn't look any friendlier than it did through the glasses," said Jerry, scanning the forbidding structure. "But it's in pretty good shape for an abandoned house. The only damage I can see is a little break in one of those double-hung windows on the second floor."

"Remember what I said," Frank reminded him. "Everybody's scared of this place."

"It'll take more than a ghost to scare a Morton away," Chet asserted.

Frank and Joe glanced at each other and smiled.

"You're pretty brave, Chet," said Phil, in feigned admiration.

"It runs in my family," Chet assured him. "Did I ever tell you about my ancestor Thaddeus Morton?"

"The horse thief?"

The others snickered.

"No, buffoon—the Revolutionary War hero."

"Oh, yeah—the one who changed sides when he saw the red-coats coming."

The others laughed.

Chet shook his head. "I can see I'm just wasting my time talking to you skeptics."

He tapped Joe on the shoulder. "Drive on, my man."

"I think we'd better," said Joe, looking up at the raindrops that had begun to fall.

He started his engine, and Frank and Biff started theirs.

Frank pointed ahead. "We can put the bikes in there."

At the far end of the turnaround, quite a distance from the house, stood a garage with double sliding doors, the right one of which was open.

"Just in time!" yelled Frank, as they sped toward the garage through the rapidly increasing rain.

There was a flash of lightning, then another.

As the motorcycles pulled inside, a tremendous clap of thunder broke overhead and the shower suddenly became a downpour.

The hammering of the deluge on the old roof was almost deafening as the drivers turned off their machines and leaned them on their kickstands. Everyone quickly dismounted.

"Let's get out of here before we lose our hearing!" Frank shouted.

Joe pulled a flashlight from his saddlebag and turned to the others.

"Ready to roll!" he yelled.

Biff stepped to the door and raised his arm to lead the charge. *"To the house!"*

With Biff in the lead, the explorers sprinted to the door of a lattice-enclosed service porch at the left front corner of the house.

Biff ran up onto the stone stoop and rattled the old porcelain doorknob. "It's locked!" he cried.

"Let's try the front door!" yelled Jerry. He started running.

"You didn't seem so eager to get inside before, Old Scout!" Phil called to him from behind. "Did something change your mind?"

"You bet!" the new leader shouted back, rain streaming down his face. "The old fortress doesn't look so bad, after all!" He jumped up onto the stoop, pushed open the unlocked door, and stumbled inside. "Or does it?" he added, as the others came up behind him.

In the large entrance hall, long spider webs hung down like ghostly banners, illuminated by flashes of lightning from the windows beyond. Undisturbed dust lay thick upon the floor. High above, a dust- and cobweb-covered crystal chandelier sparkled faintly in the beam of Joe's flashlight.

"Well, go on," said Chet, from the rear of the group. "*Ghosts* can't hurt you!"

"That's easy to say from where *you* are," Jerry replied.

With Biff and Frank leading the way, the dripping, silent company advanced through the hall and past a stairway on either side into a spacious, empty living room dimly lit by the tree-filtered, stormy light coming in through its windows.

"That's odd," Frank remarked, looking down at the wooden floor.

Long streaks, such as would be made by a pushbroom, were visible in the dust.

"Someone's swept the floor!" Joe exclaimed, coming up beside his brother and shining his light on the boards.

He turned and pointed with the flashlight beam. "From below the stairs—"

The shaft of light swung back and zigzagged across the floor.

"—all the way over, from wall to wall!"

"He didn't sweep it very *well*," Phil observed sarcastically. "It looks like a plowed field!"

Biff chuckled. "Someone just pushed the dust around."

"Why," asked Frank, "would anybody sweep the floor of an abandoned house?"

"*Part* of the floor," said Joe with a grin. "He missed the front hall."

Frank took the flashlight, went to the foot of the south stairway, and ran the light along the steps.

It showed a thick layer of undisturbed dust.

He moved to the north stairway.

There the light revealed the marks of a very uneven broom.

"Someone swept here, too," Frank said thoughtfully, as the others came up to him. "I wonder why."

He knelt and, tilting his head sideways, put his face close to the first step. Holding the flashlight almost horizontally, he moved the light and his attention along the board.

"Footprints," he announced. "Made by more than one kind of shoe."

He started up the stairs on his knees, examining each step in the same manner.

"Why look at them sideways?" asked Chet, after a while.

"That's a trick Dad taught us," Joe answered. "If you're tracking someone over difficult terrain, it helps to look at the ground sideways. Little differences are more noticeable that way."

He laughed. "It's also useful when you're trying to find something small you dropped on a carpet."

Jerry looked at Phil. "We could apply that in the Scouts."

He looked at the stairs. "It must be great to have a father who's a private investigator."

"It is," Joe replied. "When he's around."

"Why are you so interested in some *footprints*?" Phil asked Frank impatiently.

"Because," Frank answered, looking at the floorboards of the landing halfway up, "someone tried to hide them."

"Maybe he was just doing a quick cleanup. Or what he *thought* was a cleanup."

"Then why didn't he sweep the other stairway?"

"You got me there, kiddo."

Frank stood up, went to the left handrail, and shone the light on it. Studying its dusty surface, he walked to the top of the stairs, crossed to the right handrail, and examined it on his way down. On the bottom step, he returned to the left handrail and, studying it, walked up to the landing. Then he turned away and walked down.

"The stairs have been swept more than once," he told the others as he descended. "There're some traces of footprints I can't make out. But the last set's still readable, thanks to all the dust that was left and the sloppy sweeping."

At the foot of the stairs, he turned and shone the light up the steps.

"There were three men here last. One, with large, smooth-soled shoes, kept to the center as he walked up, then backed down. So he must've been the one who did the sweeping. He swept each step with two passes—a long one to the left and a shorter one to the right."

"Which means," said Joe, "that he had long arms. And he was probably left-handed."

"And lazy," added Frank. "Or in a hurry. He missed the center of the steps half the time, and he didn't put enough pressure on the broom."

"You sound like Aunt Gertrude," said Joe teasingly.

Frank turned his head and smiled. Then he looked back at the stairs and continued:

"The other prints were made by two pairs of shoes. Each went up once and came down once. One pair had large soles with lines across them. The other had smaller soles with a crinkled pattern."

He pointed the flashlight beam far to the left of the center of the bottom step, then moved it up the stairs.

"Going up, Lines was on the left."

The beam moved far to the right and returned. "Coming down, he was on the other side—his left, the same as going up."

Frank turned off the light.

"Since Lines and Crinkle Soles went up and came down on the

sides of the steps, I figure they were here at the same time, walking alongside each other. Otherwise, they'd have walked in the middle. One of them left handprints on the railing—kind of small ones—with his right hand going up and his right hand coming down."

"Crinkle Soles," said Joe.

"He grabbed hold at nearly every step. The railings haven't been brushed off, so I could see three or four handprints at practically every place he grabbed. Each man was well over to the side, but Lines didn't put his hand on a railing once, as far as I could tell. Which probably means—"

"They were carrying something between them," Joe suggested, "so they had to walk far apart. And Lines was strong enough that he didn't need to hold onto a railing for support."

"Or," countered Frank, turning, "they were *each* carrying something—Lines using both hands and Crinkle Soles using just one."

He switched on the flashlight. "I want to see what's up there. Anyone want to come along?"

"You bet," Joe replied.

"Let's all go," said Biff.

"I'll stay here," volunteered Chet, "and guard the door."

"Nervous?" Joe asked, grinning.

"Nervous?" Chet drew himself up to his full height. "Why, when danger appears, Chet Morton laughs. When evildoers threaten, Chet Morton laughs. When—"

"When the homework assignments are written on the board," Phil interjected, "Chet Morton laughs."

"Strictly," agreed Biff. "And when the teacher says, 'Chet, you're staying after class,' Chet Morton laughs."

"And when his mother says, *'Chet, I wish you wouldn't eat so much,'* Chet Morton laughs."

"Chet Morton laughs," Biff concluded. "That's all he ever does."

"Fellas . . ."

"Remember, Chet," said Biff, "*ghosts* can't hurt you."

"It's not the ghosts that worry me," Chet admitted. "It's the footprints."

Joe glanced around. "There must be plenty of them down here."

11

"And keep in mind," said Phil, "that although the footprints go up . . ." He raised his hand in increments. "They come *down* again." He lowered it the same way.

Chet shrugged. "Okay—lead on."

Frank climbed the stairs, with the others close behind him.

On one of the top steps, he crouched down and studied the floor ahead in the beam of the flashlight.

"It's been swept, too," he announced. "Once over lightly with a pushbroom."

He crawled along the floor for a few feet, examining the dust-streaked boards. Then he looked up at an open doorway across from the head of the stairs. "Crinkle Soles and Lines went over there."

He stood up and followed the footprints into a spacious, empty, east-facing room with two widely spaced windows.

The others waited at the doorway.

"They stopped here," Frank told them, kneeling by the window on the right. "Okay—you can come in now."

Joe, the first one in, walked over and knelt beside his brother.

"Look at these," said Frank, shining the light on the floor beneath the window.

Close to the wall were four clusters of round, three-quarter-inch marks in the lightly swept dust. One in each group was more distinct than the rest.

Frank pointed with the flashlight to each of the four clearest marks in turn.

The two nearest the wall were about a foot and a half apart. The two farther back were the same distance from each other and about a foot from the first two. All together, they formed a rectangle.

"Probably made," said Frank, "by the rubber feet on a box of some kind."

He moved the flashlight beam back and forth in the same area.

Here and there at irregular intervals in the dust were larger round marks, some more distinct than others, each about an inch and a half in diameter. All together, they formed a large, rough circle.

Frank stared at the floor.

"Those look as if they were made by a cane," he said, perplexed. "But that doesn't make sense."

Joe reached down and drew lines connecting the three clear-est marks.

The lines, each over four feet long, formed an equilateral tri-angle.

"A tripod," Joe suggested.

"Maybe they were photographing from the window," offered Chet. "With a big camera."

Joe got to his feet and looked out. "Nice view of Walton Point. And a whole lot of ocean."

He went to the other window. "Nice view of a tree."

"My guess," said Jerry, "is that this is the only window with a clear view of the ocean. And maybe the only one with a view of anything that anybody'd want to photograph."

"There's one way to find out," declared Biff, walking to the doorway.

The investigators went from one upstairs room to another, looked through the windows, and called to each other:

"Nothing here but branches!"

"More branches!"

"There's the coast, looking north through the trees!"

"Over here's the turnaround!"

"Yeah—and the trees beyond it!"

"I'm not so sure about the photography theory," said Phil, when everyone had returned to the room with the marks and footprints. "If *I* were photographing the ocean from this house—and I don't know why I would, since there are lots of better places to photo-graph it from—I'd choose the view up the coast from that north-east bedroom window."

"There's not much to choose from," Chet remarked. "Consid-ering that only two windows up here have an ocean view."

"The other view's more photogenic. *This* one has all that rock smack in the middle of it."

"What it amounts to," said Frank, "is that we don't know what those men were doing."

"What else *could* they have been doing?" Joe asked querulously. "They were hauling up and using a big camera—a view camera, probably—and a bag of photo equipment."

13

Frank stepped to the right window and looked out through the rain-blurred glass.

"Why do all that sweeping," he asked, "just to hide signs of *photographing*?"

"Telescopes mount on tripods, too," Phil remarked thoughtfully. "Maybe they were looking for something."

"Looking for what?" Frank mused aloud, peering out at the storm.

Beyond the tops of the trees just below the window and the ends of the branches of the taller trees encroaching on the left and right was the long, broad spine of Walton Point. Like the foredeck of a ship, it appeared to be cleaving its way through the choppy, storm-tossed waves rolling in from the horizon, under a sky darkened by thunder clouds and rain, lit here and there by jagged streaks of lightning.

Frank turned to the others. "We've found *one* end of the trail. Maybe we ought to take a look at the *other* end."

"Yeah," agreed Joe, "and see where those two *came* from. They sure didn't come through the front door!"

"And you can bet," added Biff, "that they didn't come from the *spirit* regions."

He and Phil turned and headed for the doorway.

"Watch out, house haunters!" Chet announced loudly, as he followed them from the room. *"The ghost trackers are on their way!"*

The group of investigators, eager for further discoveries, noisily descended the stairs.

As the leaders reached the landing, Frank called to them: "Don't walk around down there until—"

His words were cut short by a scream of maniacal laughter from somewhere above their heads.

A Disturbing Presence

For an instant, the boys stood as though frozen in place, as the insane laughter echoed through the empty house. Then, simultaneously, they turned to look up at the head of the stairs—all except Chet, who stood without moving, wide-eyed and stiff-shouldered. With a mighty *"Lemme outa here!"* he started down the remaining steps on the run.

The others, seeing a dim, moving shadow on the wall above them, started after him.

At the foot of the stairs, Chet slipped on the dusty floor and fell, as another shriek of laughter rang out, sounding louder and closer than the first.

"It's coming after us!" Jerry shouted.

Now thoroughly panicked, all rushed through the entrance hall.

In the stampede, Joe was thrown against the wall by the front door. Attempting to recover his balance, he pushed against a double switch plate.

One of the pushbuttons clicked, and the walls were suddenly bathed in brightness.

Joe looked up in amazement. The light bulbs of the dust-covered chandelier were glowing.

"The light!" he shouted. "The *light*'s on!"

"Well, turn it off!" exclaimed Biff, returning to retrieve the straggler.

He pushed the two protruding buttons and yanked the mesmerized boy's arm, pulling him out into the rain.

"Frank!" Joe called, as he and Biff ran from the house. *"Frank!"*

His brother, almost at the garage, stopped and turned.

"The *electricity*'s on!" Joe shouted, as he came up to him.

Biff didn't stop to discuss the matter.

Frank stared at the now-illuminated lamp hanging from the underside of the small roof over the front door. Then he called to the others, who by then were inside the garage: "Hold on! I'm going back in there! I want to find out what this is all about!"

"Sorry—wrong number!"

"Gotta go!"

"Let's give this place the Fuller!"

"Come on!" yelled Frank. "Someone's just trying to scare us off!"

"He's doing a pretty fair job of it!" Biff shouted, climbing onto his already turned-around motorcycle.

An upper-story window flew up, raised by unseen hands. From the opening came torrents of psychotic laughter.

As each outburst ended, an echo, like an answering voice, reverberated faintly out through the open front doorway.

"Let's ride," urged Joe. "We can come back later."

"I'm going to," Frank replied, glaring at the open window. "No one's going to run me off again with a lot of crazy laughter!"

He and Joe turned and walked quickly to the garage. As they stepped inside, Frank stopped and stared to the left.

"My bike!" he exclaimed.

"What's the matter?"

"I didn't put it over there—it was here!" he declared, pointing to the middle of the right half of the floor. "Somebody moved it!"

"Don't look at us!" said Jerry, climbing onto the back of Biff's motorcycle. "It was there when we ran in!"

"Let's move 'em all!" shouted Biff, starting his engine. "Ten miles down North Shore!"

Although the rain had diminished, it was still falling steadily as the motorcyclists neared Bayport.

About a mile from town, Frank's engine began to sputter. Then it stalled.

"Uh-oh!" exclaimed Phil from the rear seat. "As my grandmother would say, a good time for walking this isn't!"

Frank coasted the motorcycle to the side of the road as the other two drivers, having gone past, circled back.

"Out of gas?" Phil asked.

"No, I think the fuel line's blocked. It got crimped yesterday, and I straightened it out in a hurry and forgot about it. It probably needs replacing."

They dismounted, pushed their vehicle under shelter of a roadside tree, and leaned it on its kickstand.

The other motorcyclists pulled alongside, switched off their engines, and dismounted.

"Gas line again?" Joe asked.

"It sounds like it. But the tools're in the bag. This won't take long."

Frank reached into his saddlebag and pulled out a jacket. "Boy, I'd forgotten this was here. I sure could have used it!"

Suddenly he stiffened.

The pockets had been pulled inside out.

Frank pushed them back in, then turned the jacket over, examining it.

"Somebody's gone through my jacket!" he exclaimed in disbelief.

He put it down on the seat absentmindedly. "And moved my bike."

"Why would anybody do that?" asked Biff.

Frank stared at the jacket without answering.

Joe bent over Frank's motorcycle.

"Take a look at these. On the handlebar, here. And the gas tank."

On the silver metal, repelling the rain that dripped on them, were what appeared to be grease marks.

Frank looked closely at a translucent oval spot on the left handlebar. A smile crept over his face.

"A *thumbprint*," he announced.

"What do you know!" remarked Jerry. "A ghost with greasy fingers!"

A Well-Organized Crime

Dessert was almost over at the Hardy residence, a white, two-story Victorian house on South Bayview Street, on a hill overlooking Barmet Bay.

Gertrude Hardy—a thin, nervous, middle-aged woman with graying brown hair—stirred a spoonful of sugar into her tea.

"If they catch a severe cold," she remarked, with a stern look at her nephew across the dining table, "they *might* learn *not* to go on long motorcycle rides in the rain."

Joe looked cheerily back at her. "You're the English teacher, Auntie . . . Don't you mean severe *colds*? One cold each?"

"Hmmph."

"We didn't plan to ride in the rain," Frank pointed out.

"It came up when we weren't looking," Joe added. "Just the way it left—once it finally decided to."

He took a final bite of pie, chewed it fast, and glanced through the window at the clear, still-light sky. "To look out there now, you wouldn't think it'd been pouring down for hours. Except that it's cooled down quite a bit."

"Where did you boys go?" asked Evelyn Hardy, an attractive blonde with alert, inquisitive eyes.

Joe leaned back in his chair. "We went out—"

On the other side of the table, Frank, chewing a last mouthful, made a slight side-to-side motion with his head.

18

"We went out quite a ways on North Shore, Mother," Joe began again, "to get away from the heat. Frank's engine conked out, and it took a while to fix it."

"All the more reason to worry," insisted Aunt Gertrude, glad of the opportunity to voice her concern. "Those motorcycles—"

"Speaking of motorcycles," interrupted Joe, eager to change the subject, "what's this case you're working on, Dad?"

He turned toward his father—a handsome, athletic-looking man with gray-streaked brown hair.

Fenton Hardy laughed. "Well, speaking of motorcycles, Joe, I can tell you that I've been retained by a major New York pharmaceuticals house—"

"I'll wager you boys don't even know how to *spell* 'pharmaceuticals,'" remarked Aunt Gertrude.

Frank smiled. "*Pharmaceuticals*—p-h-a-r-m-a-c-e-u-t-i-c-a-l-s."

"Also spelled d-r-u-g-s," said Joe.

"This firm has hired me," Mr. Hardy continued, with an amused smile at his older sister, "to investigate the disappearance of boxes of drugs from their New Jersey warehouse, from distributors' warehouses, and possibly in transit—something that's apparently been going on for quite some time."

"Isn't their insurance company investigating the losses?" asked Frank.

"They're at work, all right. But the head of the pharmaceuticals house wanted an independent-minded operator involved, as well—considering the lack of progress being made along the regular channels—and it seems that I was the most independent-minded one the directors could come up with.

"This isn't a matter of a few missing boxes—it's known by now that the operation is not only interstate but international. So the FBI and U.S. Customs have been brought in, too."

"Big time!" said Frank, impressed.

"Strictly!" Joe exclaimed.

"Decidedly big time," their father replied. "Some of the stolen drugs have shown up in port cities on the other side of the ocean. Therefore, one can deduce that—" He took a bite of pie and looked expectantly at his sons.

"They're being smuggled out of the country by ship," responded Frank.

"The FBI and Customs," contributed Evelyn Hardy, "are watching the large ports up and down the coast. They believe the drugs are being hidden among the heavy shipments that go through those areas."

"That sounds reasonable," said Frank.

"It *is* reasonable," Fenton Hardy agreed. He smiled. "That's what started to bother me after a while. I began to wonder if the smugglers weren't counting on us to look in the reasonable places and overlook the *un*reasonable ones."

"You're working with the FBI?" asked Joe.

"We're sharing information. Beyond that, I'm on my own. I have my approach—"

"Which, as you two ought to know by now," Gertrude Hardy interjected, pushing aside her empty dessert plate, "is to do pretty much the opposite of what everyone else is doing—"

"And that's why I've come back to home territory for a while—to do a little backyard investigating, so to speak."

"Do you mean," asked Frank, "that there might be smugglers in *Bayport?*"

"Possibly. Or in some other small town on the coast."

"But wouldn't they be *noticed* around here?"

The detective exchanged glances with his wife. "That's what most people—your mother included—would think: Big criminals avoid small towns. But that's not what *I* think—in this case, at least. These people are slipping through the net. They wouldn't need a very big hole to do that."

"But why a place like Bayport?"

"According to my theory, the smugglers *could* be using small boats to deliver the goods to passing freighters. If that's how they're operating, they would have an easier time away from the major ports and shipping lanes—but not too far from either for collaborating ships to rendezvous with them, once their legitimate cargoes are on board. Doesn't that sound like Bayport?"

"I still think they'd be noticed here."

"Wherever they are, they haven't been noticed yet. Oh—there's one other thing I might mention. I've just received a tip that a smuggler named Oscar Volchek may be in the area. *May* be. I don't know yet."

"Would you recognize him if you saw him?" Joe asked.

"I certainly would. And before long, so will merchants up and down the coast." Mr. Hardy took another bite of pie.

"Fenton is going to be circulating his photograph," Evelyn Hardy added in explanation. She pushed her empty plate aside. "And information from his record."

"So," Frank said to his father, "if somebody around here tells you he's seen this Volchek—"

"I'll be fairly certain there's funny business afoot."

"Where are the drugs going?" asked Joe.

"To countries devastated by the war."

"But that would *help* people."

"For a price. An exorbitant price—far higher than anything the legitimate outlets would charge. With no controls of any kind. On the black market, anything goes." Mr. Hardy finished the last of his pie, put his fork on his plate, and pushed it aside.

"The smugglers are victimizing the victims," commented Mrs. Hardy, shaking her head. "They're in business to help themselves, not anyone else."

"Lovely people," said Frank.

"*Dangerous* people," replied his mother.

Fenton Hardy nodded. "In all likelihood, anyway. So—if you two happen to see anyone or anything suspicious in the area, I'd appreciate it if you'd let me know."

"There *is* something I've been wondering about," said Joe. "Why would an abandoned house have—*ow!*"

"Sorry," said Frank. "My foot slipped."

"What was that, Joe?" his father asked.

"Oh—nothing, Dad. Just a riddle. Frank thinks it's stupid."

"It's our turn to wash the dishes," said Frank, pushing back his chair.

Joe put the dried dinner plate on the shelf. Then he turned down the volume of the countertop radio.

"Another long underwear gang," he remarked scornfully. "Clock punchers."

He took another rinsed plate from the large drying rack and began wiping it with his dishtowel.

"They *started* solid," said Frank, with a regretful glance at the radio. He picked up the last rinsed cup and ran his towel around its interior.

"Okay, big brother," Joe began. "Now that we can hear each other . . ." He put the dried plate on top of the previous one. "Why not tell Dad what happened at Polucca's?"

He picked up a third plate.

"Because," answered Frank, putting the cup away, "there's a very small chance that what we saw might have something to do with the smuggling operation he's investigating."

He hung up his dishtowel.

"That's just what I mean." Joe put the dried plate on the stack. "Why not—"

"We don't *know* there's a connection, do we?" Frank took the sponge from its dish on the counter and began wiping the drainboard.

"No, but it's worth looking into."

"That's what *I* think. So what will happen if we tell Dad now?"

"Well . . . He'll notify the authorities, and—"

"We won't be allowed near the place." Frank dropped the sponge back in its dish. " 'Sorry, boys—just stay out of our way. We don't want you to get hurt.' "

Joe put the plate on top of the others and took the last one from the rack.

"That sounds like Aunt Gertrude," he said, staring grimly at the plate and rubbing it hard.

"It sounds like most of the adults in Bayport."

Frank leaned against the counter with his back to the sink, put his hands in his pockets, and frowned.

Joe stopped rubbing and glanced at his brother. "But if there *is* something crooked about the old house, looking into it could get dangerous."

He put away the plate, then hung up his towel.

"Look into it is all we'll need to do," said Frank. "If we find a sure sign that something slippery's going on, we'll tell Dad."

"Okay," Joe replied, leaning against the counter by the radio. "I'll go along with that."

"If we were to tell him now, and he got the authorities involved, and they found out there was nothing to it . . ."

"We'd look pretty silly."

"Exactly," said Frank. "You know what people in this town think—we're just a couple of juveniles who like to play detective. That's bad enough. What if we sent everyone on a wild goose chase? Who'd take us seriously after *that*?"

"No one, probably," Joe admitted.

"There may be an aboveboard reason why the power is on in that house. There may be an equally legit reason why the 'ghost' scared us away."

Joe laughed. "Such as insanity?"

"Or something else that's strange but legal. That's why I want to photograph those fingerprints on my bike and try to get them identified. If whoever made them has a record, we can be pretty sure we're onto *something*."

"I set up the lights before dinner. I just need to bring down the camera and the lifting kit. We can start—"

The front doorbell rang.

"—as soon as Chet arrives."

Frank went to answer the ring.

Joe turned off the radio and followed, switching off the kitchen lights as he walked out.

"I hope he brought the Duchess!" he called to Frank, as he entered the living room.

"He *said* he would," Frank replied.

"We'll get it," he announced to his parents, who were sitting listening to the radio, and to his aunt, who was on her way to the front hall. "It's Chet."

Aunt Gertrude stopped and turned. "Did Joe say *duchess*? *What* duchess?"

Frank walked to the front window. "Yep—there she is."

Joe came up beside him and looked out. "What a doll! She's just as beautiful as he said she was going to be!"

"A *duchess*?" Aunt Gertrude asked again. "In *Bayport*?"

"Take a look," said Joe.

Mr. and Mrs. Hardy exchanged amused glances.

Aunt Gertrude hesitated, a glint of suspicion in her eyes. "I scarcely know when to believe you boys," she remarked.

She stepped to the window and peeked out.

Parked across from the house, visible through the porch railing, was a gleaming black 1934 Ford four-door sedan with chromed wire wheels, white-sidewall tires, and a low stance.

"Chet's just finished rubbing out her paint," Joe explained to his aunt. "Isn't she classy? That's why he calls her the Duchess."

Gertrude Hardy sniffed. "That's not a *duchess*," she declared. "That's a *dustbin*." She walked back to her chair.

The doorbell rang again.

"We can look at the car later," Frank said softly to his brother. "First, the fingerprints."

"I'll get the camera," Joe replied in a low voice. He turned from the window and hurried away.

Frank went to answer the bell.

"Good evening, madam," Chet began, as the door swung open. "I'm working my way through reform school, selling subscriptions to defunct magazines." He took a step forward. "And I wondered if you might be—"

"Meet us out back," Frank said with a smile, as he closed the door in Chet's face.

A Ghost of a Chance

Chet joined Frank in front of the garage by Frank's motorcycle, the front end of which was parked between two slender tripods holding unlit photoflood lamps. A more substantial, unoccupied tripod stood to the side.

Joe descended the stairway from his father's above-the-garage laboratory, carrying an attaché case and a camera with a lens extension.

"You're too late!" he called down. "We've already eaten!"

Chet sighed. "You wound me deeply. Do you think that all I care about is food?"

"Yes!"

Chet gave a long-suffering groan. "As I told you this afternoon, I want to watch you photograph those fingerprints."

He looked up at the cloudless sky. "It sure seems hard to believe that it *was* this afternoon."

Frank laughed. "You sound like someone remembering a bad dream."

"Something of the sort. First that unpleasantness at the house, then that ride home . . ."

"The ride home wasn't bad," said Joe, walking over to the motorcycle. He laid down the attaché case. "A little wet, that's all."

"A *little* wet? I haven't felt so drenched since Biff pushed me into the pool at the May Day Fête."

"Well, it was your idea to go see the house," Joe pointed out, as he fastened the camera to the waiting tripod.

"That's an odd-looking camera," remarked Chet, trying to guide the conversation in another direction.

"It's an investigator's camera," Joe told him.

"A modified press camera," Frank added.

Frank opened the attaché case and pulled out a magnifying glass. Then he switched on the lights and bent over the gas tank.

"I hope you have your father's permission to ruin his equipment," said Chet.

"We asked if we could practice with it," Joe replied guardedly.

"Remember what we agreed," Frank cautioned the visitor. "Don't tell anyone what happened today. Including Dad."

"Whatever you say, Lieutenant. The Morton mouth is sealed."

"For once," Joe commented sarcastically.

Frank glanced up at his brother. "*You're* a fine one to criticize. *You* nearly blabbed twice already."

"Well, I—"

"There's a great thumbprint here," said Frank, returning his attention to the top of the tank by the filler cap. "On a nice flat surface. Tented arch."

Joe took a soft-bristled brush from the attaché case, pointed it down, and rolled its round handle quickly back and forth between his palms.

"Fingerprint brush," he explained to Chet. "This is the way to clean it and fluff out the hairs."

"What's all that other stuff?" asked Chet, pointing to the case.

"Lifting tape," recited Joe, looking down at the contents. "Black, white, and clear. Background cards for the clear tape—the other tapes have their own backing. Cotton gloves. Scissors. Two camel's-hair brushes—one in hand. Flashlight—to locate hard-to-see prints by shining light on them at an angle. Magnifying glass—removed by investigator. Black and white cards for background when shooting prints found on glass. Two jars of dusting powder—black and gray."

He took out the jar of black dusting powder, turned it over, and shook it. Then he turned it right-side up, tapped the lid with the end of the brush handle, unscrewed it, and put it aside.

"The fingerprints are really greasy," he told Chet, "so we might not use this stuff. Greasy prints are tricky to dust, because the powder sticks to the lines *and* the spaces. We'll photograph them as they are, then decide if we want to try to dust them lightly and lift them with the tape. But I thought you might like to look at these."

He handed over the jar and brush.

Chet flicked the hairs of the brush with his finger, then held up the jar and looked closely into it. "Mmm. Sure is black."

A hint of a smile crossed his face. He lifted his head slightly. "*Aah—aaah—*"

Frank looked up from the handlebars.

"Do you have any idea what we would do to you," he asked, "if you sneezed that powder all over the place?"

"No," said Chet, immediately recovering.

Joe pointed his thumb toward the house. "We'd turn you over to Aunt Gertrude."

Chet looked stunned. "You're nothing but sadists."

He returned the jar and brush to Joe, who replaced the lid and put them back in the case.

Frank straightened up, held out the glass, and pointed to the gas tank. "Here, Chet—take a look."

Chet bent down and peered through the magnifying glass at the well-defined thumbprint.

"You're in trouble, Mr. Ghost." He chuckled ominously. "Frank Hardy's on your trail."

Joe looked over Frank's shoulder at the tide table illuminated by the desk lamp.

"June 30—low tide, eleven-ten P.M."

He sat on the desk.

"Why don't we go in the middle of the day? We'd see a lot better than we would tomorrow night."

"Yes," Frank replied, leaning back in his chair. "And anyone in that house could see *us* better."

"If there's anyone there to see us."

"We'd better assume there might be."

"But why do you want to go by *boat?*"

"Because," answered Frank, "I've been asking myself some questions."

"Such as?"

"Why are people being kept away from the Polucca place?"

"I'll pass—next question."

"Could smugglers be using it?"

"Possibly—for a lookout, maybe."

"If so, wouldn't that mean they're operating in the area?"

"I suppose."

"Where in the vicinity of Bayport could they be hiding out?"

"Nowhere."

"Why not?"

"Because wherever they might put themselves, sooner or later someone would notice their cars and trucks. And boats."

"Good reasoning," said Frank. "But what if they only used boats, running the goods in and out late at night when most people are asleep?"

"They'd still have to *hide* the boats, and the goods, and themselves," Joe insisted. "Day and night. Someone would notice."

"If they were in that lonely area along the coast by Walton Point—"

"There's no place there to hide their stuff."

"Except the Polucca house."

"Yeah, but they're not using *that* to—"

"And the point."

"There's nothing there."

"*Nothing?*" asked Frank. "There's a big stone promontory with rocks screening the end of it—screening it so well that no one, as far as I know, has ever *seen* it."

Joe sat up straight. "Hold the phone. There could be a *cave* at the end of the point! Is that what you're getting at?"

Frank nodded.

"Caves exist here and there," he said, "up and down the coast. There're bound to be one or two that haven't been noticed. If there *is* one there, who'd know about it? Boats stay well away from those rocks. Not many people would be eager—or foolish enough—to try to find a way through them."

"Especially," said Joe, reflecting, "with a 'haunted house' to discourage anyone from prowling around."

"Yeah," agreed Frank. "Very convenient. Anyway, that's why I want to look at low tide, when a cave would be most visible."

"Visible if we can get past those rocks."

"Right."

"I hate having to wait until tomorrow night to find out," said Joe, getting up from the desk.

"We'll have things to do before then," Frank replied. "Tomorrow's Monday. We can show those prints to Chief Collig and ask if he can have them identified—"

"Without telling him any more about them than we have to."

"Yeah. And we'll need to get a boat."

An Explanation

Bayport Chief of Police Ezra Collig—a heavily built man in his mid-fifties, with short-cropped, grizzled hair—looked up from the fingerprint photographs Frank had just placed on his desk.

"I wish you boys would tell me more about this," he said.

"There isn't much to tell," Frank replied, returning to a chair in front of the desk and sitting down.

"You say someone fooled around with your motorcycle—"

"And went through my jacket—"

"Out on North Shore Road."

"That's right."

"So whoever-it-was looked through your jacket for something to steal, started to take your motorcycle, but then changed his mind and left it. Is that how you see it?"

"I don't know." Frank turned to Joe, seated in an adjacent chair.

Joe shrugged. "Search *me*," he said.

"We don't know what to make of it," said Frank. "It just doesn't make sense. Why would somebody move a motorcycle a few feet?"

"He heard you coming back, probably—got scared and ran off." Chief Collig absentmindedly drummed his fingertips on the desk. "Whereabouts on North Shore was this?"

"At the Polucca place."

The chief smiled and leaned back in his swivel chair.

"Bayport's infamous haunted house." He laughed. "Let me guess—you boys were doing a little *investigating*."

30

"We were curious," said Joe. "There've been so many stories—"

"Yes—stories. As far as we've ever been able to determine, that's all they are."

The chief looked at one of his visitors, then the other.

"Well?" He smiled. "Did you find anything?"

"We found someone who scared us away," Joe answered cautiously.

"Oh? Who was it?"

"We don't know," said Frank. "We—Joe, Biff Hooper, and I— put our motorcycles in the garage, to get them out of the rain. There were three other fellows with us. The front door of the house was unlocked, so we went in. After we'd looked around for a while, someone we couldn't see started screaming and laughing like a maniac. We left in a hurry after that."

Chief Collig frowned. "I shouldn't have to remind you two— considering who your father is—that the Polucca place is private property."

"We thought it was just an old abandoned house," said Joe. "We didn't mean any harm, or cause any damage."

"I'm sure you didn't. But it *is* someone else's property, just the same."

The chief leaned forward. "If it makes you feel any better, I think I might know who scared you away. In all probability, it was the caretaker."

"Caretaker!" Joe exclaimed. "That old mausoleum has a *caretaker?* What does he do—count the weeds and cobwebs?"

"That I can't say. I haven't the slightest idea what he does, or if he does anything. Or even who he is. I've never seen a trace of him. But, according to the owner, someone comes around now and again to maintain the old pile."

"The owner . . ." Frank began. "Just who *is* the owner, Chief?"

"Old Leo's nephew, Alex Polucca. He could be his *grand*-nephew, he's so young. He inherited the place. He lives in New York City. I met him after Leo died. He came around to clear out the house and put everything in good legal order. He's stopped in two or three times since then."

"What does he intend to do with the property?"

31

"Oh, he's been saying for quite a while that he's going to move in any day now. He works for his family part time, but he's a footloose bachelor with spending money who could live practically anywhere. One thing or another just keeps getting in his way."

"Why would he want to live in that lonely old place?" asked Joe.

Chief Collig laughed. "Who knows—he probably doesn't realize how it is here, away from the diversions of New York City. And he probably doesn't realize how heavy a maintenance job a house like that can be."

"Maybe he doesn't have enough money to—"

"Oh, he's got plenty of that. He's willing to spend it, too. He certainly spends a lot when he's here."

The chief laughed. "He even sends a check every month to the power company, just to keep the electricity on. That way, he says, the house'll be ready when *he* is."

The brothers looked at each other, and shifted uneasily in their chairs.

Chief Collig looked down at the photos, then looked up again. "Anyway . . . It may have been the alleged caretaker who scared you off. Or—just as likely, considering the stories I've heard about the old shack—it may have been someone playing a joke."

"An odd sort of joke," Joe remarked.

"Tell me," said the chief, his eyes narrowing. "Was *Chet Morton* out there with you?"

The boys laughed.

"He sure was," Joe replied. "But he turned as pale as the rest of us when he heard that laughter."

"I know what you're thinking, Chief," Frank said with a smile. "But that's one joke Chet didn't pull on us." The smile faded. "If it *was* a joke."

Chief Collig shuffled through the photographs. "This business of some greasy-fingered tamperer going through your jacket and then starting off with your motorcycle . . . That doesn't sound like the work of a mad caretaker or a prankster. Still, I don't see that these photographs are likely to give us much help."

"Dad," said Frank, "mentioned that the FBI has fingerprints on file of every—"

The chief looked up. "Oh, I should have known these were Fenton's idea."

He leaned back and smiled. "Our renowned private investigator covers every possibility. That's all right, then—I'll send these on to Washington." He winked. "Just to be certain, you know. And I'll let Fenton know the results."

"Just tell us," said Frank, "and we'll tell Dad."

"We'd rather not bother him for a while," Joe added. "He's pretty wrapped up in a case."

"Fine," replied the chief. "I won't mention it to him. After all, you're the ones filing the complaint."

He slapped the arm of his chair. "Come to think of it, there's an FBI agent in Bayport today—Lane Anderson, from the New York field office. He telephoned a few minutes ago. He's here to see your father, he said, and then he's heading for Washington. He told me he'll stop in on his way out of town. I'll give the photos to him then."

He smiled. "You can't get better service than that. And I'll see that he doesn't bother Fenton with our little mystery."

"Thanks, Chief."

"Yeah, Chief—thanks for taking the trouble."

"It's no trouble at all, boys. I know *you* aren't pranksters or cranks. Not like *some* young people I know."

The brothers looked at each other and smiled. They knew what was coming next—a tirade on the tormentor of the Bayport Police Department, the freckle-faced instrument of mischief named . . .

"*Chet Morton.*" Chief Collig rolled his eyes. "Did I tell you two about the time that rascal phoned here about his cat?"

"I don't think so," said Frank, trying not to smile.

"Well, it was like this. One night, Con Riley's on duty, as usual, when the telephone rings. It's Chet Morton, wailing about his lost cat. Con calms him down and humors him along, thinking maybe it's a joke but maybe not, for once: 'Sure, Chet, we'll be on the lookout for your cat—just take it easy.'

"Well, Chet goes on and on—Con taking notes all the while—about this blessed cat. He describes him in the most minute detail—his right front paw has a white spot on it, and so on."

33

"Did Sergeant Riley believe him?" asked Joe.

"He wasn't sure what to think. Chet's past performance was against the likelihood of a truthful story, if you know what I mean. Still, he *sounded* convincing. Anyway, Chet finishes babbling and blubbering, and hangs up. Two minutes later, the phone rings and Con answers. Guess who it is."

Frank laughed. "What did he say this time?"

"Calm as anything, he says, 'Sergeant Riley—I just remembered. I don't *own* a cat.'"

The brothers laughed.

"He owns one *now*," said Joe. "So you'd better watch out."

"You know my nephew, Terry, the fireman," the chief went on. "He was on duty a few evenings ago, when the firehouse phone rang. He answered. At the other end of the line, some young hysteric yelled, *'My house is burning! My house is burning! Send a fire truck!'* And then he hung up. No name. No address.

"A minute or two later, the telephone rang. It was the lunatic again. *'My house is going up in flames!'* he yelled. *'Can't you get here any faster? Send two fire trucks!'* Then he hung up.

"After a minute or so of calm, the phone rang. This time the crackpot screamed, *'I'm on the roof of my house—the flames are licking my toes! What's the matter with you people? Send three fire trucks out here before I—'*

"By then, Terry thought he knew who the madman was. 'Is that you, Chet?' he interrupted. The voice said, 'Chet? Who's Chet?' Then he hung up. He sounded just like you-know-who.

"So when Terry went off duty an hour or so later, he fetched a fizz-water dispenser and drove out to the Morton farm. And when Chet came to the door—"

"Terry put out the fire," Joe concluded for him, with a grin.

"That he did, that he did. But enough about that menace to society. We've all got better things to do than talk about *him*."

Chief Collig picked up the photographs. "I'll let you know as soon as I learn something about these."

"Thanks, Chief," said Frank.

The boys stood up and started for the door. Then Frank stopped and turned.

"By the way," he said, "was Leo Polucca ever involved in shipping or importing?"

"No, not old Leo." The chief shook his head and smiled. "That sort of business would have been beyond him, I'm afraid."

"Why? What did he do for a living?"

"Oh, he worked for the Highway Department, blowing rocks out of the way so roads could be put through."

"That's a strange occupation," said Frank.

"I thought I heard a rumor," Joe casually remarked, "that he once had some connections with a smuggling racket."

"*Smuggling?*" The chief laughed. "Our Leo?" He chuckled. "Now there's a rumor that's *way* off."

"We'd always heard he was pretty peculiar," Frank said cautiously.

"Oh, he was an odd number in one or two ways, I'll grant you, but . . .

"Well, first of all, Leo just wasn't the criminal *type*. Second, he was too busy earning an honest living. Dangerous, I'm telling you, but honest. It certainly paid him well. And, according to his nephew, he gained quite a large inheritance, which he squirreled away in various banks. He had a *lot* of money—enough to build that big house and retire while he was still fairly young. Why would he have risked a prison sentence for some *dis*honest money?"

"I don't know. I just thought I heard—"

"Leo had an *artistic* temperament," the chief said thoughtfully. "If you know what I mean. He made some nice sculptures, even sold a few . . . He came from a big family, a close one—I remember one or more of his brothers or cousins or whoever they were would always be staying at his place. They even helped him build it—to save money, he said. Leo didn't like *spending* money, just *saving* it. Family aside, though, he was pretty much of a loner. And once he retired, he hardly left the house or had anything to do with anyone."

The chief laughed again. "Leo Polucca a *smuggler*! That's a good one!"

Second Thoughts

The sky was turning cloudy as the brothers left the police station. A light mist was blowing in from the bay, carrying the scent of the ocean and a few drops of rain. But Frank and Joe didn't seem to notice.

"So much for *smugglers*," Frank remarked bitterly, as they reached their motorcycles.

"Let's go for a walk."

"Yeah. And do some thinking."

"Are *we* in danger of looking stupid!" Frank exclaimed, after they had gone a short distance. "The owner of the house is keeping the electricity on . . . He's hired someone to guard the place . . ."

"That was a pretty crazy way of guarding it," Joe replied skeptically. "And I'll bet that was no caretaker who scared us away."

"If it wasn't, then . . . Well, I hate to admit it, but Chief Collig's suspicion of a Chet Morton prank might have something to it. Frightening people is one of Chet's favorite occupations. Remember the time he and Night Owl Thompson woke up Stu Davidson's family by running around outside their house, making noises like a police raid?"

"Yeah, but—"

"And it was Chet who suggested that we go to Polucca's. He might've gotten some friend to—"

"Chet's not *that* good an actor. He was scared. And have you ever known him to keep quiet after pulling off a joke?"

"No, I guess not."

Joe snickered. "Caretaker, huh? What about those things we saw?"

"It may be possible to explain every one of them."

"Okay, try."

"The caretaker was in the house—"

"Where? He wasn't upstairs—we looked in every room. And if you think he was hiding in a closet or something, just tell me how he could've gotten up there without leaving footprints on the steps."

"He might've sneaked up when we were in that room."

"That would've been a pretty good sneak, with all of us right there across from the head of the stairs, with the door open."

"Even so, he could've done it. He could've taken the other stairs. He could even have climbed up from outside."

"In that storm? Awful slippery climb. And a lot of work for someone who doesn't seem to like doing any."

"Wherever he was to begin with, he heard something, got up to the second floor, realized we didn't belong there—"

"Or realized we'd discovered something—"

"—and then did what he could to make us leave."

"Yeah—scream like a lunatic."

"Well, by all appearances," said Frank, "he's a pretty odd care-taker."

"That's for sure. The only visible thing he does is sweep two floors and one of the stairs—apparently to hide footprints."

"Maybe he didn't want his employer to know that anyone had been in the house."

"That sounds *almost* reasonable. But if he's so protective of the place, why was the front door unlocked?"

"Maybe he'd just unlocked it and was about to go in when he heard us coming."

"So he left it unlocked? And how about the motorcycle being moved? How does the caretaker fit in there?"

"He, or somebody with him, started to steal it—"

"But it was put way over to the *side*. Funny direction for someone to go, if he was trying to steal it."

Frank stopped and stared ahead of him.

"Yes," he said thoughtfully. "That's true."

Joe walked in front of his brother, stopped, and turned to face him.

"Just remember what Dad says about the way detectives need to look at situations," he admonished. "As if they haven't a clue to what happened. No snap judgments, no preconceived ideas . . ."

"Sure, but—"

"And remember what he says about people who're mentally lazy, 'conservative-minded.' They want a life of easy, predictable patterns. They aren't *intrigued* by disturbances to those patterns, they're *bothered* by them. So when something they don't understand comes along—something that disturbs the pattern of what they know, or *think* they know—they immediately try to reassure themselves and other people by explaining it away. And once they've made a habit of doing that, they're no longer able to *see* clearly."

Joe pointed to the police department. "Chief Collig's a great example. He's slow at coming up with solutions because he's fast at jumping to conclusions. He's more concerned with explaining than with investigating."

He tapped Frank's chest with his finger. "*Investigators* don't respond with knee-jerk explanations. They *investigate*, instead."

Frank took a deep breath, then let it out. He smiled and patted Joe on the shoulder. "All right, Professor. Let's go see Tony."

In the alley alongside Prito's Produce, the Hardy boys talked with the owner's son, a muscular teenager with dark, curly hair, as he lifted crates of fruit down from the tailgate of a truck.

"That's it, Tony," said the driver, as he stepped out with the last crate and put it down.

"It's just as well I wasn't there," Tony replied to Frank.

He slid the crate off the edge of the tailgate and put it on top of two others on his hand truck. "I'm allergic to maniacs. All of a sudden, I'm glad Pop needed me here yesterday afternoon."

The driver closed the back of the truck, then gave Tony a bill of lading. Tony signed and returned it. The driver handed him his copy.

"Thanks, Tony."

"Yeah—thanks, Jimmy. See ya."

As the truck drove off, Tony remarked to the Hardys: "I've never seen Polucca's up close. Maybe I can take a look at it with you later on—when no one's there but ghosts."

He tilted the hand truck back, turned, and started toward the side entrance.

"We're hoping to go out there tonight," said Joe.

The hand truck returned to upright with a *clunk*. Tony swung around and looked from one face to the other. "You're foolin', right? You wanta go to that spook hotel at *night*, with a *madman* on the loose?"

Frank smiled. "We're not going to the house. We want to try to get to the end of Walton Point at low tide, to see if there's a cave there. We think something illegal might be going on."

"I never heard of a cave, but that doesn't—illegal what?"

"Smuggling."

"*What?* In *Bayport?*"

"Dad's investigating a smuggling racket that may be operating somewhere nearby. We're looking into it, too—in our own way. But we need a good pilot, and a good boat. Like you and *Napoli.*"

"Is this for real?"

"It sure is."

Tony looked from the alley to the misty street. "Sounds like the New York gangster stuff Pop tells me 'bout."

"Do you know if it's possible," asked Joe, "to get through those rocks and reach the end of the point?"

Tony came closer and scratched his head. "I suppose anything's possible. If you're crazy enough. And if you don't mind putting a hole in your boat."

"It's that bad, huh?"

"Lemme put it this way," Tony answered. "There're two kinds a boaters—the sane ones and the *in*sane ones. Pop and I like ta think we're in the first category.

"One of the things that determine whether you're gonna be safe and sound or wrecked and ruined is how ya deal with *rocks*. If you're sensible and wanta stay afloat, you keep away from 'em whenever possible. And you learn where they are below the surface. 'Cause it's the ones you can't see that'll get ya."

"Are you familiar with those big rocks off the point?" asked Joe.

"I've had a good look at the outside of that hodgepodge. But there's the *inside*, too. I don't know anyone who knows anything 'bout that. And at low tide, in the dark . . ."

He walked a few steps away, rubbing his neck. Then he turned and walked back.

"Why not go out at high tide?" he asked. "In daylight?"

"Because," answered Frank, "if there *is* a cave, it'll be more visible at low tide."

"And," added Joe, "*we'll* be *less* visible at night."

Tony nodded. "Figures."

"So you think it's too risky," Frank said glumly.

"One problem is *rocks*," Tony replied. "Another one is *Pop*. If he says uh-uh, we won't hafta worry 'bout rocks."

"Could you ask him now?"

Tony laughed. "Sure. Lemme practice first.

" 'Hey, Pop—how 'bout letting me take *Napoli* out tonight, with Frank and Joe Hardy? We wanta find out if we can make it through those rocks off Walton Point. We'll be there and back before you can say *extensive hull damage.*' "

"*Napoli* has a pretty shallow draft," said Frank. "With us watching carefully and using the spotlights—"

"We'd sure need 'em if *that* keeps up," interjected Tony, glancing up at the overcast sky. "No moon."

"Well, even so—"

"Just remember something: We're not wealthy. Pop paid for that boat by scrambling for the money, all those years he spent in New York. I don't wanta damage it."

"Neither do we," said Joe. "For his sake or ours."

40

"Tell your father . . ." Frank hesitated. "That we're working on one of Dad's investigations."

"Yeah," said Joe. "That ought to help soften him up."

"Better yet," suggested Tony, "have your father tell him."

"We can't," said Frank. "We don't want him to know we're working on this."

"Huh?"

"We don't want *anyone* to know," Joe emphasized. "Just you and the other fellows. And your father, if he needs to be told. We don't want a word of what we're doing to get back to Dad."

"Oh, fine." Tony rolled his eyes.

" 'Hey, Pop—lemme have *Napoli* tonight. Frank and Joe and I are working on one of Fenton Hardy's investigations. *But don't tell Mr. Hardy 'bout it.'* "

He laughed. "You two're funnier'n Chet Morton!"

Smiling, he glanced from one dejected-looking face to the other. "Okay, okay—I'll go ask 'im now. I'm afraid it won't do any good, but I'll ask. You better wait here. And cover your ears."

Tony, looking slightly dazed, stepped out into the alley.

"Well?" Frank asked anxiously.

"I can't believe it," Tony replied. "Pop must be in a good mood or something. I told 'im the idea, in a general sorta way. I said the place you wanta go could be a tricky spot for a boat but that I'd take a good look at it and use my best judgment 'bout whether or not to try ta navigate through."

"So what did he say?"

"It's more like what he *didn't* say that surprised me," Tony answered, shaking his head.

"What I expected was an explosion, followed by lettuce in the face. You know—'*You wanta WHAT?*' he yells, and then I duck. But he just said, 'Only if it's clear. No overcast. Tonight, tomorrow night, whatever—only if it's clear.' Followed by the usual remarks 'bout what happens to me if anything happens to *Napoli*. So I guess it's okay."

"Attaboy!" cried Joe, slapping him on the back.

41

Frank settled for looking relieved."If we go tonight," he said, "low tide's at eleven-ten. So when—"

"We better leave no later than nine-thirty. *If* it's clear. What we need ta do out there's gonna take some time."

To the Point

It was nearly nine-thirty when the Hardy boys pedaled their bicycles up to a small green boathouse behind the Prito residence on South Edgewater. Tony sat waiting by the open door.

The sky had cleared, and a nearly full moon shone down on the slow-rolling water of the bay.

"Nice night, huh!" Tony called, rising to his feet.

"Yeah!" Joe called back. "Great night for a ride!"

He and Frank laid down their bikes, then walked up the ramp to the door.

"This is the soonest we could get here," Frank said apologetically, taking a pair of binoculars from around his neck.

"We told everyone we were turning in early," said Joe. "After we'd waited in our rooms for a while, we sneaked out."

Frank smiled sheepishly. "I feel as if we're on our way to a life of crime."

Tony laughed. "Well, let's get outa here before the cops arrive."

Inside, Tony switched on the overhead lights, then passed quickly along the narrow, U-shaped walkway to the port, or left, side of the *Napoli*—a green-and-white, two-seat runabout with red trim which sat, rocking gently, facing the bay.

Through the open sliding doors at the far end of the boathouse, moonlit ripples lapped and shimmered.

"What exactly did you tell your father about what we're doing?" Joe asked, as he and Frank walked to the *Napoli*'s starboard side.

"I told 'im you two wanted to look in ta something to help your father," Tony answered, casting off the port lines. "Something that nobody's supposed ta know 'bout."

He walked quickly to the starboard side. "I guess the helping-your-father business is why he said yes."

Tony pulled the *Napoli* to the edge of the walkway and held her steady so the others could climb on board.

" '*Okay, kid,* '" he said loudly, mimicking his father's deep, growly voice. " '*As long as ya get up on time. But if ya wreck* Napoli, *you'll pay what eva it costa fixa.* '"

"*We'll* pay," said Frank. He climbed into the front seat and slid to the port side.

"In more ways than one," Joe added grimly, following him.

Frank placed his binoculars on the seat beside him. "What are these things?" he asked, poking some slender wooden poles with his foot.

"Those," answered Tony, casting off the starboard lines, "are the sections of a sounding stick. It's an awkward thing ta use, but it's better than a lead line for feeling our way 'round those rocks."

He climbed behind the wheel and started the engine. When it had warmed up, he turned on the running lights and eased the throttle lever forward.

With a low, powerful rumbling, the *Napoli* moved slowly out into the bay.

Before long, they were racing up the coast. The light of the moon was reflected in the low waves all around them—waves that slapped against the starboard side and prow of the speeding run-about, splashed white, then fell behind in an ever-widening wake of silver.

"Boy oh boy, this boat can run!" Joe shouted above the noise of the engine.

"We need ta make as good time now as we can!" Tony shouted back. "Once we're near the house, we'll hafta go slow and quiet!"

In the distance on their left lay Walton Point, dimly illuminated by the moonlight.

Tony switched off the running lights, then pulled back on the throttle and steered landward.

"I wanta get close in!" he explained. "To stay as much as we can outa direct sighta the house!"

Nearing land, he brought the *Napoli* parallel to the shore, her bow pointing to the seaward edge of the stand of trees hiding most of the house. "That's close enough!"

He gradually pulled back on the throttle. The sound of the engine dropped in pitch.

Like the side of a dark ship, the rocky promontory grew steadily larger ahead.

"We're near enough for a look," said Frank.

Tony slid the throttle to neutral and the *Napoli* came to a halt, rocking gently on the waves.

Frank picked up the binoculars and stood. Leaning on the top of the windshield, he examined what little he could distinguish of the house.

"I don't see any sign of life up there," he said shortly.

"Hold on." Tony nudged the throttle. "And keep watching."

The *Napoli* moved steadily forward, the power of her chugging engine overcoming the outward pull of the retreating tide.

"There's the window we looked through!" Frank announced after a while. "We've moved past the trees south of it that were in the way!"

"It's the only window," Joe explained to Tony, "with a clear view of the ocean."

"*Most* of the ocean, maybe," Tony replied. "But not close ta the shore, south of where we are."

Visible now over some shorter trees in front of the house, the second-story window looked dark, vacant, lifeless. Its glass dully reflected the moonlight.

"It's nice and dark," said Frank. "I can't see anybody behind it. But from this angle, I probably wouldn't, anyway."

The *Napoli* continued slowly along the shore.

As Walton Point loomed ever higher ahead, the window and then the roof above it disappeared behind a barrier of seemingly rising evergreens.

"There goes the house," Frank announced. He sat and put the binoculars down beside him.

Tony switched on all the lights. "You handle the port spot, Frank," he directed, aiming the starboard spotlight straight ahead.

Frank shone his light forward.

The sudden brightness temporarily disoriented the occupants of the *Napoli*, accustomed as they were to the soft light of the moon.

The wall of rock before them, which had been waiting in shadow, now appeared to glide toward the boat, which seemed to be standing still, waiting for its approach.

Tony turned the wheel, and the *Napoli*'s bow swung seaward. As it did, the wall of the point seemed to pull alongside and move past them, heading toward shore.

"Weird effect, huh?" Tony remarked to the others, noticing their dazed looks. "Don't let it get ya."

Joe blinked and shook his head. "I don't know which is moving—the rock or the boat."

"The boat. Okay, while we're put-putting to the enda this thing, lemme tell ya 'bout what's coming up.

"Those rocks off the end musta once been parta the point. Now they're a maze of smaller, worn-down Walton Points with channels between 'em that the water runs through.

"Some of those channels're probably deep enough for us, but others won't be. Some'll be wide enough, some'll be too narrow. It's treacherous territory. That's why anyone with any sense stays away from it."

"Does that include you?" Joe asked, grinning.

"Pretty much. But I *have* come close a few times, just outa curiosity."

"It's a good thing you're not a cat."

"Yeah—especially tonight. Anyway, that helter-skelter maze is made up a the outer rocks that you can see and a lotta inner ones, some of which you can see and some of which you can't. Close in to the enda the point are two stone monsters. Each one screens half the end, more or less. Let's call 'em North Rock and South Rock. We're gonna hafta get by at least one of 'em to reach the end—if that's possible, and nobody knows. Nobody *I* know, anyway."

"Sounds like a nice puzzle," Frank commented.

"You betcha. Okay, North Rock looks sorta like a huge octopus head with a big bite out of it. It tapers down to a wide base, like tentacles spreading out. The side that faces South Rock, as much as I could ever glimpse of it, appears to be a vertical wall.

"South Rock sits a good deal lower in the water. It looks like a long, thin, giant-size potato.

"Between the two is a passage of water running roughly northeast to southwest. It's hard ta tell how wide it is. To make things nice'n difficult, there's a whole graveyard of rocks, big and small, between it and the open sea."

"Any other possibilities?" asked Joe, frowning.

"Two more—a curving channel between South Rock and the point, and a twisty-looking one on the back side of where we are, between North Rock and the point."

"So there're three channels," summarized Frank. "South, middle, and north."

"And the south one," said Tony, lifting his left hand from the wheel to indicate it, "is just up there."

The Maze

The *Napoli* had been brought around. Ahead to the left of her foredeck light, the nearly vertical end of Walton Point curved away into shadow. About three boat widths to the right of it was the rounded end of an enormous rock.

A low incoming wave spilled into the gap between the two, raising the water level slightly. Then, with a sloshing, sucking sound, the water pulled away and the level returned to what it had been.

"And now the fun begins," said Tony, reaching below the seat. "Help me put this together."

They hauled out three sections of a wooden pole with a series of lines on it and a weight on one end. Tony fitted them together by way of metal sleeves on the ends of the middle section.

"Okay, Joe," he said, "we need ya ta kneel out on the enda the foredeck with this thing."

He pointed to a thick dark line on the pole.

"From the weighted end to this mark is the distance from the bottom of the propeller to the deck, plus a foot. That's as close ta rock as we can go."

He pointed to a thinner line a couple of feet farther from the end. "That's the warning line. Lower the stick each time till that's 'bout level with the deck. If ya touch anything at that depth, holler."

"Gotcha."

"We'll take it nice'n slow. As we go along, drop the weighted end in, lower the stick to the warning line, lift it out, drop it in again. Let the weight do the work—release the stick, let it go down, then grab it with both hands ta stop it. Pull it out hand over hand. Don't try ta drag it through the water from one spot to the next. If we get in a tight area, check each side—otherwise, just the middle."

"Aye, aye, Cap'n."

Joe climbed around the windshield and took the boat cushion that Tony handed him. He placed it at the bow, then turned and accepted the end of the pole from Frank.

As Joe knelt and started sounding, Tony eased the throttle forward.

The *Napoli* crept into the channel, the *chug-chug* of her engine echoing from the rock on either side. The sound of the waves grew fainter behind her.

Foot by foot, yard by yard, the stone walls slipped by, drawing nearer ahead, narrowing the passage until the barnacles in the high-tide zone were nearly within reach on both sides of the boat. The water dripping from them made eerie *plops* closer and closer to the *Napoli* as she moved slowly forward.

"I'm gonna get it," Tony said uneasily, watching the rock come ever nearer. "Just one scrape, and—"

"It's shallower now!" called Joe. He held up his hand. *"Whoa!"*

Tony reversed the throttle momentarily, and the *Napoli* rocked to a halt.

Joe plunged the sounding stick in as far ahead as he could reach. A couple of feet down, it stopped.

Joe hauled out the stick, turned, and waved his arm.

"Too shallow! Go back!"

"Hang on!" said Tony, as he nudged the throttle into reverse.

In a few minutes that seemed like hours, the *Napoli* was clear of the rocks.

"My nerves!" Tony exclaimed, shaking the tension from his hands. "If this is the way the other two're gonna go, we'll be out here all night!"

49

At a comfortable distance, they cruised slowly eastward along the side of South Rock, looking for an opening ahead on the left.

Just past South Rock, they came to a long, lower rock pointing east. Its western third was several feet higher than the *Napoli,* but beyond that it plunged down to just below the top of her windshield.

As the barrier dropped away, Frank and Tony stood and anxiously scanned what they could see of the jumble of inner rocks.

In the moonlight, the sea-carved stones resembled a scattered collection of fantastic sculptures.

"See what I mean by a *maze?*" asked Tony. "There must be all kinds a twisting passages going every which way 'round—"

"Hey!" Joe yelled from the foredeck. He pointed to a large, high rock ahead on the left.

"Between that one up there and the end of this one, I think there'll be some room!"

As the *Napoli* passed the end of the long rock, Tony slowed her and turned in.

"Uh-oh!" cried Joe.

Tony, seeing what had startled him, stopped the boat.

Farther on lay a small, low rock just northeast of the one they were coming around. A short distance east of it was another low rock, a bit bigger and higher than the first. Just east of that was a larger, slightly higher rock and then, southeast of that, the much larger and higher one Joe had pointed to.

"Come on!" Joe shouted, waving his arm. "I think there might be enough room between the two low ones! This might be our only chance to get in there!"

Tony, looking doubtful, nudged the *Napoli* forward.

"Those two're awful close together!" he yelled to Joe.

"They are, aren't they!"

"*Close* is right!" exclaimed Frank, as the dubious gap drew nearer. "Ready to admit you were wrong?" he called sarcastically.

"Not yet!" Joe probed the water ahead. "Keep coming!"

The *Napoli* was just short of the gap when Tony stopped her.

"Boy, I don't know 'bout this," he said worriedly, leaning on the edge of the windshield. "From where I am, it looks awful tight!"

"It looks possible from here!" Joe replied, probing near the rocks. "And it's plenty deep!"

Tony stared at the space between the rocks. Then he looked beyond it and studied what he could see of the maze, like a chess player planning his next few moves.

"All right," he told the others at last. "I think I see a way 'round the rocks up ahead. But these first two're squeaky tight. I don't wanta go *too* slow between 'em, or the waves might push us against one. So, Joe—lie down, put the stick in as far in front as ya can, and brace it and yourself against the bow. If ya touch anything, scream your head off."

Joe made himself ready.

"Okay!" he yelled.

"Hang on!"

As Frank gripped the edge of the windshield, Tony set his jaw and eased the throttle forward.

The *Napoli* entered the gap, then slid past the rocks with only a few inches of clearance on either side.

"*Wowee!*" Tony shouted, turning to look behind him as the rocks glided astern. "It's a good thing Pop's not here! He'da had heart failure by now!"

He brought the *Napoli* to a halt and gazed down at the water.

"It looks deep here," he called to Joe, "but we'll be zigzagging around, so who knows what we'll find! Don't spare the stick!"

He moved the throttle slightly ahead.

Joe pushed himself up to his knees and resumed sounding.

The *Napoli* slowly passed one inner rock after another, turning left, right, left again . . .

An enormous shadowy form shaped like the head of a gigantic octopus grew nearer above the rocks on the right.

The eastern end of its huge, lower-profile neighbor loomed ever larger over the rocks on the left.

As the last of those rocks passed by, the tip of South Rock swung into full view, like the prow of a ghostly ship.

The final intervening rock on the right slipped away, revealing the eastern end of towering North Rock and part of its vertical inner side, which angled away to the left and disappeared from sight behind South Rock.

Between the giant stones was a narrow, but apparently adequate, passage of water.

"We *made* it!" Tony exclaimed softly.

All gazed ahead, fascinated, as the *Napoli* approached the passage . . . reached its entrance . . . and slipped inside.

Dead End

The chugging of the *Napoli*'s engine reverberated from the huge rocks as she made her way between them. By all appearances, it was they and not the boat that were moving. Slowly, majestically, they glided past, as if under some strange power of their own.

One eerie optical illusion succeeded another as the world narrowed to a long hallway of seemingly still water and moving rock. The spotlights, manned by the *Napoli*'s standing pilot and navigator, swept back and forth across the stone surfaces, illuminating protrusions and indentations that seemed to change places with each other as they slipped by—pushing forward in light, pulling back in shadow . . .

And then the "head" of North Rock glided away above on the right, the echoes of the engine noise grew softer, and the world widened.

The crew of the *Napoli* found themselves on a broad pool of slowly moving water. The "tentacle" base of North Rock angled off to their right without any apparent break between it and the point. Curving dramatically away to their left was the side of South Rock. Ahead—pulling back in a wide, concave depression to form the far edge of the pool, then closing in diagonally on the left to almost join the western tip of South Rock—was the end of Walton Point.

"There it is," Tony said in a hushed voice. He slid the throttle to neutral, then leaned forward on the top of the windshield. "I can hardly believe it."

"It's like a dream," Frank replied quietly. "I wonder how many people have seen this."

"I wonder if *anybody* has."

Joe turned his head slowly from side to side, taking in the scene before him. *"Unbelievable,"* he remarked at last.

"But," said Tony, "I don't see any sign of a cave over there."

Frank reached down and aimed his spotlight at the concave wall at the far end of the pool. As he swept the beam from left to right, just above the water, a vertical shadow appeared on the rock. He swung the light to the left. The shadow moved to the right and vanished. He swung the light back, and the shadow reappeared.

Tony directed his spotlight to the same area. As he raised the beam, sweeping it back and forth, an edge defined itself.

The vertical line of shadow seemed to reach all the way up the rock face.

"The wall must curve around behind itself to the right," said Frank.

"Looks like the water goes back in there, too."

"Let's find out."

As the *Napoli* drew near to the end of the point, Tony turned his spotlight, illuminating the area to starboard.

There the rock curved inward suddenly for a few yards, forming a shallow cove.

"Take a look at *that*," said Tony, pointing.

In the previously hidden rock face, beginning below the water level, was a flat-backed indentation about two feet deep, not much wider than the *Napoli*, and a few feet higher than the top of her windshield. Its irregular edges were smoothly shaped, as though they had been formed over centuries by the relentless action of water. Its high-tide zone, like that on either side, was covered with rockweed.

"Take her in close," directed Frank, staring at the depression.

Tony turned the wheel and eased the *Napoli* to starboard.

"It's *mucho* deep here!" Joe called, pulling up the sounding stick.

Tony brought the *Napoli* to a halt when her bow was a few feet from the rock.

"I've seen formations like this before," he remarked.

He sat down and shone his light on it.

"They always look weird. They're made of rock within rock. The inner rock—the flat area, there—is tougher 'n the outer. So as the softer stuff wears away—"

"That could almost be the entrance to a cave," said Frank, gripping the top of the windshield as he peered intently at the recess. Then he relaxed his grip, sat down, and sank into the seat, defeated. *"Almost,"* he repeated bitterly.

Kneeling on the foredeck, Joe glared at the unusual formation.

"We made our way past all those obstacles," he said angrily, "just to find *this!*"

Raising the sounding stick like a spear, he jabbed hard at the center of the indentation.

The weighted tip landed with a soft, damp *thud.* The indentation, with its rockweed attachments, moved slightly with the blow, like a heavy curtain of wet canvas.

For a few seconds, the three seekers, struck dumb by what they'd seen, stared at what once more appeared to be solid rock.

Joe slowly pulled back the stick and jabbed again at the indentation. Again it moved with the blow.

"Whoopee!" Joe shouted, waving the sounding stick over his head. "Whoopee-whoopee-*whoopee!*"

"I don't believe it!" Frank gasped, sitting up straight and blinking. "It really is . . . It really is . . ."

"You better *believe* it is!" declared Tony, laughing.

"We'll be famous!" shouted Joe. "There'll be—"

"Hey!" Frank shouted over him. *"Be quiet!"*

Alert now to the possibility of danger, the boys waited anxiously for a sign that they had been heard. One long, slow minute passed, then another. But nothing happened.

Still holding the stick, Joe scrambled to his feet and began to dance a jig, causing the boat to roll and dip.

"We found it!" he proclaimed. "We *found* it!"

"Stop!" said Tony, laughing. "You'll swamp us!"

Joe laid the sounding stick across the foredeck cleats, staggered aft on the rolling deck, knelt, and stuck his right hand over the windshield.

"Slap that skin!" he exclaimed, as he slapped, and then shook, hands with his companions. "Slap that skin! Love it, love it!" He wiggled his arms. "Reen*yaakka!*"

Tony leaned back and laughed.

"We're all crazy!" he declared. "There's a gang a *smugglers* in Bayport, says Frank! I think they've got a *cave* at the enda Walton Point! Right, says Tony—I believe ya! Just squeeze between those rocks, says Joe—never mind the damage! Yeah, sure, says Tony—anything ya say! Okay, Tony, says Pop—you can borrow the boat! Sink 'er and you'll be paying for the resta your life! Thanks, Pop, says Tony—I really *appreciate* it!"

He laughed again. "We're all *nuts!*"

"Hey," said Joe, laughing so hard he was starting to cough. "Just imagine what *Chief Collig* would say about us!"

Frank laughed, slid down in the seat, and threw out his arms. "'Chet, my boy! Welcome to the station! I hope you didn't bring those troublemaking *friends* of yours!'"

"'Not me, Chief,'" mimicked Joe. "'I don't *believe* in smugglers!'"

Smiling, Tony looked through the windshield at the camouflaged curtain. His smile vanished.

"I suppose you realize," he said, eyeing the canvas warily, "that somebody *could* be behind that thing."

"No one's come out," Joe replied, staring at the curtain. "Despite all the noise we've been making."

"Yeah, but they could be hiding in there, waiting for us ta—"

"*Look!*"

Startled, Joe and Tony turned to see why Frank had shouted.

He was on his feet, his left hand clutching the top of the windshield, his right hand pointing to the sky.

The others followed his gaze upward, and their mouths dropped open.

High above their heads, a powerful beam of light was piercing the darkness—a yellow-white ray of dazzling intensity, shining out to sea from somewhere on Walton Point.

Then suddenly it was gone. The only light in the sky was that of the glowing moon.

A Light in the Darkness

Frank, Joe, and Tony stared up at the moonlit sky, stunned by the appearance and disappearance of the mysterious light.

"What in the world—"

"Did we really *see* that?"

"Where'd it come from?"

"The house—it must've come from there!"

"Of course!" yelled Frank. "They're signaling to someone! We've got to get out of here!"

Joe lunged for the sounding stick, yanked it apart, and handed the sections to the others. Then he grabbed the cushion from the foredeck. Clutching it, he half climbed, half fell over the windshield and into the seat.

Tony reversed the throttle, and the *Napoli* backed from the cove.

As soon as she was clear of the rock projection, he shoved the throttle full ahead and turned the wheel hard to starboard. The water churning against the side of the angled rudder pushed the *Napoli*'s stern landward.

As her bow swung toward the channel entrance, Tony brought the wheel back around. Her rudder straightened and she sped forward.

They raced across the pool, into the channel, and through it to its far end. There they decelerated quickly, the drag of the water acting as a powerful brake, and began the awkward process of maneuvering around one rock after another—speeding and slowing, speeding and slowing, their wake catching up with them, jarring the stern, then falling behind again.

Accelerating around the last rock, they saw ahead the narrow gap through which they'd entered.

Just before they reached the opening, Tony slowed the *Napoli*, calculated how she could come to the rock on his side, then pushed the throttle forward.

As the boat slid between the rocks—with little more than a hand's width of clearance on the starboard side—he switched off the lights.

Then they were clear of the rocks, bouncing in the waves.

Tony pulled the throttle to neutral, then looked around, blinking to accustom his eyes to the moonlight.

"Where are they?" he asked. "I don't wanta get us any farther out in the open till I know which way we gotta go."

"I don't see anyone out there," said Frank, scanning the waves.

"We risked smashing *Napoli* to pieces for *no one?*"

"*Someone's* going to show up," said Joe. "They didn't shine that light just for the fun of it."

Frank looked to his left at the rocks east of the entrance. "We can see only half the ocean from where we are, with those in the way. Somebody might be coming from north of the point."

"The local crew, maybe," said Joe. "But if the house lookout's signaling to a freighter, it'd be coming from the south."

"So now what?" Tony asked. "Get outa here while we can?"

"Let's move down the shore," Frank suggested, his eyes on the horizon. "Close in, so we'll be harder to spot. If we can get back to where we were just before the window came into sight—"

"Hoping," Joe interjected, "that whoever's in the house is looking out to sea while we're getting there—"

"—then we'll be able to watch the entrance *and* keep an eye out for signals from the house."

"Okay with me," said Tony.

He accelerated smoothly and turned the wheel to starboard.

"That's good!" called Joe, studying what little he could see of the house through the binoculars.

Tony turned the *Napoli* until her bow was facing the end of the point. He put the throttle in neutral and switched off the engine. The *Napoli* settled down like a seabird, gently rising and falling with the waves.

Her crew stood and leaned on the windshield.

"You concentrate on the house, Frank," said Tony. "The two of us'll keep a sea lookout."

"I've been watching out there since we left the maze," Frank told him. He took the binoculars from Joe and peered through them at the house. "I haven't seen anyone—or an answering light."

"If there *was* an answer," said Joe, "it would've come while we were in the—"

"There it is again!" cried Frank.

Once more the powerful beam shone into the night. This time they could see where it originated—the second floor of the abandoned house.

"Now we know why those footprints led to that window," said Frank, trying to see past the screen of brilliantly backlit treetops.

"Yeah," said Joe. "And we know what that tripod was for."

The light went out.

"Maybe now we'll see some action out there," Tony remarked. "Glasses, please."

Without taking his eyes from the distant waves, he stretched out his hand and accepted the binoculars from Frank.

"There!" he exclaimed, pointing southeast.

He raised the binoculars to his eyes and turned the focusing knob.

On the horizon, a speck of light was shining. Then it was gone.

Tony lowered the binoculars. "It's a ways out, that's all I could tell. Moon or no moon, it's impossible to judge how far away a light is in darkness."

"Why would they shine those lights?" Joe asked, gazing at the horizon.

"To let each other know they're there," answered Frank, watching the house. "Or that they're ready."

60

"I mean, why would they risk someone *seeing* their signals? They could send radio messages, instead."

"If they did," responded Tony, his eyes on the far waves, "anyone with a radio set within miles of this place could intercept 'em."

"But anyone could've seen those *lights*!"

"The one at sea probably wouldn't mean anything ta anyone," Tony replied. "Us included, if we hadn't been looking for it. But the one from the *house*..."

"I'm sure," Frank said thoughtfully, "that whoever shone the light from the window took a good look around first, to see if anyone was out on the water. Maybe that's what the signals were for—to tell each other no one's in sight."

"Possibly, but—"

"It would be pretty obvious to anyone accidentally picking up radio communications that something peculiar was going on in the area—peculiar and *human*. Ghosts don't use radio transmitters. But they might shine a mysterious light."

"Ghosts?"

"That's who's supposed to be in that house."

"If somebody in a passing boat saw that light," Joe argued, "he'd *know* something weird was happening—whether or not he knew the Polucca place is said to be haunted."

"Yeah, but think it over. If he was far away, he wouldn't be able to see where the light was shining from, in the brief amount of time it'd be visible. And if he was close enough in to see where it came from, he might not believe what he'd seen."

Tony laughed. "*I* didn't believe it—and I was right *under* it!"

"Yeah, but still—"

"If," said Frank, "someone saw that light *and* saw where it came from, and was curious and ambitious enough to look for what made it, he'd go to where he thought it'd been and find . . ."

"An empty house."

"More likely," remarked Tony, "he'd go to the Coast Guard or the cops."

Frank chuckled. "They'd tell him they'd look into it, he would leave, and they'd laugh. Or they'd go out to the house and discover no source of any such light and no sign that anything of the sort had ever been there. And people would have one more story to tell about the old haunted house. And one more reason to stay away."

"Hear that?" asked Tony, turning his gaze from the horizon.

From somewhere near the end of the point came the faint sound of a slow-running powerboat engine. It was joined shortly by the sound of another engine, and then another.

Tony looked through the binoculars at the moonlit water and rocks.

"Here they come," he said, after about three minutes.

At the entrance to the maze, a light was glimmering. Then it vanished.

A vague shape, no more substantial than a shadow, moved rapidly away into the distance, heading southeast. The noise of its racing engine drifted over the waves to the *Napoli*.

"What is it?" Frank asked, squinting.

"A speedboat," Tony answered. "With a long, dark hull. The pilot had one spot turned on, aimed low. He shut it off as soon as he came out."

Like a firefly, another light danced between the rocks, then disappeared. Another shadow sped away. The sound of its powerful engine faded in the distance.

Another light glimmered and vanished; another shadow hurried into the night. The noise of its engine died away.

"That must be all," said Tony, after a minute or so. "Three of 'em." He lowered the binoculars and sat down.

"The smugglers *were* in the cave!" Joe exclaimed, staring at the maze entrance.

"I wonder," Frank remarked, as if to himself.

He sat, followed by his equally preoccupied brother.

"The boat pilots," Frank said slowly, "didn't go out after the first light we saw, or after the second light—they left soon after the *reply* to the second light. That must mean they were waiting for a reply. But if they were in the cave, how did they *see* it?"

"Yeah . . ." Tony frowned. "How could they?"

"Maybe," Joe suggested, "somebody radioed to them from the house."

Tony smiled and shook his head. "With all that rock in the way?"

"Another thing," said Frank. "If they were in the cave, why didn't they *hear* us? First we beat at their door and cheered, and then we made all that racket ripping out of there. But they went out in their boats, anyway, as if they hadn't heard a thing."

"If they were in there," Tony asserted, "they shoulda heard *something*. That canvas or whatever it is couldn't be that thick."

Frank looked up at the roof in the trees.

"What if the pilots were up *there*, in that house with thick stone walls and closed windows? Couldn't that explain why they were able to see the answering light and why they didn't respond to our noise?"

"How could they have been that far away?" Joe replied skeptically. "They left the cave only a few minutes after the reply to the second signal. We *know* that's where they were, because we saw and heard their boats coming out from the rocks."

"We don't know that's where they were a few minutes *before*."

"Well, if they weren't in the cave to begin with, how'd they get to it?"

"That's just what I've been wondering," said Frank. "If they were in the house—and that's the only possibility I can think of that makes sense—how did they get to the cave in such a short amount of time?"

Joe shook his head. "They couldn't have come from the house."

"They *must* have," Frank insisted. "There's no other explanation."

He paused, then added: "Unless there's something we're leaving out. Something we don't know about."

Joe gazed up at the house.

"I think it's time to take a good look at that place," he said slowly. "All of it—the whole property."

"Not now," objected Tony. "Not with all these crooks up and active."

"No, not tonight," said Frank. "In the morning."

"Speaking of morning," said Tony, looking at his watch, "I've gotta get up early for the produce run."

He gazed out to sea. "Also, those boys in the boats'll be back.

And when they return, they'll be looking this way, with their beady little eyes accustomed to the moonlight . . ."

"We've seen enough," said Frank. "Let's go home."

Tony started the engine and turned the *Napoli* around.

Slowly and quietly, she headed south.

Complications

"A car and a truck," said Joe, crouching at the entrance to the Polucca driveway.

He looked up from the marks in the dry, partly shaded soil to the late-morning sun shining through the treetops. Then he looked down again. "Made yesterday, I'd say."

Running past him in the dirt were the overlapping impressions of two designs of tire tread. One track was wide, with a complex pattern of diamonds and parallelograms. Partially obliterated by it was a narrower one consisting of straight lines alternating with short, angled cross-lines.

Both sets passed over the narrow tracks—faint, washed-out impressions going in, and deeper, sloppier ones coming out—left by the boys' motorcycles two days before.

Joe pointed to the car tire impression. "The car drove in first, then the truck." His finger followed two adjacent overlapping tracks. "The car went out, came back . . ." He put his finger on a wide uppermost track shallower than the first. "Then the truck left."

He stood and looked down the driveway. "The car must still be here."

Frank crouched down nearby and examined the ground.

"The truck's back," he said.

He pointed to where a faint truck-tire track ran over the better-defined one Joe had put his finger on.

"Uh-oh," Joe remarked, staring down at the feeble track. "Someone got up a little earlier than we did."

"It's good we hid the bikes," said Frank, standing. "Let's make sure *we* aren't spotted."

He picked up a fallen pine branch and brushed away their footprints.

They started toward the house, walking cautiously through the vegetation along the left edge of the driveway, watching as they went to make sure they left no signs of their presence.

Frank looked up, nudged Joe, and pointed ahead.

The clumps of grass and weeds they'd driven around had been cut down.

"Hey!" Joe said softly. "Maybe there *is* a caretaker!"

Before the final bend, they left the driveway and moved from tree to tree until they could see the turnaround.

There the invading vegetation had been cut away, as well.

In front of the house sat a large, dark-blue, unlabeled moving van and an unusually long, silver, four-door automobile with graceful, sweeping fenders and running boards, whitewall tires, and chromed wire wheels. Both vehicles had New York license plates.

Four rough-looking men were unloading furniture from the van, supervised by a man in his late twenties or early thirties wearing a charcoal pinstripe suit.

"A Packard Twelve!" Joe exclaimed, in as quiet a voice as he could manage, as he and Frank knelt behind a tree. "Seven-passenger Touring Sedan. Suicide doors in back, standard in front—must be a '37. Great year for Packards!"

"Never mind the car. Take a look at Mister Fashion Plate."

The young man in the pinstripe suit was tall and strikingly handsome, with dark, slicked-down hair. His posture, movements, and voice had an unmistakable air of authority. Although his hands were idle, his eyes were busy, taking in the scene before him in quick shifts of focus and attention.

"I'll bet that's the owner," Joe said quietly. "Alex Polucca."

"What do you make of him?"

"Good-looking—in a too-smooth way. He looks as if he hasn't done a day of physical work in his life."

"No tan," said Frank, "for someone with hair that dark. He must stay indoors."

"He looks like a high-class salesman."

"With those sneaky eyes?"

"Yeah, I see what you mean."

"He looks smart."

"Cunning."

"Cunning enough," asked Frank, "to be part of a smuggling network?"

"To me, he looks cunning enough to be the boss."

"He's too young for that. But he may be *one* of the bosses. If there're more like him in the organization, I can understand why they haven't been caught. I'll bet things're going to tighten up around here now—no more ghost tricks and sloppy sweeping to hide what they're doing."

Joe struck the tree shielding them with his fist. "What rotten luck! He's moving in just when we come back to take a good look at the place!"

Frank frowned. "Doesn't that seem like a little too much of a coincidence?"

"What else could it be?"

"The long-absent owner shows up," Frank said slowly and reflectively, "shortly after we go through his empty house." He paused. "But other people have come out here. Why would *we* have made anybody nervous? Because we went inside and saw some funny marks in the dust? Why would a successful gang of smugglers worry about some teenage haunted-house tourists like us—unless . . ."

He turned away and stared into the distance.

"Yeah. That must be it."

"What?"

"My jacket. Someone examined my jacket."

"What's that got to do with this?"

Frank turned back. "My name's on the label."

"So what?" asked Joe. "What's important about the name *Frank Hardy?*"

His brother smiled.

"Nothing's important about the *Frank*," he answered. "But something's important about the *Hardy*."

"Oh. Yeah."

"Seems pretty likely, doesn't it?"

"So now they're making things look aboveboard, in case anyone comes around to investigate, tipped off by the son of Fenton Hardy."

Frank chuckled. "It's becoming clearer all the time, isn't it?"

"What do we do now? This moving-in business is going to keep us from getting into the house and searching around outside."

"Then we'll look in the garage."

"Huh?"

Frank regarded the empty-looking structure with the slid-open door. "I'm glad they haven't put anything in it. And I hope they don't."

"Why?"

"Because I want to look for something."

"But there's nothing *in* there."

"That's why I want to look there."

"Talk sense. If there's nothing in the garage—"

"Then why would someone move a motorcycle that was parked in it?"

"Why, indeed?"

"People don't do things like that without a reason," said Frank. "Maybe it was in the way."

"In the way of what?"

"I'm not sure. I have an idea, but I can't say for certain until we look inside."

"How are we going to, with all these people around?"

"I don't know. Things're getting a little complicated."

"Let's call a conference," said Joe. "We haven't told the others what happened last night. And we need to let them know about this, too. I can phone Chet, and—"

"And he'll tell everybody." Frank laughed softly. "Oh, well—that'll save *us* the bother. Just remind him not to mention anything to people who aren't in on the secret."

"Right. And we can all meet this afternoon, at Thayer's."

Help Wanted

The jukebox was playing Francis Craig's piano-boogie introduction to "Near You" as Frank and Joe entered the soda fountain in the back of Thayer's Pharmacy.

The seats were empty, except for the large corner booth, in which Biff and Chet were sipping milkshakes with two girls.

"Well, well," said Frank, as he caught sight of the group. "Callie's here!"

"Yeah," Joe replied. "And *Iola*," he added grimly.

"She likes you."

"Don't rub it in."

"Late to your own party!" Biff scolded, shaking his finger at the brothers as they approached the booth.

"That's all right," remarked Chet, stirring his milkshake. "*They're* paying."

"Hi," said Frank to Callie Shaw, an attractive girl with long, wavy auburn hair sitting in the near end seat.

She smiled and moved over to make room for him beside her.

"And how's Iola?" Frank addressed to the freckle-faced redhead with a ponytail sitting next to Callie. Attractive in her own pixielike fashion, she looked like a slender, feminine version of her older brother, Chet.

"Peachy, Frank," Iola replied pleasantly as he sat down.

She gave the younger Hardy a radiant smile. "Hello, Joe."

"Uh—hi," Joe managed to reply, as he slid into the seat beside Chet at the other end of the booth.

A thin, balding man dressed in gray slacks, white shoes and shirt, and a pharmacist's jacket emerged from the front room and walked over to the group. He dropped his chin and peered over his rimless glasses.

"Well, *Hah*days," he said to the newcomers. "What's yo-ah *plez*ah?"

"A strawberry shake," Joe replied.

"Vanilla for me, Mr. Thayer," said Frank.

The pharmacist went behind the counter and started mixing the milkshakes.

"Where's Ernie?" Joe called to him.

"*Fetch*in' somethin' at the *d*epot," Mr. Thayer answered. "Soda business was slow. Always *is*, 'bout this *tah*yum. Ernie was lookin' *bo*ahd. So I told 'im I'd take *ov*ah."

He carried two glasses and drinking straws to the booth and set them down on the table.

"How ah the in*ves*tigatahs?" he asked, looking over his glasses at Frank, then Joe. "Keepin' outah *mis*chief?"

"So far," Frank answered, a bit coolly.

"But summer's just beginning," added Joe with a grin.

"Feels as if it's been around *he*ah a long *tah*yum," Mr. Thayer replied, waving his arm at the soda fountain's two whirling, pole-mounted fans as he headed back to the milkshake machines.

"Your *fath*ah was in *eh*lier," he informed the brothers as he poured the thick liquid into the glasses.

He slid the glasses to their proper places and put the half-full milkshake containers in the center of the table.

"He had a *pick*chah. *Ug*ly fellah." The pharmacist chuckled dryly. "The *pick*chah, that is—not your *fath*ah. A man he was lookin' *fo*ah, he said. Wanted to know if I'd *seen* 'im. Said I hadn't, and didn't *kay*ah to."

Mr. Thayer scanned the faces in the booth. "If you want somethin' *mo*ah, just *hah*lah."

71

He returned to the front of the store.

"Yes," said Callie, in answer to Frank's questioning look. "Chet told us."

"And yes," added Iola, "we'll keep your secret."

She glanced around the table. *"Do any of you rinky-dinks know what you're getting into?"*

The boys laughed nervously.

"I mean it!" Iola declared. "Any and all of you could end up in the morgue!"

"They're smugglers," Joe retorted, stirring his milkshake. "Not murderers."

"How can you be certain of that?" asked Callie. "You don't know who they are, or what they might do."

The brothers looked at each other uneasily.

"Whoever they are and whatever they might do," Frank said evasively, "this is our chance to show what *we* can do."

He took a long sip of milkshake.

"The people in this town," Joe contributed, "always think we're just fooling around—playing detective. But now we have an opportunity to change their attitude."

"The police," asserted Frank, "haven't a clue about what's going on out on the point. If we told them what we've seen, they'd laugh."

"Are you sure?" Callie asked.

"Who'd care to bet," inquired Joe, looking around the table, "that we could talk Chief Collig or any of his policemen into taking a boat ride through those rocks to see a secret cave?"

No one spoke.

"At best," remarked Frank, "they'd go to the house, poke around, find nothing suspicious, tell Alex Polucca what we'd told them, apologize heartily, and leave."

"After which, the crooks'd move their operation to who-knows-where in the middle of the night."

"We want to get something more on these people," said Frank, "before we tell anybody what we've seen."

"Why not tell your father right now?" Iola asked. *"He'll* believe you."

"We were going to tell him this morning," Joe said to her. "But then we talked things over. We concluded that what we've discovered so far could be discounted as lucky guesswork and being in the right place at the right time. There's not much merit in that. So we decided to go one step further and find out something that can't be discounted. Frank thinks he can manage that."

Callie frowned. "It sounds dangerous. Very dangerous."

"It won't be," Frank assured her, "if we're careful. We need to come up with a safe way to examine what we need to at the Polucca place. That's why we're asking for everyone's suggestions."

"Where's Phil?" asked Joe, looking around. "And Jerry?"

"On their way to a campout," Chet answered. "It seems that Scoutmaster Campbell asked them a couple of weeks ago to help him educate the younger generation for a few days."

"Fine timing!" Joe exclaimed bitterly. "And Tony's working . . ."

"We won't need them," Chet said airily.

He made a loud *slurp* through his straw, then pushed his empty glass aside.

"I have a plan," he announced grandly.

Iola groaned. "*Please*, Chet. I'm trying to digest this milkshake."

Chet looked at her in disgust.

"Sisters," he stated firmly, "should be seen and not heard. Better yet, not *seen*."

Frank tapped the table in front of the distracted schemer. "What's your plan?"

Chet returned his attention to the matter at hand. "Well, it's like this. You want to get into the Polucca house, right?"

"Not exactly. I want to look at the inside of the garage."

"Oh, yes. The garage. Joe told me, but I forgot. Well, to each his own."

"And," said Frank, "going over it at night won't work. Anyone in the house could see our flashlights, with that door wide open."

"Slide it shut."

"Right. And wake up everybody."

"Anyway," Chet went on, "someone needs to distract Alex Polucca, and whoever else may be there moving furniture or lurking in the shadows, while you two do your investigating."

"Sounds good, so far. And how—"

"Don't rush me. So Biff and I go to the house and tell Mr. Polucca that we have a class assignment—"

"In summer?" Biff interrupted.

"Summer school," said Chet, still looking at Frank. "We have an assignment to study historic houses in Bayport—"

"The Polucca property isn't *in* Bayport," Biff pointed out.

"Close enough. And when he lets us in—"

"Why should he?"

"And when he lets us in . . ." Chet turned to Biff. "Well? Aren't you going to interrupt?"

"Go on," said Frank. "Then what?"

Chet turned back to him. "Then we distract Mr. Polucca and his sinister friends by asking questions about the historic house, while you two scour the garage for footprints or whatever you're looking for. Maybe we can even do some sleuthing of our own."

Chet pointed his thumb at the wall behind him and called to an imaginary person across the room: *"Say, Mr. Polucca—are there any secret passages in this house that could be used by smugglers?"*

"Blabbermouth," said Joe. "You'd get your head blown off."

Biff sighed. "No one would notice any difference."

"There's one thing wrong with any of you trying to carry out that plan," Callie remarked.

"What's that?" asked Frank, turning to her with interest.

"Whoever scared you away probably saw what all of you look like."

"Yes . . ." responded Frank, considering the point. "I'll bet he did."

"Whether anyone got a good look at us or not," said Joe, "they'll be suspicious of *any* boys who show up there now."

"They haven't seen Iola or me," Callie pointed out. "And why would they suspect *us*? We could appear on Alex Polucca's doorstep carrying our sketchbooks and ask his permission to draw the house. Then we could keep him away from the garage with a lot of questions and small talk while—"

"Hold on," Frank interjected. "A little while ago, you said the

74

situation is dangerous. It certainly *would* be for you two, if you were to try something like that."

"Oh, I'm not saying it wouldn't be dangerous. But any attempt the two of you might make to get into the garage would be a good deal *less* dangerous if we were there."

"What makes you so sure of that?"

"Reasoning. *Alex Polucca* is supposed to be the new resident, not a gang of smugglers. He wouldn't want visitors to see any of his henchmen. So he'll keep them out of sight. Therefore, they'll be less likely to see *you*."

"Oh, they'll be around. Watching from an upstairs window, as likely as not."

"If they are," put in Iola, "I'll bet they'd rather watch *us* than an old *garage*."

"*Oh,* "said Chet, a wide grin on his face. "So now *you* want to participate, too!"

"Well . . . *Maybe*."

"If the other men are there," asserted Callie, "they'll be hiding. From us, from you, from everybody. Alex Polucca's the real danger."

"Maybe, but—"

"And he wouldn't be any more likely to harm us innocent visiting girls than the others would. Anything of the sort would destroy his facade of respectability—and he has everything to lose if that happens."

"*Facade* is all it is," Joe insisted. "Frank's right—it's too risky. Alex Polucca and crew may well be desperate to keep up appearances. But that wouldn't necessarily stop them from doing whatever they liked to you and then getting rid of you at sea with the next load of stolen drugs."

"They wouldn't be very likely to try," replied Callie. "They'd risk their entire operation if they did. As insurance, we could mention to Mr. Polucca that our art teacher had recommended a few hours before that we draw the house—"

"But even so—"

"—and that our big, strong boyfriends would be dropping by later on to fetch us."

"After playing a little summer football," Iola added helpfully.

She closed her eyes and smiled dreamily. "I can see them now. They're *much* bigger than you boys. Good-looking, too."

She opened her eyes and turned to Callie.

"Frank and Joe could take us out there on their motorcycles," she said, warming to Callie's idea. "They could sneak through the woods to the garage, getting tired and dirty, while you and I sashay down the driveway to the house, getting the attention we so richly deserve."

"It would be better," suggested Callie, "if Chet were to drive the four of us to the area in his car and hide somewhere. If Frank and Joe took us and then were caught, we couldn't handle those motorcycles. If Chet were there and the rest of us got into trouble, he could go for the police."

Everyone looked at one another.

"Well," said Frank, "if Chet was there to go for help . . ."

"With that safeguard added," said Joe, "it's not so bad. Yeah. Not bad."

"It sounds like a pretty good plan," Biff commented. "Aside from the possibility that all of you could be killed, and one or two other minor points."

"There's one more thing," said Callie. "We ought to give the furniture movers or whoever they are time enough to finish their job and leave—"

"Or hide under the sofa," Iola interjected.

"Then Mr. Polucca will be indoors, settling in, and we'll have an easier time keeping him out of sight of the garage."

"How long do you think it'll take those men to unload that truck?" Biff asked Frank.

"Another hour or two, probably. Maybe longer. It wouldn't be safe to go back today."

"Let's go tomorrow morning," Joe urged.

"What if two loads of furniture aren't enough," asked Chet, "and they come back to deliver some more while you're snooping around?"

"It was a large van," Frank replied. "Large enough that it cut corners and scraped trees getting in. And the way they were pulling things out of it made it look as if they'd packed it as full as they could. Still, it's a big house . . ."

"We don't want to waste time," said Joe. "Let's just assume that two loads'll do it. If we get there and find the truck again, we'll leave and return later. And if it comes while we're—

"To be safe," said Iola. "How about tomorrow afternoon?"

Frank, Joe, and Chet exchanged glances. Chet shrugged. Joe nodded.

"Tomorrow afternoon," said Frank.

"Trumpet Blues" by the Harry James band blared down at Evelyn Hardy as she called up the stairs, a few minutes before dinner.

"Boys! Someone wants to speak with you on the telephone!"

Joe passed his brother's open door on the way to the upstairs phone.

"Put the mute on Harry!" he shouted.

He picked up the receiver.

"I've got it, Mother!" he yelled. *"Frank!"*

The music stopped.

"Hello?" Joe spoke into the receiver. "Sorry about the shouting."

There was a click on the line as the kitchen phone was hung up.

"Joe?" asked a familiar voice.

"Yessir. At your service."

"Joe—Chief Collig. Listen, I've just received a call from Special Agent Anderson, at the FBI. We've got some very interesting news for you."

"Oh—you do, do you?"

Joe turned to wink at Frank, who had joined him. He put his hand over the mouthpiece.

"Chief Collig," he whispered.

"It seems," continued the chief, "that those fingerprints you boys picked up on North Shore belong to Ivan Slovacic—known to some of us as Ivan the Terrible."

Joe laughed.

"*Ivan the Terrible?* What is he—a grand prince?"

"Not yet. And he probably won't ever be anything of the sort, considering that he can't keep out of trouble."

Joe laughed again. "Ivan the *Terrible?*"

"Don't blame me—someone else gave him the title. He's earned it, though. A nastier customer you wouldn't care to meet."

"Are we talking about a big-time crook or—"

"No, his nickname's due more to his personality than to his deeds. They're nothing outstanding—mostly petty stuff. But the potential for criminal greatness is there. Along with a rotten disposition. Shyster lawyers love him. Nobody else does."

"No bank robberies or anything like—"

"No. The latest charge against him was *receiving stolen goods.* About a year ago. He got out of that one."

Joe smiled.

"Mind you," the chief went on, "there's nothing illegal about him putting his greasy paws on Frank's motorcycle—if that's all he was doing, and we can't prove otherwise at this point. But we'll be on the lookout for him, just the same. Where Ivan goes, trouble surely is a-lurking.

"By the way," he added, "Alex Polucca started moving into his inherited house yesterday. He stopped in to see me. With him around, Ivan isn't very likely to return to the scene. But I'm sending a couple of the boys out, anyway, to warn Alex that he was reported in the area and to take a look around. We're far more likely to find that no-good in town, though, in one of the rough spots."

"I suppose so."

"The FBI's wiring me a photograph of the little darling. Drop by the station in the morning, and I'll give you a copy. A souvenir of your adventure."

"Will do, Chief."

"Be seeing you."

Joe hung up the receiver and smiled at Frank.

"The chief got I.D. on those fingerprints." He laughed. "They belong to some bad dream named—"

"Ivan the Terrible." Frank smiled.

"He's sending a couple of boys in blue out to Polucca's, to peek in the bushes and warn Mister Slick that Ivan's been there."

Frank frowned. "He'll probably ask them how they can be sure a criminal was on the property and how they know who it was— and they'll tell him about the fingerprints on the motorcycle. *My* motorcycle. And then he'll *know* we're trouble for him."

"It can't be helped," Joe replied, shrugging. "He knows it already, if he's as smart as we think he is. But I wonder if the police'll notice anything suspicious when they drop in on him."

"They won't," said Frank. "They'll be looking for a little crook, not a big one."

He paused, then added: "Even if they suspected Alex Polucca of harboring a criminal, they wouldn't know where to look for evidence. But maybe *I* do."

Hiding Place

"What kind of car is this, Chet?" Callie called from the middle of the back seat of the Duchess—trying to be heard over the band on the radio—as Frank and Joe, their two accomplices, and their chauffeur sped up North Shore Road in the midafternoon heat.

"That's hard to say!" Chet yelled in reply.

He reached over and turned down the pounding of "Back Beat Boogie."

"It's a little of everything," he added, in a quieter voice.

He lifted his hand from the volume knob and pointed. "Surrounding us, a Ford body of excellent vintage. Up front, a bored-out Cadillac V-8. Out back, a modified Ford rear end. And in between, some of the finest parts that anyone ever scrounged off—"

"I mean, what's it *called?* Don't cars like this have some sort of name?"

"Junk buckets," Iola suggested.

"Before the war," replied Chet, ignoring his sister in the back seat, "they were called 'hop-ups' or 'hot irons.' Now they're called 'hot rods.' "

"What does that mean?"

"Low and fast," answered Joe, looking out the open left rear window at the trees racing past.

"I hate to interrupt this intellectual discussion—" began Iola.

"Then don't," said Chet.

"—but I've been thinking."

"That won't get you anywhere."

"Might there be some way to prove that the Polucca house is hiding a smuggling operation, and that Frank and Joe deserve full credit for dicovering that, *without* them risking their necks?"

Frank turned around in the front seat to answer her. "We could go to the power company and ask how much electricity has been used there lately. Or we could get the numbers off the house meter and ask someone to translate them. That light we saw must burn a lot of power. And any amount they used would register."

"But that wouldn't work," Joe pointed out, "if they managed to reset the meter. And I'll bet they did."

"We could also do some inquiring at the telephone company. There's probably a connected phone somewhere in the house, with long-distance bills run up on it for calls to New York City."

"Unless they called collect."

"But none of that," Frank said, "would prove anything. Even if we could find people who'd be willing to answer our questions."

"Which wouldn't be very likely."

"Alex Polucca could just say that he or some friends stopped in or stayed there a few times and used the phone and the electricity."

He paused thoughtfully, then added: "There's another problem with that approach—we're the sons of Fenton Hardy."

"The Hardy boys," said Joe. "Local snoops."

"And if we—"

"Or our friends—"

"—go around asking nosy questions, we'll draw attention to what we're doing, without being able to demonstrate that what we've learned means anything. Asking Chief Collig to identify those fingerprints was risky enough. If we talk to more people, the story'll spread all over town. This *is* Bayport, you know."

" 'TOWN GOSSIP TIPS OFF CROOKS,' " Joe pretended to read from an imaginary newspaper.

"Or," said Frank, " 'NO CRIMINAL ACTIVITY FOUND IN POLUCCA HOUSE. LOCAL BOYS LOOK STUPID.' "

"And how will you look," asked Iola, "if someone hits you over the head with a monkey wrench?"

Frank smiled. "Well, it's your job to make sure no one does."

"Coming up on our left, ladies and gentlemen," Chet announced, "is the first stop on our tour, the delightful Olsen residence. Often overlooked but well worth a visit. Within easy walking distance of the famous Polucca House of Horror."

"*How* easy?" Iola asked dubiously.

"Above Olsen's," Frank answered, "there's a fairly short, straight bit of road, a long curve to the left, a short one to the right, and a long straight stretch."

"That's easy?"

"You'll love the Olsen estate," Chet continued, slowing the Duchess for a curve. "Antique atmosphere. Rural charm. Nice secluded parking."

"There's a dead-end side road just beyond Polucca's," Joe told Iola. "That's the only other place around here to hide a car. But if we put the Duchess there, she could be seen by someone passing by."

About a hundred feet past the curve, Chet brought the Duchess almost to a stop, then cautiously steered her into a gap in the trees on the left.

Ahead, beyond a thick carpet of roadside vegetation that obscured its beginning, lay a long-neglected, deeply rutted dirt driveway.

Leaning out the window, Chet steered the left front tire onto the wide, grassy center strip, then accelerated slightly.

The Duchess moved slowly and awkwardly forward, her hood ornament centered over the right-hand rut.

"Golly!" Callie exclaimed, looking around. "What a mare's nest!"

At the end of the long driveway, each side of which was paralleled by a dilapidated wooden slide-rail fence, stood the fire-blackened remains of what once had been a farmhouse.

To the right beyond the house, behind a short surviving section of fence, was a large, faded-red barn with a collapsing roof.

Attached to the right end of the barn, facing away from the driveway, was a long, slightly less decrepit equipment shed, painted green.

Saplings and grass, the long stalks of the latter bent to the ground by the recent heavy rain, filled the long-abandoned fields.

"*Secluded parking* for sure," Iola commented with a shudder.

Frank pointed to a grove of oak trees in the field on the right. "We can put her back in there. Then no one on North Shore'll be able to see her."

"That *sounds* easy," Chet said skeptically.

He stopped the Duchess and cast a wary eye over the ground between the driveway and the trees. He sighed. "After all the work I went through to lower this car . . ."

Frank got out and walked ahead.

"It's flatter here," he called, pointing to a higher part of the driveway.

At the high spot, Chet carefully steered the Duchess across the now-shallow right-hand rut as Frank slid the rails from a section of the fence.

The Duchess passed regally through the gap, then waited, her engine rumbling.

Frank kicked the car-flattened grass in front of the fence this way and that to match the bent and tangled growth around it. Then he slipped the rails into place and returned to the car.

"May I see those pictures again?" Callie asked, as the Duchess came to a halt in the shade of the trees.

Frank handed two photographs to her.

The first showed a wizened face with thick eyebrows, large ears, and deep lines around a wide mouth.

"That's Oscar," said Joe. "Chimpanzee gone bad."

The face in the second photograph was long and narrow, with a prominent forehead, deep-set eyes, and a mouth like a straight line.

"And that's Ivan. The man Dr. Frankenstein put together after practicing on the first one."

Iola took the photos from Callie, stared at them, and frowned.

"They don't look any better the second time," she remarked.

"You told us there were four men in the moving crew at the house . . ." Callie began.

"That's right," Frank replied.

"Were these two among them?"

"No. Unfortunately."

"So if those four are in the local end of the gang, and these two are, as well, there are at least six men—"

"Seven," said Joe. "Don't forget Pretty Boy."

"The movers weren't necessarily local," said Frank. "A moving-company van can have a state's license plates on it without the load it's carrying coming from that state. But the van at Polucca's was unlabeled, which means it's privately owned, and it had New York plates. So New York's most likely where it came from, along with the driver and possibly one or two men to help unload. With luck, whoever arrived with the truck's gone by now."

"On the other hand," Chet cautioned, "Alex Polucca might've brought someone with him in his car. Someone who might still be there."

"It takes three men to pilot those speedboats," said Frank. "So there are at least that many local gang members. Four, with you-know-who."

"In other words," said Joe, "there could be four, five, six, seven . . ." He shrugged his shoulders.

Frank looked at Callie. "Want to back out while you can?"

"No," Callie replied with a thin smile.

She ran a hand through her hair. "If I'm right, there won't be anyone but Alex Polucca to worry about."

"And if you're *not* right," Iola remarked philosophically, "there *will* be."

She opened her door and stepped onto the running board and then into the field. Wearing a sly look, she turned and gazed in the direction of the Polucca house.

"Watch out, Tough Boys," she warned her imagined adversaries. "Here come the Gangbuster Girls."

She gave a coy smile and curtsied. "Escapades. Tomfoolery. Razzmatazz."

Visitors

"Fools rush in, where angels fear to tread—"

"Sing softer," Frank cautioned his brother, who was walking quickly behind him alongside the Polucca driveway.

Both wore rubber-soled tennis shoes. A pair of binoculars hung from Frank's neck.

"Sorry." Joe lowered his voice. *"And so I come to you, my love, my heart above my head . . .* You know, we'll need to check all those windows before we make a dash for the garage."

Without answering or looking back, Frank held up the binoculars.

"Yes, you're prepared. *Although I see the danger there—"* Joe halted suddenly to avoid a collision.

"What's the matter?" he asked.

Frank stood staring down at the soft, perpetually shaded soil at the edge of the driveway, in which were the overlapping impressions of two automobile tires.

"It's just the Packard," Joe remarked, after a glance.

"Look closer," Frank admonished him.

The Packard's straight line/angled line tire track passed over an unfamiliar one, the discernible part of which was made of zigzag lines.

"Some detectives *we* are," grumbled Frank. "We saw the truck's exit tracks—because they were the only tracks we were looking for—and missed *that!"*

"There it is again," said Joe, pointing.

A foot over from the first track was a fainter but complete tire impression consisting entirely of zigzag lines.

"Some car we haven't seen. Two sets. It drove in, drove out."

"And then the Packard came through." Frank pointed ahead to where its track, having passed over the first unidentified track, ran over the second, as well.

"I wonder if it was leaving or arriving," he said, surveying the various impressions.

"Come on," Joe said impatiently. "Let's find out."

When the brothers had worked their way to a clear view of the turnaround, they saw the Packard, conspicuous and alone, parked in front of the house.

"Boss Man's here," Joe said quietly, as they hid behind a tree. "At least, his car is."

Frank looked toward the garage, then made a choking sound.

Both sliding doors were closed.

"Oh, that's great!" Joe exclaimed bitterly, staring at what had caused the reaction. "We're shut out, and Callie and Iola'll be here in a few minutes!"

Frank studied the front of the garage. "No lock. It should be okay. If we can slide the left door open a crack, get in, and close it without being seen—"

"Or heard—"

"—then we'll be all right."

"They'll have forty-five minutes," Callie reminded Iola as the two sketchbook-carrying beguilers walked quickly up the driveway. "Starting the moment we coax Alex Polucca out of sight of the garage."

"They could have made it longer," Iola commented disdainfully. "They thought we'd lose his attention."

"Forty-five minutes ought to be long enough for them to find whatever it is they're looking for and get away. That's a long time

86

to keep someone from looking in a certain direction. Especially someone like the man we're going to be encountering."

"We'll be here sketching the house for an hour and a half after that, anyway."

"Just to look authentic. We'll need to concentrate on drawing, then—not on Alex Polucca. So we can finish, say good-bye, and get back to the car—"

"By three hours and five minutes from now," said Iola, glancing at her watch. "At the latest."

"And if we haven't shown up by then, Chet'll go for the police."

"If he's still awake. He looked pretty *comfortable* stretched out on the back seat."

"It's better to have him wait there," said Callie, "than to have him wait here and risk getting caught."

"I guess."

Iola thought for a while. "But it'd be just like him to fall asleep when we—"

"There it is," announced Callie, clutching her sketchbook tighter as the house came into view. "What a creepy-crawly old—"

Iola stopped and stared at the garage.

"Holy Mother of Trouble!" she exclaimed. "The garage doors are shut! What do we do now?"

"Just keep going," Callie replied without stopping. "And don't look at the garage. Someone may be watching."

"Righto, dearie!" said Iola cheerfully.

She caught up with Callie, swinging her sketchbook and herself with it. "Knock 'em dead!"

The front door swung open.

Alex Polucca, dressed in clean, stylish work clothes, looked in surprise from one attractive visitor to the other.

"Hello," he said, breaking into a smile. "This must be my lucky day!"

"Mr. Polucca?" asked Callie.

"Yes, indeed."

"My name is Callie Shaw. And this—"

Iola gave Alex a dimpled smile.

"—is Iola Morton. We're in Mr. Buchanan's summer art class at Bayport High. He's an admirer of this house, and this morning he suggested that we come out here and draw it."

"Some friends dropped us off," contributed Iola, "on their way to play some summer football. They wanted to get in two or three hours of mayhem before coming back to pick us up."

Alex, clearly captivated by the human-size female pixie before him, nodded. "I see."

"Would it be all right," inquired Callie, "if we made one or two drawings and asked you a couple of questions?"

"Absolutely," answered Alex, with a smile. "I'd be delighted."

"We were hoping," said Iola, beaming at him, "that you could give us a tour of the house."

Between the Lines

"So far, so good," Joe said softly as he squeezed inside.

Frank slid the garage door shut behind him.

"Oiled rollers," he remarked quietly. "*That's* a surprise."

"Yeah—how about that. Boy, it's hot and stuffy in here!"

"And dark."

Frank felt along the wall, located the old round light switch he'd noticed on his way in, and turned it.

Two bulbs in the ceiling lit up.

"Step softly," Frank cautioned. "And keep your voice down."

"In case someone walks by?" inquired Joe.

"That's one reason," Frank answered cryptically.

"It's a good thing there aren't any windows," he commented, looking from one solid wall to another.

"Isn't that kind of strange?" Joe asked, glancing around. "A garage without windows?"

"It'll make sense if we find what I'm looking for."

"I suppose it's silly to ask . . . But what *are* you looking for?"

"Two straight lines."

"Right—two straight lines. Makes perfect sense. So where might they be?"

"Where my bike was, before somebody moved it."

Frank walked quietly to the middle of the right half of the garage, turned, and gazed down at the floorboards—wide planks of greatly varying lengths—running toward the rear wall.

Looking perplexed, Joe walked over to join him.

"Notice anything unusual about the floor?" Frank asked.

Joe looked down and laughed.

From wall to wall, the boards had been swept clean.

"No, nothing *unusual*. It's like most of the floors around here. They did a better job on this one, though. They got rid of the motorcycle tracks and our muddy footprints."

"And the footprints of whoever moved my bike," Frank said distractedly, running his eyes up and down the boards. "Nuts. The ends don't line up anywhere."

"You're searching for a *trapdoor*! Now I get it!"

"Well, *I* don't get it. If there's a door here, where's its forward edge, and its rear edge?"

Joe stared at the boards.

"Maybe you're looking in the wrong direction," he said shortly.

He turned to face the right wall and pointed his toe at the near edge of a board.

"Let's say this is the front edge, and over there—" He took a few steps forward and tapped his toe on the far edge of another board. "—is the back edge."

"But a door has to have a *left* edge and a *right* edge!" Frank said irritably, gazing along the floor. "So we're back to where we started, because the board ends would have to line up to form those edges!"

"Why?" Joe asked.

Frank looked up to answer, then stopped, lost in thought.

"That's right!" he said. "Only the rear edge—the *hinged* edge—has to be straight!"

"So look for hinges."

Frank removed the binoculars from his neck and placed them on the floor. Then he pulled a flashlight from his pocket, turned toward the rear wall, stepped back a few feet, and stretched out face downward. He switched the flashlight on and ran its beam along a crack.

"The hinge pins couldn't be far down," he said, "or the door wouldn't open."

"Look in a *wide* crack," Joe suggested, walking toward the right wall and scanning the floor.

"How about that one?" He pointed to a crack near the wall.

Frank slid over and shone the light into the gap between the boards. Then he got to his knees and crawled forward, watching closely.

"There's one!" he softly exclaimed. "Painted black."

Joe knelt beside him and ran a fingertip along the top of the nearly invisible hinge.

Frank crawled slowly onward. "Here's another one . . . And another . . . And another . . ."

He stopped. "Four of them. About fifteen inches apart."

He switched the flashlight off and put it in his pocket. Then he looked to his left across the boards.

"A handle," he muttered. "Some sort of handle . . ."

At practically the instant Frank saw it, Joe noticed a large knothole, about six feet from the hinges, centered between the first hinge and the last.

Both lunged for it; Frank reached it first.

"Look out," he said, motioning Joe aside.

Both boys moved quickly but quietly around on their knees to face the apparent front edge of the door.

Frank put two fingers in the hole and pulled upward. A very irregularly-sided five-foot-by-six-foot section of the floor ahead of him rose slightly. He immediately pushed it down.

"The lights!" he hissed. "And no noise!"

Joe got to his feet, stepped softly to a switch on the right wall by the door, and turned it off. He took a flashlight from his pocket, switched it on, and stepped softly back to the trapdoor. He knelt and switched off the flashlight.

Frank raised the door a couple of inches. The warm glow of electric light shone up through the crack.

The brothers listened attentively for a few seconds but heard no sound from below.

As Frank lifted the door a few inches higher, Joe put his flashlight in his pocket, lay down on the floor, and peeked over the forward edge of the opening.

He saw a long, wide wooden stairway leading down toward the house, all but a narrow center strip of which was covered with plywood to form a ramp.

He motioned Frank to lift the door higher.

On a slight pull, it swung smoothly and silently to a nearly vertical position.

Joe lowered himself into the hole by walking his hands down the top seven steps. He looked around, then pushed himself back up, rose to his knees, and said quietly: "There's a tunnel running to the house—or maybe a bit to the left of it. There's no one there."

Frank pointed below the hinged edge of the trapdoor where hung two iron weights, each at the end of a bent pipe attached to a rear corner brace.

"Counterbalanced," he said. "For easy lifting."

He pointed to the floorboards extending unevenly beyond the side edges of the underbracing of the door.

Each board end was several inches longer or shorter than its neighbor. No two lined up.

"Who would know those formed a trapdoor?" Frank asked. "Clever, eh?"

"You bet. Whoever built this knew what he was doing."

"The Poluccas must be a pretty creative family."

"Yeah—too bad they've got a few screws loose in the *ethics* department."

Frank stood up, hurriedly retrieved his binoculars, and walked quickly back to the opening in the floor.

"I'm going down there," he said.

"That's like stepping into a goblin's lair, isn't it?" Joe remarked.

He got to his feet and looked at his watch. "Besides, we have to be out of here in thirty-four minutes."

"Then let's not waste any time."

Frank put his foot on the top step and looked at his brother. "Coming?"

"What do *you* think?" Joe replied, grinning.

Putting a finger to his lips, Frank started quietly down the steps.

As Joe descended the stairs after him, he pushed up on one of the counterbalance weights.

Like a large piece of jigsaw puzzle, the hinged section of floor slipped silently back into place.

Goblins' Lair

The brothers saw before them a gently downward-sloping, cement-floored tunnel about eight feet in width and height, constructed of thick wooden beams and pillars and heavy-looking planking. Just above their heads, dimly glowing light bulbs spaced at ten-foot intervals dangled from a wire running along the roof boards. On the wall by the stairs hung three hand trucks and a few coils of rope.

"Boy, is *this* weird!" Joe exclaimed in a subdued voice, as he looked around. "But it's nice and cool down here!"

"Yes," Frank replied softly, gazing down the tunnel. "Nice change from the garage."

As they walked on, the sound of their footsteps echoed from the floor, walls, and ceiling.

"These shoes aren't quiet enough," Frank said worriedly.

"Let's take them off," said Joe. "We need to speed—and the faster we go with these on, the more noise we'll make. We can *run* in socks and still be quiet."

They quickly removed their shoes, tied the laces together, and hung them around their necks.

Then they began to run.

After about sixty feet, they came to an intersecting passage on the right.

Peeking around the corner they saw, about thirty feet away, a door set into a concrete wall.

"That must be the foundation of the house," Frank said softly.

"So there's a basement!" Joe remarked in a low voice. "I should've thought of that!"

"A very *tall* basement, I'd say. We're far enough below ground level by now that there must be lots of headroom."

"Or lots of room for soundproofing."

"Wait here," said Frank.

"Gladly," Joe replied.

Frank ran to the door, put his ear to it, and listened for a few seconds.

He frowned, turned away, and ran back to where Joe waited, just around the corner.

"Did you hear anything?" Joe asked.

"Men's voices. I couldn't make out what they were saying. It sounded as if there might be something between them and the door."

"Let's go. If someone comes out of there, we're dead!"

Frank pointed to the side passage ceiling.

Running alongside the lights' wire was a large electrical conduit. From a hole over the door, it led around the corner and down the tunnel.

"They must need a lot of juice down there," Joe remarked.

He turned to Frank and smiled. "Well, you got it—the boat pilots go from the house to the cave, all right."

He gazed around. "What a layout!"

"And what a lot of *work*."

A few feet from where they stood, the wooden walls began to give way to drilled and blasted rock. A few yards beyond that, the pillars, beams, and ceiling boards ended and a roof of stone began.

About sixty feet from the side passage, the last light bulb glowed.

"I wonder why the lights end there," Frank mused aloud, peering down the tunnel.

He lifted the binoculars to his eyes.

"Well, the *tunnel* couldn't end there," Joe replied. "Maybe they switch the rest of the lights off."

Frank lowered the binoculars and shook his head in irritation. "It's too dim to see."

"They must have a real scramble farther on, in order to get down to the cave," Joe commented. "This tunnel doesn't slope a whole lot, and we're quite a ways above sea level."

"I want to run down to where the lights end," Frank said determinedly. "Just to make sure this *does* go to the cave."

Joe sighed and looked at his watch. "Okay, Danger Man. But let's hustle."

About thirty feet beyond the side passage entrance, they ran past a narrow door recessed into the rock wall on the left.

"*Now* what?" whispered Joe, as they went back to investigate.

Frank listened at the door. No sound came from behind it.

Joe lay down and peered through the large, uneven crack beneath it.

After a few seconds he rose to his feet, held his finger to his lips, and beckoned to Frank. They retreated a short distance up the tunnel.

"What's in there?" Frank whispered anxiously.

"There's a man sitting behind the door!" Joe whispered in reply.

"What?"

"I couldn't see much. There's a light on, but that crack doesn't give a very tall view. Dead ahead, I saw the bottoms of some cloth sacks and a shelf of canned food."

"So where was—"

"On the left, close to the door. All I could see was the lower part of the right front leg of a chair, and a shoe, a bit of sock, a pants' cuff . . ."

Frank frowned. "I don't know what to make of *that*."

"We're skating on thin ice, brother. There are too many doors around here with people behind them."

"Just remember Chet and the Duchess. They'll go for help if we're not back in time."

"How will any rescuers know where we are? You didn't tell anyone about the possibility of a trapdoor—the *disguised* trapdoor I *closed behind us.*"

"You *what?*" Frank swung around and looked anxiously up the tunnel.

96

"Yeah—that was *my* mistake. But if the crooks catch us, they'll make sure it's closed, anyway. Then it's back to *your* mistake. But let's not waste time thinking about it. We don't have much farther to go."

They walked past the door in the wall, then started running.

Under the last light bulb, they stopped and caught their breath.

There the floor rose slightly to level off, then ended. Abutting its edge was a five-foot-wide, eight-foot-long, level wooden platform with high metal side railings.

Frank and Joe stepped onto the platform, walked to its far end, and gasped.

Down at an abrupt angle dropped the narrowing tunnel, with three metal rails descending along its floor into darkness.

"I can't believe it!" Joe exclaimed.

"So that's how they did it," said Frank, a quiet thrill in his voice. "That's how they got down there so quickly."

"You *knew* this was here, didn't you?" Joe said admiringly.

Frank laughed. "Not *exactly*. Coming back in the boat, I remembered what Chief Collig told us about how Leo Polucca made his living. So then I thought there might be some sort of tunnel to the cave. But—"

"And a passageway from the garage?"

"Yeah—after I started wondering again about someone moving my bike. Why would anybody do that? Because he wanted to get to something, and the bike was in the way? But there wasn't anything to get to, except the floor."

"So you thought there was maybe a trapdoor . . ."

"Right. And if there was, what would it go to? A room beneath the garage? A passage leading to the house? If there *was* a passage, I thought, that might explain the 'ghost.' Maybe a gang member came through, saw the bikes, decided to scare us away, and sneaked to the house by way of the garage. Of course, that wouldn't explain how he got to the second floor without—"

"Anyway," said Joe, "you figured out this tunnel was here."

"Sort of," Frank replied, looking around. "But *this*—"

"It's like a mining operation!"

97

"Yeah. Maybe it *is* one. For these people, it's probably a gold mine."

Frank pulled his flashlight from his pocket, switched it on, and pointed it at the rail bed below.

The light revealed a floor about seven feet across, topped with a smooth, flat layer of cement, to which were bolted six-foot ties about two feet apart. On top of these were fastened two narrow outer rails and a wider middle rail perforated by two rows of long, narrow, rectangular holes.

Joe took the shoes from around his neck and put them beside him on the platform. Then he lay down and hung his head over the forward edge.

Frank did the same, aiming the light beneath them.

They saw a strongly built steel frame, slightly smaller than the platform. Its vertical members were much longer on the downhill end than on the uphill, allowing the floor above to remain level. The corner uprights ended in ball-bearing sleeves, through each pair of which passed an axle with flanged wheels.

Above the axles was a sloping, heavily reinforced metal deck extending the length and width of the frame. To the right of its center was bolted a large electric motor. From the left side of the motor projected a drive shaft, which was connected by sprockets and chains to a rugged double cogwheel, the teeth of which engaged with the slots in the center rail. Secured to the left side of the deck, connected to the motor by two heavy electrical cables, were four truck batteries with linked terminals. At each end of the deck was a small headlight and a large generator, the latter coupled by a belt and pulleys to the axle below.

Joe whistled appreciatively. Then he rose to his feet and looked around the car. His eyes came to rest on the downhill end of the right-hand railing.

Projecting from the inside of the top rail were a small two-position lever and a slide switch.

On the uphill end, on the opposite side of the car, was an identical set of controls.

Joe stepped to the railing and put a finger on the lever.

Frank got to his feet, switched off the flashlight, and turned to see what Joe was doing.

"Don't start it up!" he exclaimed. "That cogwheel must make as much noise as a small machine shop!"

"I'm not *that* stupid," Joe responded, grinning. "I just wanted to figure out how they work this thing."

Frank picked up his shoes. He turned the flashlight on and pointed it down the tunnel.

The beam projected a few yards, then disappeared in the blackness.

"Seven minutes to go," Joe announced, looking at his watch. "Let's run for it."

Joe glanced at the front of the house, squeezed past the end of the garage door, and sprinted for the trees.

Frank exited, slid the door shut, then backed quickly away in a crouch, erasing all traces of footprints with a branch until they faded out in the vegetation.

The Gangbuster Girls

"We could spend the rest of the afternoon in here!" Callie said appreciatively, studying a small painting on the wall.

"This is much too grand for a living room," Iola remarked. She stroked the head of a stone horse displayed on an end table. "It's really more like an art gallery!"

Alex Polucca smiled. "I guess it *is* pretty much an art gallery."

He walked to the large fireplace, leaned against the mantelpiece, and looked around. "This is the only part of the house that's set up. The other rooms are mostly in boxes—the few that I have furniture for, anyway. Most of those on the second floor are going to stay empty until I have some use for them."

Callie approached a three-foot-high bronze statue of a man standing on a tall wooden base. The figure wore a beret, a cloak, a ruffed jacket, tight breeches, and pointed shoes. His right hand held out, as though he'd just removed it, a large mask set in a wide grin. On his face was a half mask with a demonic, scowling forehead and thick eyebrows. Below the half mask, the mouth wore a tight, mocking smile.

"Scaramuccia," said Alex, seeing Callie's look of admiration for the sculptor's craftsmanship turn to puzzlement over the statue's meaning.

"I beg your pardon?"

"Better known as Scaramouche. A character in the *commedia*

dell'arte—the Italian comic theater of the late Renaissance. Scaramuccia was, or appeared to be, a cowardly, bragging servant. Beneath his buffoonery, he was a covetous, intrigue-plotting rascal—a Renaissance con man who always managed to escape the consequences of his plots by swindling or implicating an innocent bystander. The French and English turned him into a clown— Scaramouche. But they left out half his character. Scaramuccia had two faces, you see. But not on stage. Those masks are Uncle Leo's addition to the stock character."

"Your uncle made this?"

"He sculpted it in clay over wire, built the mold, and poured the bronze. He carved all the stone pieces in here, as well."

"Your uncle," said Callie, "must have been a very talented man."

Alex shrugged. "He loved his carving. And his cooking."

"Hot smoking cheesecake!" Iola exclaimed, as she followed Callie from the hall past the swinging door that Alex was holding open. "This is the biggest kitchen I've ever seen!"

She gazed across the expanse of white-tiled floor to a long food-preparation table in the center of the room. Hanging above it was a large oval pot rack. In the corner beyond it lay stacks of opened and unopened boxes.

"You could rent this house out as a convention center!"

Alex laughed. "That's what it was—a convention center for the Polucca family. That's why Uncle Leo had two of those."

He pointed to a large refrigerator by the counter against the south kitchen wall on the right, then to its twin between the floor-to-ceiling cupboards and chest-high food bins that took up most of the windowless outer wall across from it.

Callie wandered casually around to the left and looked past a propped-open swinging door into the pantry, glimpsing more floor-to-ceiling cupboards and rows of almost-empty shelves.

"Surely *you* don't need two refrigerators," she said. "And all this shelf space."

Alex laughed. "Not with *my* food intake. But I hope to do quite a bit of entertaining, once I get this place set up. Maybe I can lure my cousins out here, so the old shack can be the center of festivities it was before."

"How many cousins do you have?" Iola asked, smiling at her host.

"*Lots.* Most of them are in New York. To them, New York's heaven. But I think this area has its possibilities."

Alex sauntered past the stove and counter, followed by Iola. "I stored all the equipment and appliances after Uncle Leo died. No one else wanted them. When I decided to move here, I thought I might as well put everything back where it used to be."

He opened the refrigerator door with a flourish, revealing a nearly bare interior.

"As you can see," he addressed to the north wall, "there is hardly anything of consequence inside."

He grandly held out his hand to Iola. "And now my lovely assistant will step into the box, and I will demonstrate the world-famous Polucca disappearing act."

Iola tilted back her head dramatically and put her hand to her temple. "I'm afraid I can't just now. My head hurts awfully."

Alex raised his hand to his heart. "Ladies and gentlemen, I'm truly sorry. Perhaps at the next performance."

He closed the door and smiled at his visitors. "Well, so much for the old kitchen. Would you care to see the rest of the place?"

Callie and Iola stood among the trees, drawing the back of the house. From behind them came the loud whispering of the relentless waves. Through the open windows ahead of them came the drone of electric fans and the occasional distant sound of Alex Polucca moving boxes and furniture in a front second-story bedroom.

"Isn't Alex a solid sender?" asked Iola, glowing with admiration for their host.

"Yes," Callie replied grimly. "A real charmer."

Her pencil stopped.

"That's odd," she said, staring at the four kitchen windows.

"What?"

Iola looked at Callie, then at the windows.

"The space between the northernmost kitchen window and the end of the house," Callie answered. "When we were in there, I could've sworn that window was closer to the wall."

"Stone walls," said Iola, returning to her drawing. "They're thick, so they make the inside smaller than it would be otherwise. So naturally—"

"I'm sure of it—that kitchen window was a good deal closer to the end of the house than it is out here. The walls can't be *that* thick."

"Optical illusion."

"I wonder."

Callie looked up to the second floor. She ran her gaze all the way across from right to left, then back again, stopping at the northernmost window.

It, like the kitchen window below it, was set farther in than were the windows at the other end of the house.

"Did you notice," Callie asked, staring upward, "the closet along the north wall of the bedroom above the kitchen?"

"The deep one in the northeast corner?" Iola replied, still drawing.

"Mm-hmm."

"Inconvenient place for a closet, if you ask me. Coming in the door, you'd have to walk over to the far corner to put your things away."

Callie continued staring, lost in thought. Then she looked down and resumed drawing.

A minute later, she stopped and studied the windows again.

"I'm through with the front," Iola announced, looking across the turnaround to the house. "As soon as you finish, let's show Alex. He's still up in his bedroom. Don't you think he's sweet?"

"*Sweet?*" Callie said with a grimace, her eyes on her nearly completed drawing.

"For a slimy, filthy, rotten criminal." Iola paused, then added: "If he *is* one."

"And why *wouldn't* he be?"

"Oh, I don't know . . ."

Callie stole a glance at the Packard, parked to the left of the front door.

"I want to get inside his car," she confided.

"You don't care for him but you love his car?"

"When we walked by it, I noticed a hat on the back seat. A brown one—it wouldn't be his. I want to see if it has a name inside."

"Chimpanzee's, maybe, or Frankenstein's?"

"Or some other name that could be useful to the authorities."

"I can call Alex outside again and distract him—"

"While I open the car door, look the hat over, and close the door—all without him noticing."

"Okay, I can go ask him something and keep him away from those windows."

"We've asked him enough already. He'll get suspicious."

"So how shall we work it?"

"Let's walk toward the car now, while we're drawing."

"Let's do that."

They strolled absentmindedly up to the Packard, as though they were concentrating on their drawings.

"Now we notice it," Callie said softly, lowering her sketchbook, "and look at it admiringly."

"Like this? *Oooh—killer-diller!*"

"Not so loud, Zeal Girl. The idea is to look as if we're marveling over the car—not to draw attention to us."

Iola glanced casually up at the open third and fourth second-story windows from the south end of the house.

"I don't see him," she announced. "And I don't think he's likely to hear us, with that loud fan going."

"Just the same . . ."

Callie ran her hand along the edge of the car roof, then gazed up to the right, beyond it.

"Look up there," she said, pointing to the eaves at the end of the house.

Iola looked.

"You draw what I'm pointing to," Callie instructed.

"Watching the windows of Alex's bedroom—"

"While I get to the hat."

Callie lowered her eyes and swept her vision appreciatively over the left rear fender, the doors . . .

Iola turned to a fresh page. Her pencil moved sketchily across it as she nonchalantly studied the bedroom windows.

"We're funny, aren't we?" she remarked. "First we want to be noticed . . . Then we want to be ignored . . ."

"Do you see him?" Callie asked, peering in the driver's window.

"No," answered Iola, watching and drawing. "I'll let you know if I do."

Callie put her sketchbook and pencil on the roof of the Packard, quietly opened the front door, and looked at the dashboard with as much visible envy as she could simulate.

"Why don't you just open the rear door," Iola asked anxiously, "and grab the hat?"

"Because," Callie answered, "someone else might be watching."

She quickly studied the plush front seat, then quietly opened the rear door and admired the jump seats folded against its back. Leaning in, she put her hand on the rear seat cushion and looked up, inspecting the luxurious headliner. Her hand slid to the hat. Looking down at the seat, she turned the hat over and glanced at it in passing. She surreptitiously turned it back as she looked around the interior. Then she withdrew.

She gently closed both doors, then picked up her pencil and sketchbook.

"Let's leave," she said softly.

"Leave? Our drawing time's not up! And when it is, we'll still have a little bit of—"

"We need to go. Let's say a quick good-bye to Alex and get out of here."

"What in the world's the matter?"

"We need to get to the car. *Fast.*"

***

105

Frank, Joe, and Chet were sitting on the Duchess's running board discussing the afternoon's discoveries when Callie and Iola came racing up to them.

"You're a bit early, aren't you?" Joe asked. "I thought—"

"Callie saw something," explained Iola, catching her breath. "So we hurried away."

Frank studied Callie's face. "You look as if you'd seen a ghost."

Chet laughed. "She picked a good place for it!"

"Not a ghost," said Callie, breathing deeply.

"Well, what *did* you see?"

"A hat—on the back seat of Alex Polucca's car. I examined it on the sly. It had caught my attention because it was brown."

The brothers stared at her uncomprehendingly.

Iola looked at Callie. "They're boys," she said. "They don't know about complexion and clothing."

She turned to the others. "Brown isn't Alex Polucca's color. Therefore, it was someone else's hat."

"All right," said Frank to Callie. "What bothered you about it?"

"There were initials on the sweatband, and they . . ."

"Yes?"

"Oh, Frank—the initials were *F.H.*!"

Patterns

Frank stared at Callie. "*F.H.?*" he asked incredulously. "Are you *sure?*"

Callie nodded. "And the hat looked like the ones your father wears."

"Does he have his hats monogrammed?" asked Iola.

"Yes," answered Frank, a worried look on his face. "He does. His hats and his handkerchiefs. So he can use them as markers."

"What do you mean, *markers?*" Callie inquired.

"If he gets into a situation he hadn't anticipated, he leaves something to indicate which way he went. He puts it in an inconspicuous place, usually, so a casual passerby won't see it and take it. Then whoever he's working with can find him."

"Or, if he's on his own," said Joe, "searchers will know where he was last, in case something happens to him."

"Could your father have gone to the house to investigate?" Callie asked Frank.

"Maybe."

"Did he say anything about suspecting it, or Alex Polucca?"

"Not a word. Not to us, anyway."

"If he did go there," said Chet, "and he did leave something to show which way he'd gone, where would he be likely to leave it?"

"In the ditch by the entrance," said Joe. "Hidden in the grass."

"People rarely look very far up or down," Frank told the others. "Especially when they're driving. That's why a ditch would be a good place. Chances are, no one would notice anything there, unless he was searching for it."

"Alex Polucca would," Joe asserted. "He looks up, down, and sideways."

Frank stood and opened the car door.

"Let's see what we can find."

The Duchess stopped by the entrance and everyone got out.

Frank looked up the driveway to make certain no one was watching. Then he knelt on the pavement, surveyed the impressions in the dirt, and pointed.

"There are Callie's and Iola's footprints, coming and going. But no one else's."

"Dad wouldn't have left any," Joe remarked brusquely. "He'd have avoided the dirt, the same as we did."

Frank regarded the various tire marks.

"No new tracks," he said. "There's that pattern we can't identify." He pointed to one of the zigzag-tread impressions.

"But it's not Dad's," said Joe.

"How do you know?" Iola asked him.

"We made a cast of his tire tracks a while ago, for practice. Their tread lines are straight, with sawtooth edges."

Callie, holding her sketchbook, crouched beside Frank and pointed to a tire impression that had obliterated part of the unidentified track he'd pointed to.

"That was made by Alex's car," she said.

"Uh-huh," Frank replied, staring at the marks. "The other car must've left before—"

He turned to Callie. "Wait a minute. How do *you* know?"

Callie turned to the last page of her sketchbook and handed it to him. "I thought it might be a good idea to record that."

Frank looked from the hastily drawn tread pattern to the track she'd pointed to. They matched.

Joe walked over and looked down at the drawing.

"Nice work," he said.

Frank studied the sketch as he stood up. "It *is* nice work." He turned to Callie. "But someone might've seen you draw it."

Callie stood and smoothed out her dress. "Not Alex. He was preoccupied."

Frank looked quizzically at her as he gave back the sketchbook.

"Oh, it was safe enough. Iola called him outside to answer a question. They were facing the front of the house and I was behind them, by Alex's car. Iola had him mesmerized. A herd of cattle could have walked by and he wouldn't have noticed."

"Oh, yeah?" Joe said skeptically.

He turned and looked at Iola. She grinned impishly at him. He turned back and looked at the ground.

"Could you draw this one?" he asked Callie, pointing to the unidentified track.

While Callie sketched what she could see of the pattern from the two clearest impressions in the dirt, the brothers examined the ditch on either side of the entrance.

"I don't see any disturbance in the grass," said Frank from the right side.

"And I can't tell if anything was put here or not," Joe replied from the left.

Callie closed her sketchbook. "Got it," she announced.

Joe looked around. "Well, Dad didn't *drive* in. So if he *did* come here, where did he park his car?"

"Let's try the side road," Chet suggested.

The Duchess slowed to a stop about fifty feet north of the Polucca driveway.

"Nothing," Chet told the others, looking out his window at the entrance to a narrow, unpaved lane on the west side of the road.

"Let's take a closer look," said Frank.

All got out and walked to the entrance.

"That's a funny sort of road," Iola remarked.

"It looks as if it started out to be a driveway," said Joe, "and then someone—one of the Poluccas, maybe—changed his mind."

They looked down the weed-invaded lane to where it ended, about seventy feet farther on.

The dusty surface was covered with tire tracks, each of which appeared to be formed entirely of zigzag lines.

"The other car from the driveway!" Callie exclaimed.

"Somebody drove it to the end and back," observed Joe, a puzzled expression on his face. "Over and over and over . . ."

"Why," asked Chet, "would anyone do that?"

Frank pointed his chin at the empty lane.

"Do those tracks remind you of anything?" he asked in return.

Chet looked up and down the lines in the dust.

"Now that you mention it, they sort of resemble those broom trails on the floor of the house."

He turned his head and gave Frank a crooked smile.

"Could it be," he asked, "that somebody's trying to *hide* something?"

"I don't know what else it could mean," Frank replied, staring down at the tracks.

He turned to Joe. "We'd better phone home, to find out if Dad's there—or if he said anything about where he was going today."

"And if the answers are negative?"

"Then we'd better go see . . ." Frank put his hand to his forehead and rubbed hard. "I hate to say it."

"We don't have much choice, do we?"

Joe watched intently from the open left rear window as the Duchess very slowly passed the entrance to the Polucca driveway.

"I don't see anyone," he announced, gazing as far as he could down the winding drive.

As the car gradually accelerated, he leaned out the window and looked back.

Just before they entered the first curve, he shouted: "The Packard's pulling out of the driveway! It's *following* us!"

"Well, it won't *catch* us!" Chet declared.

He braked going into the curve, then put his foot on the gas pedal.

Questions

Chief Collig leaned back in his chair and started rolling a pencil between his palms. He looked from one to the other of the four anxious young people standing in front of his desk.

His eyes settled on Frank. "Do you *know* it was your father's hat?"

"No," Frank admitted. "Callie's the one who saw it."

"It was brown," said Callie, "and it had the initials *F.H.* on the sweatband."

"So why do you suppose Fenton's hat would be on the back seat of Alex's car? If it *was* his hat. And why all this urgency?"

"*That,*" responded Iola, tightening her jaw, "is what we're *trying* to *tell* you."

"We thought," said Joe, "that Alex Polucca might've picked up the hat, which Dad might've left nearby to show that he'd been there—if you know how he does that."

The rolling pencil slowed. "I do. But why would Fenton have been in the area?"

"We thought he might have gone to the house to investigate something," Frank replied.

"And why would you think that?"

"Because suspicious things have been going on around there."

"Such as?"

"Such as Ivan whatever-his-name-is moving my motorcycle, and—"

"Well, *he* won't show up there again. Not with Alex moving in."

112

"There's also what we discovered today," Frank added reluctantly.

The pencil stopped. "Elaborate, please."

"While Callie and Iola kept Alex Polucca from seeing us, Joe and I examined the inside of his garage, and—"

"*What?*"

Chief Collig sat up, slammed the pencil down on the desk, and pointed a forefinger at Frank. "You've been snooping again, on private property, after I told you . . ."

He lowered his hand and glared at Frank, then at his brother.

"This detective play of yours," he said at last, "is getting decidedly out of hand."

"If we might continue?" remarked Iola, unimpressed.

"We found a trapdoor," Frank went on, "disguised as part of the flooring."

"A *what?*"

"There were stairs below it that led to a tunnel."

The chief stared at Frank. "A tunnel."

"Just *listen* to him," said Iola. "He can tell you all about it, if you—"

Chief Collig stopped her with a wave of his hand. "I'm listening," he said.

"The tunnel led beyond the house, down to where we found out is a secret cave at the end of the point."

"A secret *what?*"

"Not far down the tunnel, we saw a door on the right, in what looked like the foundation of the house. I listened at the door and heard men's voices."

"A gang of smugglers," Joe broke in impatiently, "has its hideout under the Polucca house."

"A gang of smugglers," repeated the chief, with a disbelieving smile. "And Alex Polucca hasn't heard them?"

"Oh, he knows they're there. He's the boss. The local one, anyway."

A gleam appeared in Chief Collig's eyes. He relaxed, smiled, leaned back, and looked around.

"Where's Chet?" he asked.

"Waiting outside," Iola replied stiffly. "In the car."

"Chief Collig," Callie began, with fire in her eyes. "This is not a joke. Frank and Joe found a trapdoor in the garage, a tunnel leading from it, a door beneath the house, and—"

"Callie, you've got to admit that this sounds—"

"Around midnight two nights ago, Frank, Joe, and Tony Prito saw some men off Walton Point, using speedboats without lights. By all appearances, they're the smugglers Mr. Hardy has suspected might be operating near Bayport. And now—"

"Fenton has told me his theory," interrupted the chief, "and there's a certain amount of sense to it. A good many people in town—including the Bayport Police Department—are looking out for strangers in the area. We would be very much interested in any reports of speedboats. But to suspect *Alex Polucca*—"

"Earlier this afternoon," Callie angrily reminded him, "*a hat with Mr. Hardy's initials on it was on the back seat of Alex Polucca's car.* Mr. Hardy might have gone to the Polucca house to look around, or to ask questions. Something might have happened to him there. And we're asking you to *investigate.*"

The chief threw up his hands. "All right. All right."

He leaned forward and looked at Frank. "What did your father say in response to all this about seeing speedboats?"

"We haven't told him."

The chief sat up. "You haven't *told* him?"

"We wanted to first find out—well, what we found out this afternoon. We planned to give him the whole story at once. But when Callie saw the hat . . ."

"How do you know that Fenton's not in his lab or study, right now?"

"We stopped on our way here and telephoned."

"According to Aunt Gertrude," said Joe, "Dad hasn't been home since early this morning. Neither she nor Mother has any idea where he is."

"But if you haven't told him anything," said the chief, "why would he have gone to Polucca's?"

"I don't know," Frank answered. "I suppose he might've learned something, or suspected something, on his own."

"Did he tell you anything to indicate that?"

"No."

"Had he mentioned anything to you about intending to go out there?"

"No."

"So it doesn't seem very likely that he *did*."

Iola groaned and rolled her eyes.

"On the other hand," said the chief, with a sharp glance at the scourge of Bayport's sister, "he could have been in the house talking with Alex when you arrived."

Callie shook her head. "Mr. Polucca showed Iola and me all through the house. No one was in it but himself."

"I don't suppose you asked *Alex* why the hat was in his car."

"No," said Callie. "We don't trust him."

The chief sighed and ran a hand over his stubble of hair. "Aside from the hat—the ownership of which hasn't yet been established—were there any signs of Fenton's having been in the area?"

"There were a lot of tire tracks from somebody's car—not Dad's—in the dead-end lane north of Polucca's," Joe answered. "As if someone had tried to hide another car's tracks by driving over them. The same car left two sets of tracks in Polucca's driveway."

"But there was no sign of *Fenton's* car."

"No, but—"

"There *might* have been," Frank asserted, "in the lane."

"Speaking of cars," Joe added, "there's one more thing. As we were driving away, after we'd looked at the tracks in the lane, Alex Polucca's Packard started following us. But we lost it by whipping around a couple of curves and hightailing into town."

Chief Collig pushed back his chair and stood up. "All right. I'll head out there immediately."

"Wouldn't it be good to contact the FBI?" asked Joe. "They've been investigating those crooks, and—"

"If Fenton *is* in trouble, there's no sense in wasting time waiting for the FBI to show up. I want to determine what the situation is right away. I can radio here to have the switchboard notify the FBI if I need them."

"But don't you think that what we saw—"

"What you said you saw—even the tunnel beneath the house, if that's what it was—might have something to do with a smuggling operation, or it might not. Alex may know about a tunnel, or smugglers, or he may not. But if things there look the way you say they do, I'll call for all the reinforcements I can get."

The chief took his hat from the desk and put it on.

"You won't get very far," warned Frank, "if Alex Polucca won't let you examine things."

"Very true," the chief replied. "That's why I want to handle the situation *my* way—friendly-like, without letting Alex know what I'm doing. And without mentioning any of you, or what you've told me. If he *is* involved with something criminal, I don't want to put him on his guard. If he starts getting obstructive, I'll go for a search warrant and assemble a search team. But that'll take time, so it's not the way I want to start. We'll find out about the hat. We'll look for the trapdoor. Where would it be?"

"In the right half of the garage," said Frank, "in the middle of the floor. It lifts toward the house. The handle's a large knothole. The hinges are hidden in a wide crack near the right wall—there're four of them, painted black. It's hard to see there's a door there because the board ends forming its side edges don't line up."

"Wait here," the chief instructed. "If you haven't heard from me by dinnertime, go on home and I'll communicate with you there.

"I'll have the dispatcher put the men on standby," he added as he walked away. "There's no telling what might happen."

116

Answers

Alex Polucca, wearing soiled work clothes, came around the right front corner of his house and walked up to the two policemen who were looking in the windows of his car.

"Chief Collig!" he exclaimed cheerfully. "What a pleasant surprise!"

The chief turned and smiled.

"Hello, Alex," he said cordially.

He jerked his thumb toward his companion, a tall, strongly built young man with dark hair and eyes. "I'd like you to meet Randy Moscone."

"Good afternoon, Officer," said Alex, as the two men shook hands.

"I'm glad to meet you, Mr. Polucca."

"What brings you out this way?" Alex asked, looking from one policeman to the other. "There's no trouble around here, I hope?"

Chief Collig laughed. "Not at all, Alex. We were just passing by. I wanted to see how you're getting on."

"I'm getting on just fine, Chief. There's a lot to do, but it keeps me occupied."

The chief pointed to the Packard. "We were just admiring your beautiful automobile."

Alex smiled. "It may look a bit flashy, but underneath, it's only a car."

"I couldn't help noticing that hat on the back seat," the chief remarked.

Alex swung around and looked at the Packard, his smile gone. "Oh, *that*," he said, recovering.

He turned back to the chief and laughed. "For a moment, I didn't know what you were talking about. I'd forgotten it was there."

"It looks familiar, somehow. It isn't yours, is it?"

Alex frowned. "I wish I knew *who* it belongs to. I found it this morning, by the docks."

He opened the car door and reached in.

"How did you happen to find it?" asked Officer Moscone.

Alex pulled out the hat and closed the door.

"I'd been at Simpson's," he replied, "discussing a motorboat I'm buying from them. It must've been around eleven-thirty when I left."

He handed the hat to the chief.

"I was driving south on North Edgewater, heading toward . . ." Alex smiled and shook his head. "The street that runs up through the middle of town."

"Central."

"I hadn't gone far when I noticed a hat lying on the sidewalk on the east side of Edgewater—you know, in front of the docks."

Chief Collig turned the hat over and looked inside.

"So I stopped and picked it up. I couldn't figure out where it had come from. Some cars were parked across the street, but there weren't any nearby."

The chief looked up. "Do you know what the nearest cross street was?"

"By the rigging company . . ."

"Pope's."

"Yes—that corner."

"That'd be MacArthur."

"The hat was more or less across from where MacArthur runs into Edgewater. I didn't see anyone around to ask about it, so I put it in the car, to take to the police station. Then I drove to the hardware store—Sanderson's—and bought a shovel, had a chat with the owner . . . Then I drove home."

Alex smiled sheepishly and shrugged. "I'm afraid I forgot all about the hat."

"No harm done," said Chief Collig. "It was good of you to pick it up."

Alex held up his hand. "I just wanted to be helpful."

The chief carried the hat to the patrol car. The others followed.

"You said it looked familiar," Alex remarked. "Do you recognize it?"

The chief opened the front door, put the hat on the seat, and closed the door. He turned and watched Alex's face.

"I think I do," he said. "It looks like Fenton Hardy's. The initials inside it are *F.H.*, so it's quite likely his. Have you ever met Fenton?"

"I don't believe so," Alex answered without blinking.

The chief continued to look at him.

"A shovel . . ." he mused aloud. "Doing a little gardening?"

Alex nodded. "I'm going to put in some azaleas. I hope there'll be enough light for them back there. Come take a look."

They walked around to the right side of the house, where a shovel was sticking in the ground by a couple of two-foot-diameter holes. Beside the holes were low piles of earth and rocks.

"I haven't gotten very far," said Alex. "I had some visitors a while ago, and a couple of phone calls. And this ground is awfully hard to dig in."

He pulled the shovel up, then struck downward. There was the sound of metal hitting stone.

"It's really tough going. I guess that's why Uncle Leo didn't plant much. According to what he told me once, it gets worse the farther down you go. He said that under the house it's almost solid rock. That's why he didn't put in a basement."

"Without a basement," said Officer Moscone, "where'd your uncle store his things?"

"Mostly on the service porch and in the garage. I cleaned all kinds of stuff out of both places after his death. I left a lot of machinery parts in the garage, though, because I didn't know what to do with them."

Alex picked up the shovel. "I'll show you what I mean. I need to put this back there now, anyway."

Alex slid open the right-hand garage door, stepped inside, and placed the shovel against the wall. He turned and smiled.

"My next cleanup project," he told the policemen, sweeping his arm out to indicate the clutter on the floor.

Old pieces of machinery were grouped here and there, according to their kind. In the right half of the garage, in the middle of the floor, lay a pile of auto parts—engine blocks, transmissions, exhaust manifolds, and other heavy objects—all coated with a thick layer of undisturbed dust.

Lost and Found

Chief Collig frowned, folded his arms across his chest, and leaned back against the counter.

"Do you want me to tell it all again?" he asked angrily.

"I—I just don't get it," Frank stammered, turning the brown man's hat in his hands. "How could the garage be full of—"

"It was completely *empty*!" Joe insisted. "And swept clean! There wasn't a sign that anything had ever been in it!"

"I suppose," replied the chief, "that in the amount of time it took for all of you to drive here and tell me your story, and for the two of us to drive out there, Alex went to a wrecking yard and a machine shop, hauled a truckload of heavy metal parts home in his Packard, piled them on the garage floor, and spread a coating of dust over everything."

"Do you think Frank and Joe are *lying* to you?" Callie asked. "Do you think we *all* are?"

Chief Collig pushed back his hat and scratched his head. "Callie . . . Did either you or Iola actually look into the garage?"

"No—the doors were closed."

"Frank and I were *in* there," Joe insisted. "And we weren't *dreaming!*"

"I don't understand," said Frank, in a daze. "We told you what we saw."

"Yes," replied the chief. "And I told you what Randy and I saw.

121

That's what's in the garage. And it's obviously been there a long time."

"But it couldn't—"

"Especially after what I've seen and heard today, I would no more suspect Alex Polucca than . . . I have the highest regard for that young man. Why, I look on him practically as I would a nephew."

"Or a son?" Callie asked gently. "The son you never had?"

The chief cleared his throat awkwardly. "I don't know about *that.* But I know I'd be proud to have a son as well-mannered and upstanding as Alex."

"Well, the two of you can have nice heart-to-heart chats," Joe commented sarcastically, "when you visit him in the Big House."

Chief Collig stiffened. He pointed to the hat. "Take that home to your mother. Maybe *she* can positively identify it, even if *you* can't. I don't know how you boys are ever going to be detectives if you can't recognize something you've probably seen a hundred times or more."

Iola made a face. "Aren't we getting just a little *testy?*"

"I'm going to send a patrol car to the docks," said the chief, "to see if we can find Fenton's car. Maybe Alex discovered something amiss there. And maybe he didn't. But at least he was being help-ful—which is more than can be said at present for certain other young people in this town."

Joe threw up his hands and turned away, shaking his head.

"We'll go to the docks now," said Frank.

"No," replied the chief, "you go on home. If we find Fenton's car, we'll call you."

As he walked to his desk, he said over his shoulder: "And if by any chance you should learn something about where your father is—or where he might be—let us know."

Evelyn Hardy hung up the telephone receiver, rose from the sofa, and greeted Frank, Joe, Callie, Iola, and Chet, who had just walked in.

"That was Chief Collig," she told Frank. "The police have found

Fenton's car at North Edgewater and MacArthur. The chief said he'll meet you two down there."

The brothers exchanged uneasy glances.

Frank went over to his mother and held out the hat. "We couldn't tell for sure—is this Dad's?"

"Yes," said Mrs. Hardy, taking it from him. "It is."

She looked at it for a moment, then at Frank. "You said when you phoned that Callie saw this in Mr. Polucca's car. Was he asked how it got there?"

"We'll tell you all about what happened," said Callie, "after Frank and Joe leave."

"Have you heard anything from Dad?" Joe asked.

"No." Evelyn Hardy put the hat on the end table by the telephone. "Not a word."

She smiled at the visitors. "You're all welcome to stay for dinner. There's plenty of food, and Gertrude and I would appreciate your company."

"I'd love to stay," said Callie.

"So would I," said Iola.

"Are you sure there's plenty of food?" asked Chet.

"There most certainly is, Chet," Mrs. Hardy answered, smiling.

Joe slapped his friend on the back. "Especially if Frank and I don't return by the time you start eating."

"I'd better drive you down there," Chet said to him.

"No, we'll take the motorcycles. The fewer of us the chief sees, the more he'll like it."

Frank started for his father's study. "I'll get the family fingerprints. And a magnifying glass."

"Good idea," Joe replied, heading toward the back door.

"Sit down and make yourselves comfortable," Evelyn Hardy said to the remaining young people. "Dinner will be ready in about forty-five minutes. You'd better phone your parents to let them know you're staying."

Iola went up to her. "Mrs. Hardy . . . Has Mr. Hardy ever disappeared like this before?"

"Oh, a few times." Evelyn Hardy smiled faintly. "But not in Bayport."

She put her hands on the girl's shoulders. "Iola, we don't know yet that he *has* disappeared."

"But we found his hat, and he hasn't come back or telephoned . . ."

Mrs. Hardy smiled, ran her hand over Iola's hair, and patted the side of her head. "Maybe he's just occupied."

She patted her again, turned, and walked to the kitchen, a worried expression on her face.

Frank and Joe turned left from North Edgewater onto MacArthur and parked their motorcycles at the curb.

They walked around the corner to join Chief Collig and two officers, who stood by a dark-gray 1940 Ford DeLuxe coupé.

"The windows were rolled down," said the chief, gesturing toward the car. "We haven't touched a thing."

"The hat's Dad's, all right," Frank told him.

The chief nodded. "I knew it as soon as I heard the car was here."

Frank took an envelope from his jacket pocket and handed it to the chief. "Dad had these on file, just in case. They're fingerprints of everyone in the family, plus the two mechanics at Denby's Garage. Those are the only prints that ought to be on the car."

Chief Collig smiled. "I guess Fenton's taught you boys a thing or two, after all."

He put the envelope in his pocket.

"We'll go through the area building by building," he said, "alley by alley. But first I wanted you two to take a look at the coupé, to see if you notice anything out of place. You ought to know this car and Fenton's habits better than I do."

"I'm glad you're taking this seriously," said Frank. "I thought that after—"

"Of course we're taking it seriously. That's our job. Besides, Fenton's a good friend who's helped us quite a bit over the years. We'll search for him all night if we have to."

"The problem is," Joe remarked, going to the driver's door, "you're looking in the wrong place."

He pulled a short section of a two-inch-diameter cardboard

mailing tube from his jacket, slipped it over the free end of the handle, and gently pushed down, opening the door. Then he tossed the tube to Frank, who used it to open the passenger door.

Joe looked at the seat. "No notebook," he announced.

"How's that?" asked the chief.

"Dad writes down where he goes, what he does, who he talks to, and when, in a pocket memo book. He leaves it open, with a pen beside it, next to him on the seat."

"Does he carry it with him?"

"Sometimes. But he usually leaves it in the car."

Frank and Joe knelt, searched the floor, and peered under the seat.

"No notebook."

"And no pen."

Frank got up, reached across the passenger seat, and pulled the driver's seat-back forward. He leaned in and looked at the rear floor. "Nothing here."

He pushed the seat-back into place.

"We'll check in the glove box," said the chief, "as soon as we dust its door."

"Do you see any dirt on the front carpet over there?" Joe asked Frank, staring at the floor by the pedals.

"Nope."

"Well, there's some here, and on the running board, and I'll bet I know where it came from."

Joe stood and looked expectantly at the chief.

Chief Collig crouched down and examined the running board, then the carpet. "It'd be pretty hard to determine the source of that stuff. Fenton could've picked up soil like that practically anywhere around here."

"Or someone else could have," Joe conjectured, "when he drove Dad's car out of the lane."

The chief stood up.

"We'll find out who drove it last when we dust the door handles, steering wheel, and gearshift."

"Maybe you won't. If a certain someone is as smart as Frank and I think he is."

"Anyone driving a car would leave fingerprints," insisted the chief. "Especially in this weather. Unless he cleaned the surfaces he'd touched, or wore gloves—which would wipe existing prints wherever he put his fingers. Which would tell us something phony was going on. And we'll soon see if anything like that was done here."

"Maybe," said Joe. "But in case you don't . . ."

He looked at his brother and clapped his hands. Frank tossed him the piece of tubing.

"While Frank was going through Dad's fingerprint files and getting a magnifying glass, I sat on my bike and did some thinking. I imagined I was a really smart crook who wanted one of his helpers to move this car without leaving any signs that he'd driven it."

Joe held up the tube. "I decided I'd tell my driver to get in by sliding something like this over the end of the door handle and then pull the door shut by doing the same with the inside handle. If the window was rolled down, I'd tell him to use the inside handle to open *and* shut the door, because that'd risk smearing prints on only one handle. It'd be even better, I thought, if he'd get in and out on the passenger side."

Joe looked at the dirt on the running board. "Which the boss didn't think of, apparently."

"And just how," asked the chief, "would you *shift gears* without leaving or smearing fingerprints?"

"By sliding a bigger piece of tubing past the column-shifter knob and operating the lever in the middle, where there wouldn't be many prints. It wouldn't be hard to work the 'fingertip' gearshift in this car that way."

Chief Collig scratched his head.

"How would you steer?" he asked, a little less skeptically.

Joe reached into his jacket and took out a two-inch wooden knob attached to a two-piece metal clamp held together with screws.

"I'd put on a steering wheel spinner. Like this one from our garage parts drawer." He spun the knob with his thumb. "Then I wouldn't have to touch the wheel at all."

Frank moved around to the driver's side of the car and pulled a magnifying glass from his pocket.

He smiled at Joe. "Nice job of reasoning, little brother."

He put a hand on the seat-back, then lifted his right foot over the running board, rested his knee on the seat, and inspected the steering wheel.

"There are a couple of new-looking scratches here," he said after a while, examining the bottom of the wheel. "But I can't tell *how* new. This glass isn't powerful enough. They might've been made by Dad's ring. Except that he doesn't hold the wheel down here."

"That'd be a good place for a spinner," Joe pointed out. "It'd be more awkward to drive with it there than at the top, but there'd be fewer prints at the bottom."

"We'll take a close look," said the chief, "when we dust the wheel."

Frank stepped out of the car and put the magnifying glass in his pocket.

Chief Collig looked across the street to the docks.

"We'll find out which boats came in or went out this morning, who was in them, and whether anyone in the area noticed anything suspicious."

He scanned the street, then the nearby buildings. "No one— not even Fenton—can vanish into thin air."

Waiting

Tick . . . TOCK. Tick . . . TOCK. Tick . . . TOCK.

The clock on the living room mantelpiece counted off the seconds, the minutes . . .

"How did Alex Polucca know we'd been in the garage?" Joe asked of no one in particular.

He and Frank were sitting in armchairs on either side of the love seat, which was occupied by Chet. On the sofa, facing them at an angle, sat Callie, Iola, and—by the telephone, trying to occupy herself by reading a book—Evelyn Hardy. Gertrude Hardy was knitting in a chair next to the tall radio console in the corner.

Aunt Gertrude put down her knitting, reached over, and switched on the set. The large dial glowed; the tubes began to warm up.

"I can think of one way he could've known," Frank replied to the question. "We tracked some dirt onto the garage floor when we went in. There wasn't any way to get rid of it, without a broom. But I smoothed over our tracks outside, and that should've kept anyone from—"

> *. . . a man is a two-face—*
> *A worrisome thing who'll leave you to sing*
> *THE BLUES IN THE NIGHT.*

Aunt Gertrude turned the volume down.

"So," said Joe, reflecting, "he could've noticed the dirt—

128

what little there was of it—and followed it to the trapdoor. I suppose."

"He wouldn't have looked inside an empty garage," Chet remarked, "unless he suspected something."

"Callie," said Frank, "you told us that when you sketched the Packard's tire tread, you were behind Alex and Iola, and they were looking at the house."

Callie nodded.

"Was Alex facing a window?"

"No . . . They were by the front door. There's no window just there."

"Nothing that he could have seen your reflection in?"

"I don't think so."

"He was totally focused on me," Iola insisted, "all the time I was talking to him."

"He made you *think* he was," Joe counterclaimed.

Iola stuck out her tongue. "Bringdown."

"Having considered what you girls have told us," said Aunt Gertrude, looking down at her work, "I know what *I* would have done, had I been Mr. Alex Polucca."

The knitting needles clicked, clicked, clicked.

"I would have telephoned the high school after you left and asked if Mr. Buchanan is teaching a summer art class."

"Which he is," volunteered Iola.

"And then I would have gotten in touch with Mr. Buchanan and inquired, in a friendly and by-the-way manner, if the two of you were enrolled in the class—"

"Which we aren't."

"—and if he had suggested that you draw the house."

"Which he didn't."

Click, click, click went the needles.

From Natchez to Mobile, from Memphis to St. Joe—
Wherever the four winds blow . . .

"And then?" encouraged Joe.

"I would ask myself why those two girls had been there. In my

129

mind I would go over what they did—not what they *said*, because I would know by then that what they said could not be trusted. What did they do? In one way and then another, they prevented me from looking out of the front windows of my house. What was out there that they did *not* want me to notice? I would look outside, and see the garage."

My mama done told me there's blues in the night.

"That's it," agreed Frank. "That's got to be it."

He stood up and went to the end table.

"So he checked on the girls. Well, we'll check on him."

He pulled the directory from the shelf below the telephone and flipped through its pages, humming along as the Artie Shaw band began its powerful, five-minute rendition of "Summertime."

His finger slid down a page, then stopped. "Here we are."

He put back the directory, lifted the receiver, and dialed a number.

"Hello?" answered a man's voice, after a few rings.

"Mr. Sanderson—this is Frank Hardy."

"Well—hello Frank."

"I'm sorry to bother you at home . . ."

"That's perfectly all right. What can I do for you?"

"You can help Joe and me settle a bet."

The voice laughed. "A bet, eh? What do you want to know?"

"Whether Alex Polucca bought a shovel from you this morning."

The voice laughed again. "I see—a matter of great significance. Well, let me think. Oh, of course—he did come in and buy a shovel, late this morning."

"Oh," said Frank disappointedly.

"I remember he made a joke about it—he's a very pleasant young man. Something about him needing a shovel for the fuller's earth he'd bought the day before."

"The what?"

"Fuller's earth. It's called that because it's used to full cloth—give it more bulk. It's also used in talcum powder, I believe, and to

130

clean tapestries and fine carpets. Alex Polucca was in the store yesterday to buy some tools, and he asked me where he could get some. He said his Persian carpet needed despotting. He hadn't treated it himself before, he said, but he wanted to because he doesn't trust professionals. He probably meant professionals in Bayport, as opposed to New York City. Anyway, I recommended that he ask at Thayer's—a pharmacy being the most likely place to find fuller's earth."

"But where *is* it, exactly?"

"An absorbent—it removes grease and such. It's a form of clay. Very fine powder."

The voice laughed. "I warned him not to open the package near an electric fan, or it'd be all over the room in no time at all, and make everything as dusty as can be."

A faraway look came into Frank's eyes. "Oh . . . Well, thank you, Mr. Sanderson."

"I hope I've been of help."

"You sure have. Good-bye, and thanks again."

"Any time, Frank."

Frank hung up the receiver and stared at the phone.

"What did he say?" asked Joe.

Frank looked up. "A.P. was in Sanderson's this morning, all right. According to Mr. Sanderson, he was in there yesterday asking where he could get some fuller's earth."

"Yeah, I heard you ask about that. What is it?"

"Fine clay. Powder. Mr. Sanderson warned him not to open the package near a fan."

Joe nodded slowly. *"Oooh."*

He laughed. "Well, there's *one* piece of the puzzle. Fake dust."

"But where," asked Chet, "did he get the machine parts to put *under* it?"

"I don't know," Frank replied, returning to his chair. "Somewhere on the property, maybe. As Chief Collig pointed out, he didn't have much time to collect a truckload of parts and put them in the garage. And how he managed *that*, I haven't a clue."

"Speaking of Chief Collig . . ." said Evelyn Hardy.

She put down her book, turned the telephone toward her, picked up the receiver, and dialed for the operator.

"Police Department, please."

The fingers of her free hand tapped the beat of "Summertime" on the arm of the sofa.

"Sergeant Riley? This is Mrs. Fenton Hardy. Is Chief Collig available to speak to? I know—I thought he might have returned. Yes—could you have him telephone me at his earliest convenience? Of course—I realize he may not be near his radio, but . . . Thank you. I'll be waiting for his call. Good-bye."

Tick . . . TOCK. Tick . . . TOCK.

Dream—when you're feelin' blue;
Dream—that's the thing to do.

"I've been thinking over what Dad said," Frank remarked to his brother.

"What about?" Joe asked.

"About the crooks counting on the authorities looking in the reasonable places. Which would include searching for someone who's missing in the neighborhood of his abandoned car."

"What about it?"

"We believe that Dad's most likely being held prisoner in the hideout—"

"If only because Smiley is trying so hard to convince the police that he hasn't been near the place—"

"But we don't *know* it, and we can't *prove* it."

"That's right, my dears," said Mrs. Hardy, looking down at her book as she turned a page. "We—that is, *you*—don't know it, and can't prove it."

She stared vacantly at the words in front of her.

"Both of you think one thing," she added, "and Chief Collig thinks another. And here we are. Not knowing. And waiting."

Dream—and they might come true.
Things never are as bad as they seem,
So dream, dream, dream.

"What if we could prove that Dad's there?" Frank asked Joe, staring at the radio.

"How?"

Frank turned to his brother.

"What color was the shoe, sock, and pants' cuff you saw through the crack under the storage room door?"

"Brown. All brown."

Mrs. Hardy looked up. "What's this? I don't recall hearing anything about a storage room, or someone behind a door."

"There was a room for storing food," Joe explained, "down the tunnel from the hideout. I peeked under the door and saw a man sitting on a chair. Actually, all I could see of him was a shoe, a sock, and a pants' cuff."

"Did they look like your father's?" Mrs. Hardy asked.

"I . . . Well . . . I don't know."

Things never are as bad as they seem,
So dream, dream, dream.

"Chief Collig's right," said Frank, frowning. "We don't recognize our own father's clothing. It's not enough to notice what's unusual or out of place. We need to see the things we're used to looking at."

"Let me get this straight," said Evelyn Hardy, tension in her voice. "You, Joe, saw what *might* have been Fenton behind a door. But we can't *know* it was he, because *you* don't know if the clothing you saw was his."

"Mother," Frank responded gently, "we didn't have any idea that Dad was in the area. We were trying to investigate the tunnel quickly, without getting caught. We'd come to one door with voices behind it, and we weren't about to open a second door to see who was in *there*. It *may* have been Dad, tied to a chair, but—"

"That foot," Joe insisted, "wasn't tied to the chair. If it *had* been, we would've gone right in."

"Nevertheless," Mrs. Hardy tensely replied, "that *could* have been Fenton. What you've just told us is the first real indication of where he might be. It seems a good deal more promising than dirt

133

in his car and tire tracks in a lane. Did you mention what you'd seen to Chief Collig?"

Joe shook his head. "He wouldn't believe us when we told him about the tunnel. Especially after Oily got through with him. We didn't even get to the part about a storage room, let alone the man inside it."

"Well, *I* will," Mrs. Hardy grimly declared. She closed her book and frowned.

Frank stood up, walked to the open front window, and looked out into the gathering darkness, down the hill to the lights on the bay.

Speak low, when you speak, love.
Our summer day withers away
Too soon, too soon . . .

"Dad couldn't have been at the docks," Frank reflected out loud, "when Alex or his thugs ambushed him. Because of the hat. They would've left it in the area, along with his car, to draw attention away from the Polucca place. They wouldn't have put it in the Packard.

"If Dad had been wearing his hat when they jumped him, they would've put it wherever they put him. But they didn't do that, so he wasn't wearing it."

Love is a spark, lost in the dark
Too soon, too soon . . .

Frank turned to the others. "The way I see it, there's only one likely reason why the hat was in the Packard: Alex noticed it in the ditch, or wherever it was, when he was driving in or out. Either he saw it before Dad was caught—and it tipped him off that someone was there—or he saw it afterward. It may have been when he was leaving to go downtown to give the driver of Dad's car a ride back—if what Joe and I believe is true, and Dad parked in the lane and they moved his car."

"I don't think he'd have given the driver a ride back," Joe

134

argued. "There was probably another vehicle to do that—remember those tire tracks in the driveway. Mister Smooth wouldn't have wanted to risk somebody noticing a stranger getting into his conspicuous, easy-to-remember car. I'll bet he went to Simpson's and Sanderson's to talk with people, so they'd remember seeing him in case he needed an alibi."

Frank returned his attention to the night view.

It's late—darling, it's late.
The curtain descends, everything ends
too soon, too soon . . .

"No matter what happened, exactly," he went on, "it's safe to assume that Alex Polucca had some very important things to take care of all of a sudden. We can assume that, because he forgot the hat. I think he put it in the back seat when he picked it up because someone was riding in the front seat. But whatever happened, he didn't think of it again until Chief Collig showed up and started asking about it."

"He sure thought his way out of *that* situation fast," Joe said admiringly.

"But his story cost him something—*time.* Dad's car could've been down by the docks for days before somebody noticed that it'd been sitting in the same spot. That was probably one of the reasons for putting it there."

Evelyn Hardy reached for the telephone. "If I can't get through to Chief Collig right now, I'll drive down in the sedan and—"

"You won't need to," said Frank, as the chief's car pulled up in front of the house.

Tension in the Air

"All right, Frank," said Chief Collig, running a hand over his stubbly hair. "I see your point. What all of you have just told me puts today's events in a new light. Of course, it remains to be seen how all that equipment got into the garage."

He paused, then leaned forward, resting his elbows on the arms of his chair. "As for your theory that the hat in Alex's car proves that your father went to the house and was taken prisoner there— and that his car therefore must have been driven to the waterfront by someone else . . ."

He shook his head and gave a crooked smile. "Remember what I said a few minutes ago: *We've found no fingerprints in or on Fenton's car that were made by anyone other than family members or the mechanics. And we've found no signs of wiping or smudging.* Other than the smudging done by the most recent identifiable prints, as I said."

"Someone else could have driven Dad's car," Joe insisted. "I showed you how it could've been done."

"But we found no signs that it *was* done," the chief sternly replied. "And the condition of the prints indicates that it *wasn't.*

"Regarding Frank's theory about the hat: I'm afraid it doesn't prove anything—any more than does the dirt in Fenton's car or the tire tracks in the lane. Alex could have put the hat in his car at the docks—but not the way he claims. The dirt could have come from anywhere. The tire tracks could mean anything. None of that provides evidence that Fenton went to the house."

"It *could*," said Joe, "if you add everything up."

"All right—just for the sake of argument, let's say Fenton *did* go out there. He could have parked in the lane, walked to the house, asked some questions, then returned to his car. That would explain the dirt. The not-yet-identified tire tracks in the lane could have been made later, to—as you suggest—hide the fact that his car had been there. After leaving Polucca's, Fenton could have driven to the waterfront—he might have waited until Alex drove away from the house, then followed him."

"Well, Chief," Gertrude Hardy said from her corner of the living room, "you seem to have thoroughly figured out what could *not* have happened. Now what do you intend to do about my missing brother, and about Alex Polucca?"

Chief Collig turned toward her and raised a thumb. "First, we'll immediately station a squad car by the entrance to the Polucca driveway."

He raised a finger. "Second, we'll send the patrol boat out to Walton Point, pronto, to guard that entrance in the rocks that Frank and Joe described."

Another finger went up. "Third, we'll expand our search for Fenton at the waterfront."

He lifted another finger. "Fourth, we'll cite what all of you have told me as 'probable cause' in an affidavit for a search warrant, which we'll submit as soon as the courthouse opens in the morning."

One more finger went up. "Fifth, once we have the warrant, we'll conduct a thorough search of the house. We'll take the place apart—garage floor and everything."

"In the *morning*," Mrs. Hardy said anxiously. "That's *hours* from now. What if it *was* Fenton behind that door in the tunnel?"

"Which it could've been," Joe added, "if Dad *did* drive to the docks—as you say he might have—and was grabbed by Alex or his men and then taken to the house."

"There is absolutely no evidence," insisted the chief. "We have to have a search warrant—and we'll have one, as I said, the first thing in the morning. Alex and crew won't be going anywhere in the meantime. I got into a good deal of trouble in my younger

137

days over no-knocks and incidents of forcible entry, acting on insufficient evidence—"

"You can go to Judge Jamieson right now," interjected Mrs. Hardy, "and ask him to issue a warrant for a night search."

"A night search for someone, without evidence, can leave us wide open to charges of harassment and unreasonable use of power. In this case, it could give Alex Polucca's attorneys ammunition that we don't want to give them. We're the police—the upholders of the law. Which means that we need to abide by the law and take every reasonable precaution in our enforcement of it. We can't operate like private investigators or a dictator's army."

"How can you believe," Joe asked angrily, "that there's no evidence that Dad's being held prisoner in the tunnel?"

"What-ifs and maybes aren't evidence. By your own admission, the man you saw—what little of him there was to see—*was not tied up.* The door had *no lock* on it. And the only thing you know about the clothing you glimpsed is that *it was brown.* There's a lot of brown clothing in this world."

"Applying similar logic," Aunt Gertrude coldly remarked, "one could say that while there are many police uniforms in Bayport, including the one you're wearing, that fact alone is no evidence that the men inside those uniforms are policemen."

"What are you—"

"If those men in uniform, yourself included, were to *behave* like policemen, that would be evidence, indeed."

Evelyn Hardy rose to her feet.

"Chief Collig," she began, her jaw tight with anger, "does everything have to be *proved* before you act?" She pointed north. "My husband may be in that room, or in that hideout, at this very moment!" Her hand swung around and pointed at the chief. "And you quibble about whether or not there's enough *evidence!*"

She turned, took a couple of steps away, then turned back.

"Your job," she continued angrily, "is not to *judge.* It's to *investigate suspicious circumstances and enforce the law.*"

"All of which involves judgment," replied the chief, his voice rising in irritation, "concerning what measures to take, where to deploy my men, and on what to concentrate our efforts."

Mrs. Hardy went over to him, folded her arms, and glared. *"What sort of hold does Alex Polucca have on you?"*

Chief Collig, his face turning red, sucked in his breath. He looked past his interrogator to the clock, then stood up and clapped his hat onto his head.

"I'll set what I promised in motion before it gets any later," he said, darting angry looks around the room. "We'll do everything we can to find Fenton, and we'll make sure that Alex and his henchmen don't escape."

He walked quickly from the living room, through the entrance hall, opened the front door, passed hurriedly through, and closed the door loudly behind him.

"So long, Flatfoot!" Iola called.

"Really, dear!" scolded Aunt Gertrude.

"He believes *now*," said Joe bitterly, "what the rest of us told him *before* about the cave, the trapdoor, and the tunnel—"

"Now that two adults have backed us up," Frank pointed out.

"So when will he get around to taking seriously what we just told him about the man in the storage room?"

"I must say," Aunt Gertrude angrily admitted, "that I *am* disappointed in our chief of police."

She took up her abandoned knitting, looked away, then put it down again.

Evelyn Hardy stood unmoving in front of the chief's recently vacated chair, staring at the entrance to the living room. She raised her right hand, clenched it into a fist, and brought it down on her opened left hand.

"I'm *furious!*" she exclaimed. "If there's any chance at all that Fenton's in that room—or anywhere else in that dreadful place . . ."

"We should've taken Dad's camera with us," Frank said regretfully. "If we'd photographed the trapdoor and tunnel, we wouldn't have lost time trying to convince Chief Collig. The police could've moved in on that place this afternoon, search warrant in hand."

"There are quite a few things that all of us *should* have done," his mother replied. "I'm going to do what *I* should have done as soon as you told me what happened at Alex Polucca's—telephone Lane Anderson."

She left for her husband's study.

With a sigh, Aunt Gertrude returned to her knitting.

"*We* ought to rescue Dad," Joe said to his brother, after a long interval of silence.

"That's what I've been thinking," Frank replied. "We can't get to the tunnel from the garage now, but we *could* get to it from the cave, with the help of Tony and *Napoli.*"

Joe shook his head doubtfully. "You remember how steep the lower part of the tunnel is. And how *long* it must be. It's designed for a car with a cog drive!"

"There's another problem," Chet remarked. "The patrol boat's going to be sitting out by the point. That thing's made for speed. It'd catch us before we got anywhere near the entrance."

Joe groaned. "Good old Chief Collig. Trying to be helpful."

"There must be a way," said Frank, "to get to the tunnel from the house. If we could find it—"

"*Ahem!*"

Everyone turned to Gertrude Hardy.

She looked up from her knitting and swept an Aunt Gertrude scowl of disapproval around the room. "In case any of you should think for one moment that Evelyn or I would *ever* permit *any* attempt at breaking into that den of thieves—"

"We wouldn't," her sister-in-law firmly stated, as she entered the room.

"What happened?" Callie asked her.

"The New York FBI operator told me that Special Agent Anderson is putting in overtime on a case. After I briefly explained the situation to her, she tried to contact him by way of his car radio. She came back on and said that he must be temporarily out of communication. Agents working overtime are required, she said, to report to the switchboard every three hours, and he last reported a little over two-and-a-half hours ago. She said that if she can't reach him by radio, she'll have him phone here as soon as he contacts her."

Mrs. Hardy sat down and looked from one of her sons to the other. "And now—what's this about an *attempt?*"

"We were discussing how we could rescue Dad," Joe answered.

"Oooh, no," replied his mother. "No one—and that includes you, Joseph Hardy—*no one* is leaving here to risk his life."

She picked up her book. "So dream on, dreamers. Dream on."

"Is there anything wrong with us *talking* about it?"

Mrs. Hardy opened the book. "You may *talk* all you want." She resumed reading.

"I noticed a couple of strange things at the Polucca house," Callie said to Frank. "I can't help thinking that they might have to do with a hidden stairway."

"What were they?"

"Well, first there was the kitchen . . ."

Callie looked beyond Frank, as though trying to see something in the distance.

"The kitchen's in the northeast corner of the house. If you were in it facing north, you'd see floor-to-ceiling cupboards with solid doors, against the exterior wall—each with two tall doors on the bottom and two short ones above—running more than halfway along from left to right. To the right of them is a big refrigerator, then some four- or five-foot-tall cabinets with bins for flour and so on. There aren't any windows in the wall, but that isn't unusual for a kitchen with a lot of tall cupboards and appliances. I wouldn't have thought anything of it, if it hadn't been for something I noticed about the other wall."

She turned her eyes to Frank.

"From the outside, the northernmost window in the kitchen's east wall appears to be farther from the north wall than it does from the *in*side."

The brothers looked at each other.

"Not counting what I estimated to be the thickness of the stone and wallboards," Callie continued, "the difference was maybe three feet. Maybe more."

"As you say," Iola put in doubtfully, "*maybe.*"

"Good observing," Frank said to Callie.

"I noticed one more thing," the latter replied. "In the bedroom above the kitchen, there's a deep, wide closet in the northeast corner, against the north wall. *That* room's wall is genuine, because there's a window in it. But I'm not sure the closet is for real. As Iola

141

remarked to me, it's in an odd location in the room. I didn't think of looking inside it while I might have had a chance to do so—only later, when I noticed the funny thing about the kitchen window. Which, along with the closet, made me think that there might be a narrow stairway between the kitchen and the bedroom."

"Could you see what's on the inside of the rest of the north wall on the ground floor?"

"Starting at the front of the house, there's the service porch. We didn't go into it, but I peeked in from the outside."

"Its north wall is mostly lattice. No room to hide a stairway there."

"Right. Then comes the pantry, then the kitchen. The pantry has cupboards along the north wall and shelves along the facing interior wall."

"Cupboards again. How tall?"

"Floor to ceiling. With solid doors, the same as in the kitchen."

"Hmmm."

"In the wall between the pantry and the kitchen, there's a swinging door with a little window. It was propped open, or I wouldn't have been able to see as much as I did of the pantry. Between the pantry and the porch is a solid door."

"What did the lock on it look like?"

"All I remember seeing is a doorknob—a metal one."

"So in all probability," said Frank, after a few seconds of thought, "there's a stairway in the wall that you can get to from the pantry or the kitchen. And the entrance to it is most likely in those cupboards."

"And," said Joe, "it must go down to the tunnel, coming out behind that door we saw. Which, unfortunately, means that it goes right to the smugglers."

"When I listened to the voices behind the door . . ." Frank paused, remembering. "Yeah—they sounded muffled. Maybe there's another wall and a door between the stairway and the hideout."

"If there is," Joe replied, "we could sneak down the stairs from wherever the hidden entrance is—"

"You very possibly *could* sneak down the stairs," remarked Mrs. Hardy, still reading. "But you aren't *going* to."

The brothers exchanged looks of frustration. Joe sighed, leaned back, and closed his eyes. Frank put his elbow on the arm of his chair, rested his chin in his hand, and stared at the floor.

"I forgot to tell you two," said Chet, "that Biff phoned while you were at the docks. I told him what happened this afternoon. He said to let you know how sorry he is that Mr. Hardy's missing and that he'll be glad to help if there's anything he can do."

Frank nodded.

"Good old Biff," Joe muttered.

Aunt Gertrude turned up the radio, which had been lowered to a whisper on the arrival of Chief Collig.

It's quarter to three—
There's no one in the place
Except you and me.
So set 'em up, Joe,
I've got a little story
You oughta know.

Joe opened his eyes and looked at the radio. "We missed the latest 'Boston Blackie.'"

"And the *new* private eye show," said Frank, "'Philip Marlowe.' Tuesday night." He thought for a moment. "Last night."

"Third episode."

"What do you think of Philip Marlowe as a detective?" Chet asked Frank. "I mean the original character, not the radio and movie versions."

Frank raised his eyes and turned his head. "I think he's a joke."

"Why?"

"He behaves like someone who's trying to be a detective but doesn't know how. And to me, that's funny."

"How could Marlowe be funny? He's such a *serious* old sourpuss!"

"He's just not believable. He's not *consistent*. In his narration, he uses two or three adjectives to describe every little thing he sees. In his conversations, he sizes people up instantly and trades wise-cracks as quickly and cleverly as a boxer exchanges punches. He makes up figures of speech that even a college professor might have difficulty thinking of. So obviously he's got enough brain-power to be a very successful investigator. But his income is pathetic, his office is a dump, the top of his convertible leaks . . ."

Chet laughed. "Petty details."

"Marlowe tells people he's poor because he's honest," Joe contributed. "*That's* a hoot. He makes untruthful statements to everyone, encourages his clients to lie, rearranges evidence to fool police investigators, removes material from crime scenes, deliberately fails to report homicides, conceals the identities of murderers—"

"No big deal."

"Another unbelievable thing about Marlowe," said Frank, "is the way he treats people. No real-life private investigator could afford to have such an offensive personality."

"The public pretty much has to cooperate with *police* detectives," Joe explained to Chet, "because they're the law. But no one has to cooperate with *private* detectives. And if any private eye was as obnoxious as Marlowe is—"

"Ordinary, honest citizens," Frank elaborated, "don't like being questioned by strangers or being pulled into investigations. Neither do sleazy types with something to hide. So a skilled investigator uses subtlety, diplomacy, and trickery to talk information out of people and to help determine who's telling the truth. But Marlowe's an angry, alcohol-guzzling bull in a china shop. He goes after information by taunting and insulting everybody—clients, contacts, witnesses, suspects, the police . . ."

"*Aha!*" exclaimed Chet. "*That's* why he's poor!"

"In the stories," said Joe, "all these people answer Marlowe's questions, even though they have no reason for doing so. In real life, they'd slam the door in his face."

"Or beat him up," said Frank. "Or shoot him."

"As if all that wasn't unreal enough," Joe added, "Old Bigmouth tips off suspects by telling them what he's found out about them!"

"That," said Chet, "*proves* he's honest."

"It proves," said Frank, "that he's a joke."

144

"Only someone who doesn't know what he's doing," remarked his brother, "would use a *convertible* for surveillance."

Frank smiled. "Or hire a *taxicab* to shadow someone."

"Or go after killers by himself—"

"And walk into traps—"

"Perhaps," Callie suggested, "we ought to change the subject."

Well that's how it goes
And Joe, I know you're getting
Anxious to close.
So thanks for the cheer—
I hope you didn't mind
My bending your ear.
This torch that I've found—

The sudden jangling of the telephone startled everyone.

On Their Way

"It's a matter of deciding the best plan of action," said the brisk voice at the other end of the line. "There's no field office in your state to draw from, so—"

"There's a resident agency in the capital," Evelyn Hardy cut in. "And another in—"

"Yes, for a total of five men. But you know how the Bureau operates, Mrs. Hardy—*preparation* and *numbers*. In this case, we don't have the one, so we need to rely even more than usual on the other. For everyone's safety."

"How will you work it, then?"

"We'll need to notify the Boston field office. They have jurisdiction over your area. They'll either send a team of their own or assemble one from the RAs nearest to you."

"Which would be faster?"

"I wouldn't want to waste time speculating. The decision's over my head, anyway. As soon as I'm off the phone with you, I'll report to the assistant director, and he'll send word to Boston. I *can* tell you, though, that at this time of night and on such short notice, it'll be a few hours before the team arrives, whichever option's exercised."

"Could the FBI save some time by flying part of the way? There's no airport nearby, but—"

"We could go by plane, or by train, to wherever we can round up enough bucars. Sorry for the jargon—I mean *Bureau-equipped cars.* There aren't any in or near Bayport, and we've got to have them."

"Is there any chance that *you'll* be sent?"

"I'm afraid not. I wish I *could* go. The NYO—the New York field office—is the office of origin for this drugs-thievery investigation, and I'm the case agent. So far our squad hasn't come up with anything substantial, and this looks like our big break. But don't worry—every one of us in the Bureau has a strong commitment to putting these people away."

"What can the FBI do," asked Frank on the kitchen extension, "about the speedboat exit in the rocks?"

"I'm sure we'll send a Coast Guard cutter to block it. They'll get to the area a lot sooner than *we* will, no matter where we'll be dispatched from. But we'll get there—it'll all come together tonight. And I'm sure the assistant director'll have surveillance started on the Polucca family immediately. All right, Frank—tell me everything you can about the location and layout of that house."

"But, Mother," Joe argued, "if they know exactly where the stairway entrance is, and exactly how to get to it, they can sneak quickly and quietly down there and have everyone's hands in the air before anybody knows what happened."

"If the crooks *have* got Dad in that storage room," Frank joined in, "and they see or hear someone—"

"Or a big team of someones—"

"Advancing on the house or fooling around with locks and cupboards—"

"Then Dad's a hostage."

"FBI agents are *professionals,*" countered Mrs. Hardy. She folded her arms and leaned back in the couch. "They know their business!"

"But we know the terrain," Joe asserted. "There are only two of us. No one's going to see or hear us coming. Dad's taught us a lot about opening locks and panels—"

"We don't know who's on the FBI team, or how they operate,"

said Frank. "As far as we know, they might smash open the front door and storm through the house. But we know *we* can get in there unseen and unheard, and find the entrance."

"That's all very well," his mother replied. "Until you're caught."

"Chet can drive us to the area," Joe proposed. "We'll hide the Duchess and go around the patrol car. Chet'll watch from the trees. If we *are* caught, he'll head right out the driveway to the police. They can radio for reinforcements and have a small army at the door in no time. And the FBI'll be showing up—"

"And then," protested Mrs. Hardy, "they'll have to rescue *three* hostages."

"Which brings us back," said Frank, "to the need for the agents to get to the hideout *quickly* and *quietly*."

"We'll make sure the house is totally dark," Joe told his mother. "We'll get inside without making a sound and find the entrance to the stairway. Then we'll slip away to the patrol car, leaving the doors unlocked behind us. When the FBI team arrives, we'll tell them how to get to the stairway. That's all we'll do—we won't go down the stairs."

Evelyn Hardy, her eyes filled with distress and uncertainty, turned to her sister-in-law.

"You *know* what *I* think," Aunt Gertrude said grimly.

Mrs. Hardy stood and walked slowly to the fireplace. She put her hands on the mantelpiece and stared at the ticking clock for a long time.

Finally she turned to her sons. "Under the conditions that you just now stated—but *only* under those conditions . . ."

In a voice barely audible over the soft music on the radio, she concluded: "All right."

Frank and Joe went to her, kissed her, and put their arms around her.

"If either of you is harmed in any way," she assured them, "I'll never forgive myself."

"In that case," Joe replied, grinning, "we'll just have to be careful."

"Come on," said Frank. "The three of us need dark clothing."

"We'll find something in the costume closet that'll fit you," Joe told Chet as they left the room. "Something really gruesome."

"With vampire teeth?"

Evelyn Hardy looked up to the ceiling and held out her hands.

"I must be out of my mind!" she declared. "My husband's been captured by smugglers, and now I'm sending my *sons!*"

"What have you got in there?" Chet asked, pointing to the black haversack Frank was carrying, as the three dark-clad figures entered the living room. Each held a pair of black gloves and a black ski mask.

Frank handed the bag to Chet, then walked to his chair and sat down.

Chet went over to the loveseat, sat, and started pulling items from the haversack.

"Two black towels . . . An old black rag towel . . . Three pairs of big black wool socks . . . A folded piece of dark-green wallpaper . . . A roll of black electrician's tape . . . A small can of household oil, looks like, with black tape around it . . . A spray can of something-or-other, also covered with black tape—"

"Shaving cream," said Joe, reluctantly sitting.

Chet shook his head in disbelief, then continued: "A thin metal ruler, painted black . . . A multifunction knife . . . Long tweezers, painted black . . . A ring of skeleton keys of various shapes and sizes, each wrapped in tape except for the working ends . . . A glass cutter . . . A small, black cloth case containing—"

"Lockpicks."

Chet looked into the haversack. "And three black-taped flashlights and some batteries."

He began putting the objects back into the bag.

"Why the big socks?" he asked, holding up a pair.

"To put over our shoes," answered Frank. "So they won't make noise."

"Tape?"

"To hold the latch bolt in, once you turn the knob and open the door. That way, you can close the door behind you without the latch clicking shut. And when you leave, or go out and come back, you won't have to risk making noise turning the knob. Electrician's tape doesn't make a tearing sound when you pull some off the roll. And, whatever you put it on, it comes off quickly and quietly, without leaving any residue."

"Sounds reasonable. Tweezers?"

"For use on an old-style warded lock," Frank replied. "What's commonly known as a keyhole lock—the kind that can be opened with a skeleton key.

"If a key's in the lock on the inside of the door, you stick the tweezers into the keyhole, grab the end of the key, turn it until it's lined up with the opening, and push it out. It falls on that piece of wallpaper, which you've slipped under the door. Wallpaper's thick enough to help muffle the sound of the falling key and stiff enough to slide quickly under the door. You pull on the paper, the key comes with it, and you unlock the door."

"If the crack isn't big enough for that," Joe added, "you attach one end of a piece of tape to the key with the tweezers. Then you push the key out and attach your end of the tape to the keyhole plate, so the key doesn't fall onto the floor and make noise. Then you pick the lock, or use a skeleton key."

"How about this ruler?"

"That's to slip between the frame and the door," said Frank, "and coax the latch bolt back. Every door frame has a strip of wood fastened in front of the door to prevent that. But sometimes it's possible to pry it loose enough with the knife tools to poke the end of the ruler through. That won't get you anywhere with dead bolts, though, because they don't push back."

"Okay. *Shaving cream?*"

"That's for old warded locks. Most of them are filthy, rusty, hard to move, and noisy. If you spray shaving cream into the mechanism, it'll foam up and soften the sound of the skeleton key or lockpick. And it's a lubricant, which makes things move a bit smoother and quieter. Sometimes it helps to squirt some oil in first."

"And the towels?"

"The rag towel," answered Frank, "is for cleaning up. The others are to stuff under the door, so the light from a flashlight won't shine through, and to put over the knob to open the door quietly—and to avoid leaving fingerprints. It's hard to pick a lock wearing gloves."

"You can also use a towel," said Joe, "to put over your hand or elbow to break a window—after you tape the glass to keep the pieces from falling and making noise."

"Tell me something," said Chet to the brothers. "Which side of the law are you on?"

"The right one," replied Frank with a smile. "We're training to become detectives, not burglars."

"That's lucky for the rest of us."

Chet put the remaining items back in the haversack.

"Most housebreakers don't bother to pick locks," Joe pointed out. "It's easier to just smash a window or cut a hole in the glass and reach through to the latch. But for our purposes tonight, the doors are a better way in. They take us right where we want to go."

"Anybody can do this sort of thing," Frank told Chet. "That's why Dad says it makes more sense for society to encourage people to be honest than to try to maintain law and order only by punishing them after they've been caught doing something illegal. It costs a lot less to promote decent behavior than it does to build more and more prisons, and pay insurance companies and police forces for more and more damaged and stolen property. And cover the fees of lawyers, judges, and juries."

"Until a lot more people think so," said Joe, "we're all in danger. Anyone smarter than a moron can break into a house!"

"Well," Chet remarked, smiling, "I guess housebreaking won't be *my* profession. I'm not mentally qualified."

He glanced at the black bag. "I thought of one thing *you* didn't, though—sandwiches."

"A very good idea," said Mrs. Hardy, getting up from the sofa. "I'll make some right away."

She left for the kitchen.

"Alex Polucca's bedroom," Callie warned Frank, "is on the upper floor, in front—the second one from the south end of the house."

"Thanks. We'll stay as far from it as we can."

"I was such a *fool*," Iola declared, breaking her long silence.

She stared ahead, oblivious to the startled faces turned toward her. "If that man beneath the house was Mr. Hardy—and who else would it have been, shut up in that room . . . Then all the time Alex was being so *charming* to us, he was holding Mr. Hardy *prisoner* down there!"

Callie turned to the uncharacteristically reflective girl beside her on the sofa. "Do you still think Alex is *sweet?*"

"No . . . No . . . No . . ." Iola answered, more softly with each repetition.

Her shoulders slumped. She began to cry.

Callie put her arm around her.

"I'm sorry," she gently told her. "I shouldn't have said that."

"If we had told Mr. Hardy in the beginning about what's going on in that house," lamented Iola, "he wouldn't have gone there all alone! What have we done to him? What have we *done?*"

She started sobbing uncontrollably.

Joe sat unmoving in his chair, stupefied by this unrecognizable and incomprehensible Iola Morton.

Aunt Gertrude put aside her knitting, rose, went to the sofa, and sat, ramrod straight, next to Iola.

"Now, dear," she said soothingly. "My brother has been in a good many situations more dangerous than this one."

"He *has?*"

"He has. And quite often, it's been his own doing. Don't consider him merely a victim of circumstances. He has free will; he exercises his own judgment. Sometimes the decisions he makes put him in jeopardy. But he has many resources to draw upon in dealing with adversity."

Iola kept sobbing.

"As a student of language," Aunt Gertrude continued, "I believe that our names influence our conduct in this world. One cannot go through life with the name *Hardy* without being shaped by it.

152

Both Fenton and I have been. One of the many lessons we have learned from that influence is that we simply cannot afford to give way to fears, sorrows, or regrets. They take away our power to *act.*"

She patted Iola's knee.

"And now, since it appears that the four of us will be up for a good part of the night while Frank, Joe, and Chet put the authorities on the proper track, I think I'll make some tea."

She stood up and paused, looking—as stoically as she could manage to—at her nephews and their driver.

"My best wishes for the three of you," she addressed them softly. "Even though I have misgivings about what you're up to."

Frank smiled.

"Thanks, Miss Hardy," Chet replied seriously.

"Yeah—thanks, Auntie," said Joe, smiling. "We'll be thinking of you."

"Hmmph," responded "Auntie" in disbelief as she turned away.

As she passed her sister-in-law returning from the kitchen, she shook her head and muttered: *"Nephews."*

Mrs. Hardy handed a well-stuffed paper bag to Chet, then walked behind the sofa and put her hands on the softly crying girl's shoulders.

"Everything's going to be all right, Iola. It's been a while since dinner, and we're all under quite a bit of stress. We'll feel better once we've had a little more food."

"We'd better go," said Frank, standing.

As the other boys got to their feet, he collected the gloves and ski masks and put them in the haversack.

Mrs. Hardy went over to him, hugged him, and kissed him good-bye.

"My big boy," she whispered.

She hugged and kissed Joe and ruffled his hair. He grinned at her. She smiled sadly in response.

After exchanging good-byes with Chet, she turned away and walked to the kitchen.

Frank lifted the haversack to his shoulder. He looked at Callie and made a slight movement with his head toward the front door. Then he beckoned to Chet.

With a concerned look at his sister, who sat staring mournfully down at her hands in her lap, Chet followed Frank out of the living room.

Joe remained standing by his chair, his eyes fixed on Iola.

Callie, her arm still around her heavy-hearted friend, watched him watching. She smiled to herself, then gave Iola a quick hug.

"You'll be just fine," she told her.

She got up and left the room.

She passed through the entry hall, opened the front door, and stepped onto the porch, where Frank waited, sitting on the railing.

Behind him in the street, Chet climbed into the Duchess and started her engine.

Frank smiled and stood as Callie approached. She put her hands up to his cheeks.

"Be careful," she whispered.

Standing on tiptoe, she touched her lips to his.

Then she was gone. The door closed quietly behind her.

In the hall, she frowned, leaned back against the wall, and shut her eyes.

On the sofa, Iola sat with her elbows on her knees, her face in her hands.

Joe walked over and stood in front of her. "Are you okay, Iola?"

Iola looked up at him. With the back of her hand, she wiped tears away. She smiled bravely and nodded.

"Well . . ." said Joe awkwardly. "I'll see you later."

Iola's smile vanished, leaving her face as sad as before.

"I hope so," she said.

Frank leaned out of the front window as Joe reached the car.

"Is Iola all right?" he asked.

Joe turned the rear-door handle and paused.

"Yeah," he answered. He looked back at the house. "She *is*." He smiled. "She *is* all right."

He opened the door and climbed inside.

"Okay, Ride Man," he said to Chet. "Let's ride."

Impressions

Chet lowered the volume of the car radio a bit as Artie Shaw's band began its slow, ominous signature tune, "Nightmare."

"Enjoying your sandwiches, boys?" he asked, wiping crumbs from his lips with the back of his hand.

Frank gave him a sideways look and stopped chewing.

"Not as much as you enjoyed yours," he replied.

He reached down with his free hand and brushed off some pieces of sandwich that had made their way to his side of the seat.

"And the two bananas," he added.

Chet laughed. "It was fun while it lasted."

As the Duchess hurried up North Shore Road, the view from her windows was alternately illuminated by the eerie light of the full moon, then plunged into deep shadow.

The minor-key melody on the radio, with its throbbing beat and swelling-then-diminishing orchestration, provided a fitting musical accompaniment.

Chet glanced uneasily at the trees flickering by.

"It's kind of spooky out here," he observed.

"The service porch door'll be easy," Joe loudly remarked from the back seat with a mouth full of food. "Rattly old warded lock. Remember when Biff shook the knob?"

"Yeah," answered Frank. "But the lock on the door behind it's probably newer."

"A pin tumbler, most likely. Like the one in the front door."

Chet turned to Frank. "I've never seen a set of lockpicks. Do you mind if I take a look?"

"Not if you stop the car first."

As the Duchess came to a halt in the empty road, Frank put the remaining piece of his sandwich aside and rummaged through the black haversack on the floor.

From the bottom of the bag, he took a flashlight. He turned it on and passed it to Chet. Then he rummaged around some more.

"Here it is," he said, pulling out the small cloth case.

He opened it and handed it to Chet.

The beam of the flashlight revealed six black slender tools, each except one resting handle-downward in its own pocket.

"That's a tension wrench," said Frank, pointing to what looked like a bent, miniature screwdriver lying loose in the case. "To turn the lock cylinder."

He pointed to something resembling a straightened dentist's pick with the end of its bent tip ground flat.

"That's a hook pick, to push the lock pins out of the way. It and the tension wrench are all you need to open the pin tumbler locks used on most exterior doors."

Chet looked up in surprise.

"Frightening, isn't it?" Frank remarked.

"You bet it is. I guess I *could* be a housebreaker."

Chet ran a finger over the other tools.

"Those," Frank told him, "are for warded and lever locks and padlocks. They're named after their shapes." He pointed to each in turn. "Large L, small L, large T, small T."

He leaned back in the seat. "There are other kinds, too—stepped Ls, diamonds, rakes . . ."

"Tools like those," said Joe, chewing, "are used by the break-and-enter boys, law enforcement officers, some private detectives, and a few investigative reporters. Not to mention spies, weirdos, and the Green Hornet. But, unless you're a registered locksmith or the law, all those funny-looking little utensils are illegal."

"I'm glad you warned me," said Chet. He clapped the case shut, switched off the flashlight, and shoved both across the seat.

He put the Duchess in gear and accelerated.

"If the police stop us," he assured his passengers, "the first thing I'll say is *I don't know what's in that bag.*'"

"What bag?"

Frank put the flashlight and lockpick case away. Then he turned up the radio and finished his sandwich, tapping his feet to the Jimmy Dorsey band's "John Silver."

"Say, Frank," called Joe, chewing his last bite. "Tell Chet how Dad opened that door at Marsden Industries!"

Frank lowered the radio volume and turned to Chet.

"Years ago in Boston, an arsonist Dad had followed into a warehouse jumped him and knocked him out."

"It was an old wood airplane hangar of a place," Joe contributed, "loaded with flammable stuff. The owner's crooked competition paid the creep to burn it."

"The arsonist dragged Dad over to a big machine," continued Frank, "leaned him back against one of its legs, and tied his hands together behind the leg with a piece of rope. Then he piled up oily rags in a couple of hard-to-find places, lit them, and left."

"The old smoldering rag trick," said Joe. "By the time the building catches fire, the torch man's elsewhere, with an alibi and witnesses."

"When Dad came to, he felt up and down the two rear edges of the leg with his wrists. He found a rough, rusty spot and worked the rope against it until it broke. Then he headed for the nearest door. But it was locked. So were the others—all padlocked from the outside."

"Windows?" asked Chet, gazing at the road ahead.

"Way up high where he couldn't get to them. There was an office shed against one of the walls, with a door but no windows. He thought there must be a phone inside he could use to call for help. So he tried the door. It was locked."

"Metal door," Joe added. "Metal frame. To prevent anyone from breaking in with a pry bar."

"Dad looked around, trying to think of a way to get into the office, and noticed the lighting—large industrial light bulbs screwed into sockets attached to the undersides of the lowest

157

beams, several feet over his head. Then he saw a stack of electrical conduit."

"Various lengths, three-inch diameter."

"Then," said Frank, "he knew he'd found his way in."

He paused expectantly.

Chet looked at Frank, then back at the road. "It may be obvious to *you* what light bulbs and conduit have to do with getting past a metal door, but it's not obvious to ol' Chet. How about giving him a clue?"

"The light bulbs," said Joe, "had bendable wires supporting the filaments."

"And," said Frank, "the conduit could help him reach the light bulbs."

Chet rolled his eyes. "Thanks for the clues."

Frank smiled. "Dad stood one of the tubes on end, pushed it up against a light bulb, and turned it counterclockwise to loosen the bulb. But the bulb wouldn't turn. So he moved to the next one and tried again. The bulb turned, came loose, and smashed on the floor.

"Dad put his handkerchief over the stem to protect his hand and bent one of the wires into a hook pick. Then, using the flat tip of the prong of his belt buckle as a tension wrench—"

"*Oh.*"

"—he unlocked the office door. There was a telephone inside, which he used to phone the fire department and the police. The fire was prevented, and the arsonist was arrested—for more than arson."

Chet nodded reflectively. "Smart man, your father."

Conversation ceased. The three rescuers, each occupied with his own thoughts, stared ahead at the deserted road.

The underside of the Duchess scraped for the second time as she moved slowly onward, straddling the ruts in the Olsen driveway.

"Why'd you make this car so low, anyway?" Joe asked peevishly.

"Because," answered Chet, "I didn't know I'd be doing anything as stupid as this. I lowered her so I could cruise smoothly along decent, paved roads and impress the girls."

Joe snorted. "Girls don't care about cars. They're nutty that way."

Frank pointed ahead. "There's the high area. Let me out and I'll guide you."

The Duchess stopped and Frank got out. He stepped onto the wide grassy center strip and walked a few yards up the driveway; then he halted and turned.

Looking down to where the ground almost flattened out, holding a hand in front of his face to block the glare of the headlights, he beckoned Chet onward.

Suddenly he started.

He looked toward the car, putting both hands in front of his face.

"Switch off the lights and come over here!" he yelled. "And bring a flashlight! But don't walk in the dirt!"

The headlights went out and the doors opened. Joe and Chet, the latter showing the way with a flashlight, stepped from the running boards to the grass, and came up to where Frank was standing.

Chet shone the light down where Frank pointed.

Running partway into and then out of the dusty soil of the shallow right-hand rut—the one nearer the oak grove—was the impression, about three feet long, of the edge of a rugged tire. About three inches across at its widest point, it consisted of large rectangles of tread with wide spaces between them. It led from, and returned to, the grass by the side of the driveway.

Chet moved the light over.

In the left-hand rut was a wider partial track with matching tread leading from, and returning to, the center strip.

"A Jeep, maybe?" Joe asked.

"A truck," Chet answered. "That's too big for a Jeep tire."

Joe took the light from him and pointed it down at the right-hand rut.

"Whatever it was," he said, "it came through here after we left."

Curving across the rut were two pairs of automobile tire tracks—a left-tire set heading toward the oak grove and a right-tire set coming from it. Each consisted of the marks of a sharply turned front tire and those of a more moderately angled rear tire. The front-tire impressions came within a foot of each other. The truck tire had run over both.

Frank took the flashlight and walked up the center strip for a few yards, shining the light into the ruts.

He turned and walked back past the intersection of tracks, studying the ruts between it and the Duchess.

Then he returned to the others.

"The driver," he said, "apparently turned the front tires back into the grass before the rear tires could follow. And without *their* tracks, there's no way to tell if the truck was coming or going."

"It wouldn't be hard to accidentally move over here," Joe remarked, "heading in either direction. Because of the way the ground rises and flattens out."

"In a truck, they didn't have to worry about road clearance," observed Frank. "They must've been keeping to the grass to avoid leaving tracks."

"But what were they doing here?" asked Chet, looking up the driveway.

The brothers looked in the same direction. Frank switched off the flashlight.

As their eyes adapted to the moonlight, the three began to take in the scene before them.

At the end of the driveway was the dark shell of the fire-gutted house, flanked only by weeds, bent grass, and a few saplings.

To the left of the house and driveway lay overgrown, but otherwise empty, fields.

To the right beyond the house was the dilapidated barn with the collapsing roof.

Attached to the right end of the barn, facing away from the driveway, was the long, somewhat newer, equipment shed.

"The equipment shed," muttered Frank, staring at it. "I wonder . . ."

"Let's hide the Duchess," said Joe, "and find out."

Hide and Seek

Accompanied by the chirping of crickets and the crunching of grass beneath their shoes, Frank, Joe, and Chet crossed the moonlit field. In the distance, a pair of owls hooted mournfully to each other.

As the investigators approached the rear corner of the equipment shed, it and the decaying barn looming darkly behind it grew clearer in the pale, diffused light.

Behind the broken glass of each rear and side window of the shed was a sheet of unpainted, moderately weathered plywood. Here and there, wood of the same relatively recent age had been used to patch holes and gaps in the old siding.

"The Polucca house isn't the only place that's haunted," Chet commented, as he came to a stop by the shed.

"Yeah," agreed Joe, stopping beside him. "Up the road, the ghosts do housework and signaling. Here, they board up windows and repair siding."

"That's not all they do," remarked Frank, looking down.

He pulled a flashlight from the haversack hung across his shoulder, switched it on, and shone its light on the ground by the side of the shed.

The grass there was flattened, as though vehicles had been driven over it.

Turning to his left, Frank fanned the flashlight beam back and forth across the grass.

It revealed an informal roadway leading to the right of a remaining section of fence, beyond which was the driveway.

"Come on," Joe urged his companions.

Walking around to the front of the building, they saw more boarded-up windows and, in the middle of the structure, two closed sliding doors, each secured to the siding by a fairly new-looking padlock, staple, and hasp. Where the doors abutted in the center, a couple of heavy steel clips, apparently fastened to the back of one of the doors, held the two rigidly together.

The roadway of flattened grass swept around in a broad curve up to the doors.

"Aha!" Frank exclaimed, surveying the scene.

Joe laughed softly. "Tell me all *that* doesn't look just a little bit suspicious!"

"Ladies and gentlemen," Chet remarked to an imaginary radio audience, "what will we find inside? Will it be the new washer and dryer that Mrs. Elmira Schlump of Crystal Springs has been hoping for?"

Frank walked up to the left door's padlock. He turned the keyway toward him and studied it for a moment in the beam of his flashlight. Then he let go of the lock and searched in his bag.

At the sound of a loud *crack*, he jerked his head up and swung the flashlight beam toward the other door.

Joe, bent double, was gripping its lower right corner, his right foot braced against the siding. The staple end of the hasp, with padlock intact, was still attached to the door. But the screw end dangled free.

Joe straightened up and grinned.

"Why waste time?" he asked.

"Isn't that cheating?" Chet asked in response.

He went over to help Joe slide the door open.

As the old door moved noisily and jerkily to the right, the searching beam of Frank's flashlight illuminated the back end of a rugged green truck with a wide steel bed, the sides and tailgate of which were made of reinforced plywood. Behind the cab was a lifting arm with a steel hook and cable. Below the tailgate hung a New York license plate.

Tracks that matched the impressions in the Olsen driveway ran up to the tires in the dirt floor.

"Dodge Power Wagon," said Chet. "With a custom bed." He regarded it contemplatively. "The sort of vehicle my father would approve of—brute force, no class."

Joe reached into Frank's bag and pulled out two flashlights. He handed one to Chet. "Let's take a look around in there."

"And let's start with *that*," said Frank, shining his light to the left of the Power Wagon.

The features of a long black sedan emerged from the darkness.

Joe gave a whistle of respect. "Chrysler Crown Imperial."

He switched on his flashlight and went up to the car. "It's a '47—no glass panel between the front and back seats. Great gangster transport."

He leaned in the open front-passenger-door window and shone his light inside.

"Dad's notebook!" he cried.

He yanked open the door and took a small memorandum book from the seat. Shining his light on it, he flipped through it to the last entries. He quickly scanned them, then held the book out so the others could read:

Volchek? Krueger's—9:04–9:22. Black Crown Imperial, muddy plate. N. on N. Shore. Polucca drive—9:47.

The brothers looked at each other.

"He *did* go to the house," said Frank.

"Let's get over there," said Joe, turning away.

"Not so fast."

Frank took the memo book and studied the last words.

"He spotted Oscar Volchek at the electric supply store—"

"Volchek *maybe*." Joe pointed. "Notice the question mark. He wasn't sure."

"Then Volchek was in disguise."

"Disguised or not, why would someone with a record like his risk being seen at a local store?"

163

"Who knows? Maybe he was the only one who could identify what they needed."

"The rest is clear enough," said Joe. " 'Black Crown Imperial, muddy plate . . . ' "

Frank turned and walked to the rear of the sedan. The others followed.

In contrast to the dusty but relatively clean car, the license plate was caked with dirt, its numbers unreadable.

Frank put the notebook in his bag and pulled out the rag towel. Bending down, he rubbed a corner of it back and forth across the bottom of the plate.

The raised letters NY appeared, in deep yellow on a black background.

Joe chuckled bitterly. "As if we didn't know."

Chet pointed to the tracks behind the rear tires. "Those look familiar."

"Yep," said Frank, looking down at the zigzag tread lines. "This is it—the mystery car."

Joe walked back to the sedan's open door. "Maybe there's something more in here."

He shone his light inside. "There's Dad's pen . . . *Hey!*"

He retrieved something from the floor.

As the others came over to see what he'd found, he held up a short piece of two-inch-diameter cardboard tubing, with a rough slit down its side.

He spread the cut edges apart.

"So they could slip it onto the gearshift without having to go over the knob."

Frank smiled. He glanced past Joe to the interior of the car, then pointed with his flashlight beam to the top of the steering wheel.

Fastened to the rim was a steering wheel spinner.

"Whataya know!" Joe exclaimed. "I must've been on Mister Slick's wavelength!"

Chet looked from the spinner to the cardboard tube, and from it to Joe's face. "That's how they moved your father's car without leaving fingerprints?"

Joe smiled and nodded.

"And you figured it out?"

"Uh-huh."

"Nice figuring."

Frank shook his brother's hand. "Well done," he said solemnly.

"Thanks," Joe replied, serious for a moment.

He turned and tossed the piece of tubing on the floor.

Chet wandered beyond the Chrysler and shone his light around.

"What's back here?" he asked.

"We'd better get moving," said Joe, closing the car door.

"Hey, fellas!" Chet called out, walking toward a boarded-up door in the right wall. "Take a look at all this!"

In the dirt near the wall, from the rear of the shed to the front, were crisscrossing footprints, a set of Power Wagon tracks, and indentations with furrows leading from them, as though heavy objects had been dragged from where they had long been sitting. Here and there lay a few well-aged mechanical objects.

Chet pointed to the nearest ones. "Tractor muffler . . . Gasket for an auto exhaust manifold . . . Lid to an air cleaner . . ."

Frank made a quick study of the footprints.

"As far as I can tell," he announced, "all of these were made by two men—Smooth Soles and Lines."

"Now where," asked Chet sarcastically, "have we encountered *them* before?"

Joe regarded the large shoe impressions. "Those two bruisers're probably the biggest members of the gang—if the size of their shoes means anything. Let's hope we don't meet up with them."

Frank looked away, in the direction of the road.

"Alex Polucca wasn't following us down North Shore," he said softly, as if to himself. "He wasn't even in the car. These two drove it here to get a truckload of parts to haul back to the garage."

"While Sneaky dug some holes," Joe conjectured, "and got things ready for his little dust-and-metal surprise."

"Come on," said Frank, heading for the door. "Let's arrange a surprise for *him.*"

Night Prowlers

"No sign of tire tracks or footprints here," said Frank, kneeling on the thick carpet of vegetation at the entrance to the Olsen driveway.

He stood and pointed across the road with his flashlight, moving its beam from one gap in the trees to the next.

"The gang must come through the woods to get to their vehicles. They wouldn't want to risk being seen on the road."

"We don't have time to do the same," said Joe, "or to find their trail. It'll be faster by pavement."

Chet held up his hand. "Listen."

From down the road, discernible now over the sighing of the waves, came the sound of an approaching automobile.

"We'd better hide," said Frank, heading for the nearest tree.

The engine's droning grew quieter as the car slowed for the curve south of the driveway. Then long, twin shafts of light appeared beyond the sheltering trees, the engine noise grew louder, and the car rushed past.

Frank ran out into the road.

"Forty Ford Standard coupé," he announced breathlessly, gazing after the receding automobile.

The distinguishing single chevron-shaped taillight diminished rapidly in size, then vanished as the coupé entered the double curve.

"Funny time to be driving along North Shore," Joe commented, as he and Chet emerged from hiding.

"Maybe it's someone who lives up the road," Chet suggested.

"I don't think so," Frank replied. "The Greenwoods—the next house past Polucca's, quite a ways up—own a Chevy. Beyond them is Mrs. Adams. She drives a Hudson. The Wallaces have a Buick . . . And old what's-his-name, almost at the junction—"

"McAllister," said Joe.

"He's got a Willys."

"Anyway," Joe remarked with relief, "it wasn't a police car."

The three trespassers-to-be came to a halt on the moonlit east side of the double curve.

Ahead of them, the road continued its sweeping turn to the left. Beyond their view, it curved back briefly to the right, then ran on in a long, straight line past the entrance to the Polucca driveway.

"We might as well pull the wool here," said Frank, reaching into his bag. "Before we get into the woods."

The three sat down and coaxed the thick socks over their shoes.

"I always thought," remarked Chet, grunting as he tugged, "that these things went on *underneath* your shoes."

"It's a good thing we're close to the ocean," said Frank. "The twigs're so limp from the humidity that they don't snap the way they do farther back."

"And the sound of the waves," Joe pointed out, "can hide a good deal of man-made noise."

"Speaking of waves," said Chet, looking uneasily around, "it's strange how much louder they seem at night."

Joe leaned toward him.

"They're calling," he declared in a deep, husky voice. "Calling for lost souls to join them in their endless journey. Calling—"

"It's creepy enough around here without that," Frank said irritably, getting to his feet.

As the others stood, Frank removed his father's memorandum book from the haversack. He handed it to Chet.

"Hang on to this. It's our proof that Dad went to Polucca's. We'll show it to the authorities when we've found the stairway entrance."

"Why give it to me?" asked Chet, blinking.

"Because if the two of us are caught, you're the one who's going to have to get us rescued."

"You know," Chet replied thoughtfully, putting the notebook in his back pocket, "there's something about that answer that bothers me."

Joe took his ski mask and gloves from the bag and put them on.

"Isn't it a bit early for those things?" his brother asked.

"I want to go around the bend and make sure there *is* a patrol car there. If there isn't, we won't need to waste time sneaking through the woods."

"That's too risky."

"If they're up where they're supposed to be, they won't see me."

"They'd *better* not. Or we won't get to the house. *You* won't, anyway."

Joe ran silently along the shaded left edge of the pavement until shortly before the curve to the right. Then he stepped into the ditch and hunched down.

In a crouch, he cautiously continued around the curve until he could see up the road as far as the entrance.

About five hundred feet away, in the shadows across from the driveway, was the dim shape of a police car, facing south.

"Hello, boys," Joe muttered. "Keeping in the dark, eh?"

He put his hands on the ground for support, swiveled on his toes, and turned to go back.

Suddenly the vehicle's headlights blazed on, and both car and road were dark no longer.

Joe flung himself face downward in the ditch.

The patrol car's engine started.

Alarmed, Frank and Chet ran for the trees, as the car sped toward the curve.

When the police car was about twenty feet from where Joe lay, shielded from the headlights by the eastward sweep of the road, it slowed to a crawl.

At each end of the windshield, a spotlight lit up and swung toward where Joe was hiding.

Looking to his right, Joe could see the lights shining into the woods just beyond him. He could hear the car coming closer . . .

168

"It was about here," said the officer at the wheel, his voice clearly audible through the open windows.

"You must have really good eyesight," said the officer on the passenger side. "To see something in the shadows from that far away!"

"I *do* have good eyesight," responded the driver confidently. "You oughta know that by now, O'Brian."

Staring past O'Brian's head, he turned the steering wheel, and the car rolled closer to the side of the road.

The right front tire left the pavement, then stopped.

Hearing the nearby crunching of gravel, Joe turned his head and looked up.

The passenger-side spotlight was sweeping forward and back, dropping lower with each pass.

"If there's something out here," said O'Brian, gazing at the lighted trees and their moving shadows, "where is it?"

"Just don't lean out and look down," Joe whispered.

He turned to his right and saw the downward-angled shaft of light stop and swing upward.

"Come on," said O'Brian. "Let's go a little farther ahead."

Hearing the engine speed increase, Joe looked back to the left.

Above him, the right front tire turned away, and the car moved on.

When its taillights were about thirty feet from where he lay, Joe rose to his knees, stared after the car for a moment, then scrambled from the ditch and ran for the trees.

He was well hidden when the patrol car halted, turned around in the curve, and drove back on his side of the road, its spotlights sweeping the trees.

The car stopped a few feet from where Joe had lain. The driver leaned out and shone his spotlight into the ditch.

"No one hiding in there," he announced.

He pulled his head back in, switched off the spotlights, and accelerated.

"Maybe it was a deer," he said, as the car pulled away.

"Yeah," replied O'Brian. "Or maybe it was your grandmother."

Two's Company

A chill breeze from the sea whispered through the branches as the three kneeling figures wearing dark clothes, ski masks, and gloves gazed at the front of the grim stone house.

All the windows were closed. On the upper floor, only two—the third and fourth from the south end—were curtained. Behind the windows, all appeared dark.

In contrast, the entire facade of the house, several feet of turn-around, and the silver Packard parked by the front door were bathed in full moonlight.

"Not so good," said Frank softly.

Joe shook his head worriedly. "With all that shining on us, we'll stand out like crows in a cornfield."

Frank turned to Chet. "We're going to make sure the rest of the windows are dark. Then we'll start picking. We'll leave the doors open behind us, so you'll be able to see if something goes wrong."

"Wrong?" Chet responded facetiously. "What could possibly go wrong?"

As his companions sneaked away to the north through the trees, he tugged nervously at his tight ski mask.

Frank bent down on the porch stoop, put his nose to the keyhole below the porcelain knob on the right side of the door, and sniffed.

He turned to Joe, who was standing on the ground to his right, shifting the haversack so it hung down in front of him.

"Oiled," he whispered.

He straightened up and wrapped the fingers and thumb of his gloved left hand around the shank of the doorknob, to prevent it from rubbing against the escutcheon. With his right hand, he tried to turn the knob. It didn't move.

He carefully lifted his hands away, removed his gloves, and gave them to Joe, who put them in the haversack.

Joe pulled a towel and the lockpick case from the bag and handed them over.

Frank hung the towel on the knob and put the case in his pocket. Then he held out his hand and imitated the turning of a key.

Joe reached into the bag, closed his fingers around the skeleton keys, and passed them to Frank's waiting hand.

Frank selected one of the keys. With the thumb and first finger of his left hand, he held the two hanging halves of the towel against the escutcheon, pinching them together around the shaft of the key as he slowly inserted its head into the keyhole.

The key met no obstruction.

Holding the towel firmly against the escutcheon, he slowly, carefully turned the key.

With a muffled *click,* the dead bolt slid into the lock.

Frank paused for a moment, listening. Then, still pinching the towel around it, he rotated the key back and pulled it out. He closed his left hand around the keys, gave them to his right hand, and returned them.

He lifted the towel, wrapped one end of it around the doorknob with his left hand, and slowly turned the knob until it stopped.

Pulling up on the knob to counteract the sag of the door and thereby decrease the likelihood of its hinges squeaking, he cautiously pushed the door open enough to admit him.

After looking around the edge of the door, he squeezed inside, picked up the other end of the towel with his right hand, and wrapped it around the inner doorknob.

Pulling up on both knobs, he proceeded by short, flatfooted

side steps until the door was wide open. Then he removed his left hand and the towel from the outer knob and waited.

Joe entered, pulled off his gloves, and tucked them into the bag. He took out the knife and the electrician's tape.

Operating by the moonlight streaming through the doorway, he cut off four six-inch strips of tape, each of which he stuck temporarily to the edge of the door. He closed the knife and returned it to the haversack. Then he wrapped two of the pieces of tape around the roll and put it in his pocket.

With his left hand, he attached the end of one strip to the outside of the door to the right of the knob and held it in place with his thumb. With his right hand, he pulled the tape around the front edge and stretched it. He pressed it down over the tip of the retracted latch bolt with his left thumb, stretched it around the rear edge, and attached it to the back side of the door. He pushed it down all around, then stretched the second piece and pressed it down over the first.

Frank relaxed his grip on the doorknob, removed the towel, and hung it around his neck.

His way lit by the moonlight shining through the doorway and lattice, he advanced slowly between stacks of boxes to the shadowed inner door, offset to his right.

At the door, he put his ear to the wood and listened.

No sound came from behind it.

He lay down and peeked through the fine crack below the door.

No light shone through.

He slipped the towel from his neck and laid it in front of the crack. Then he stood up.

"This door doesn't line up with the outer one," he whispered as Joe came up to him.

"Because of the depth of the fake inner wall and the cupboards, I suppose," Joe whispered back. "They had to offset the door."

"The trouble is, Chet probably won't be able to see into the kitchen."

"There's nothing we can do about that."

Frank looked back at the porch doorway. Then he took a flashlight from his pocket and put his left fingers over its lens. He aimed it at the door and turned it on.

The weak light revealed a tarnished doorknob with a keyway in it on the left side of the door and, about a foot above it, the newer-looking face of a deadbolt lock.

Frank switched off the flashlight. He closed his left fingers and thumb into a cone around the lens, switched the light on, and directed its small beam into the lower keyway, then the upper. He switched it off and put it in his pocket.

He reflected for a moment. Then he pulled out his shirttail, put it over the doorknob, and tried turning it.

The knob moved.

Startled, Frank hesitated. Then he slowly turned the knob all the way and gently pushed.

The door didn't budge.

He slowly rotated the doorknob back, lifted his hand from it, and tucked his shirttail in. He turned to his brother.

"Only the dead bolt's locked," he whispered.

"Maybe the knob lock's broken."

"I don't like that. It seems odd."

Frank took out the small cloth case, opened it, felt inside, and removed the hook pick and tension wrench. He returned the case to his pocket.

Operating by touch, he slipped the pick and the wrench into the deadbolt keyway and manipulated the pins. Then he removed the pick and turned the wrench.

With a faint *click,* the bolt slid into the lock.

Frank removed the wrench, put his ear to the door, and listened. No sound came from within.

He took out the case, put the tools in it, and returned it to his pocket.

Then he retrieved the towel and used it to wipe the lock face and adjacent wood.

He wrapped one end of the towel around the knob and, as before, cautiously opened the door.

All was dark in the pantry beyond.

Joe followed Frank by feeling his way along the opening door with the back of his hand, to avoid leaving fingerprints.

Inside the pantry, Joe took the roll of electrician's tape from his pocket. By feel, he pulled off the two cut strips and taped the latch open, then put the roll in the bag.

Then he nudged Frank, who removed the towel from the knob and handed it to him. He put the towel away.

"Callie said there's a swinging door next," Frank whispered. "Swinging doors have big cracks all around them—"

"And this one, she said, has a window."

"So before I shine a light to examine the cupboards in here, someone needs to check the kitchen."

"Someone meaning me."

"Yep. First let me know if it's clear in there, so I can get to work. Then you'd better look in one room beyond the kitchen, just to be sure no one's around."

"Roger." Joe placed the bag on the floor.

He slowly felt his way to the far end of the pantry, located the door with the back of his hand, felt along it to a small window in its left side, and peered through—into darkness.

He cautiously pushed the door open with his arm, took a couple of steps in, and looked around.

Ahead of him, in the east wall of the kitchen, were four windows, each made slightly lighter than the surrounding wall by the meager amount of light reaching it.

Stooping down, he saw, dimly outlined against the windows, what appeared to be a food-preparation table in the center of the room.

Joe straightened up and turned, keeping the door open with his back, and pulled his flashlight from his pocket. Holding his fingers over the lens, he flashed an "all clear" signal to Frank. Then he put the light away, stepped to the side, and eased the door shut with his arm.

"The dining room," he thought, turning and facing the windows, "must be the next room over. That means the door to it's in a wall to my right. South. And there ought to be another door from the kitchen to the rest of the house. Probably in the wall behind me."

He backed up until he touched the door through which he'd entered. Then he began moving sideways to his right past the frame, running the back of his hand up the wall to shoulder height, then lowering it as he slid his feet—feeling, sliding; feeling, sliding . . .

His hand soon touched what felt like a door frame. Sliding past it, he felt a slight movement.

"Swinging door number two," he thought.

He located a small window in it on the left, looked through, saw nothing.

He pushed the door open with the back of his hand and poked his head into darkness. "Hall, maybe."

He eased the door shut and turned to face the east wall.

"Where would *I* put a dining room door? At this end of the south wall, or the other end . . ."

Reaching the south wall, he felt his way along it and around a barely visible stove, counter, and refrigerator, before locating another swinging door with a window.

He looked through the glass, saw nothing, opened the door, and peered into darkness. He slowly closed the door.

He turned and followed the glowing window and outline of the first swinging door back to the flashlight-lit pantry.

"All clear," he told Frank softly, pulling off his ski mask and putting it in the haversack on the floor. "It's as dark and quiet as the grave out there."

Frank removed and put away his mask. Then he shone his light on the cupboards that took up the entire length of the pantry's north wall. Their tall lower double doors were open, revealing . . .

"Shelves. Nothing but shelves. There's no way I can figure that anyone could get through *them.*"

"Let's take a look at the ones in the kitchen."

"Notice anything odd about them?" Frank asked quietly, shining his light along the closed doors of the cupboards against the north kitchen wall.

"They're separate units," Joe answered, pointing his flashlight beam at the narrow gap between two adjacent cupboards. "Not like the ones in the pantry."

"Doesn't that seem like a waste of wood and effort?"

"Maybe they got them prefab."

"For a house like this? There must be some other reason for all that work."

Frank ran his flashlight beam up to where the tops of the units almost touched the ceiling.

"Why," he asked, staring upward, "do they *almost* touch? Maybe . . ."

He knelt in front of the first cupboard from the left and shone his light below its double lower doors.

The recessed kickplate, he saw, rested on the smooth, white-tiled floor.

He slowly moved the light across.

The bottom of the second unit's kickplate came within a fraction of an inch of the tiles.

Below the other kickplates there was no apparent gap.

Frank slid over and briefly examined the tiles in front of the second cupboard.

He then rose to his feet and opened the cupboard's lower doors.

Reaching across each half of the divided, shelfless interior was a rod for hanging clothes. Along each outer side at waist height was a row of tool clamps. The second clamp from the front in the right half of the unit held a broom. A dustpan lay flat on the floor. Except for these items, the two spaces were empty.

"Hold this," said Frank, handing Joe his flashlight.

He glanced to his left at the propped-open pantry door, then grasped the nearest tool clamp on each side and pulled straight back.

Smoothly, almost silently, the tall cupboard unit moved toward him.

"It's on wheels!" Joe exclaimed.

"*Rollers*, I think," said Frank. "It moves too easily for wheels."

As the unit rolled clear of the others, a tall, dimly lit opening in the wall behind it became visible. At the bottom of the opening

176

was a narrow, shallow landing—which, like what could be seen of the stairs leading to and from it, was covered with thick carpeting.

On the landing, leaning against the upper steps, sat a small man pointing an automatic pistol at the intruders. His grinning face, less haggard than it had appeared in the mug shot supplied by Fenton Hardy, roughly resembled that of a chimpanzee.

Stupefied though they were by the sight before them, Frank and Joe quickly turned at the sound of a *click* across the room, as the kitchen lights were switched on.

Blinking in the sudden brightness, they saw a tall, wide-faced, broad-shouldered man standing by the dining room door, a pistol in his left hand.

"We've got company," he said in a deep, resonant voice.

The door to the hall was pushed open and an equally tall but thinner man brandishing a revolver walked in, squinting in the light.

His face, the Hardys could see, looked as it had in the FBI photograph—long and narrow, with a prominent forehead, deep-set eyes, and a mouth like a straight line.

"Yeah, we've got company, all right," he said in a rasping voice, confronting the housebreakers. "And they've got *trouble*."

A Call for Help

A few feet from the edge of the turnaround, Chet lay on his chest, watching the house intently from behind a tree.

Suddenly he saw bright light shine into the service porch.

"Oh-no-oh-no-oh-no," he muttered.

A small man holding a large unlit flashlight stepped to the porch doorway and scanned the moonlit area in front of the house. Then he switched on the flashlight and swept its powerful beam back and forth, illuminating in turn the shadows by the garage, the nearest trees beyond the turnaround, and the dark mouth of the driveway.

Chet dropped his head as the shaft of light swung in his direction. It briefly brightened the ground on either side of the tree in front of him as it passed by.

Seemingly satisfied that no one was there, the man switched off the flashlight, put it down inside, stepped back to the door, and pushed it shut. It made no sound in closing. He pulled it open, removed the tape from in front of the latch bolt, and shut it again. This time the latch clicked.

Something rattled faintly against the door frame; then a key turned in the lock. There was more faint rattling, apparently caused by the key being returned to a hook.

The man's footsteps retreated. There was the sound of a latch being released; then the inner door closed with a *click*. Its dead bolt slid into place.

Chet stumbled to his feet.

A glow appeared in the curtainless windows of the vacant second-story rooms, as if the upper-hall lights had been turned on.

A few seconds later, the two curtained windows of Alex Polucca's bedroom lit up.

Glancing frequently at the house, Chet hurried from tree to tree until he reached the driveway. He made his way awkwardly along it in the semidarkness, watching over his shoulder until the house lights had died away through the branches. Then he halted, tore the mask from his face, pulled a flashlight from his pocket, switched it on, and broke into a run.

At the driveway entrance, he ran onto North Shore Road and stopped, breathing hard.

The road was empty.

"They're not here?" Chet asked aloud, frantically looking around. "How can they be *not here*?"

He clapped his gloved, mask-holding hand to his head. "Where would they be? Where, *where*? I know—maybe they moved to the side road, to get out of sight!" He started running.

As he came up to the lane, his jaw dropped.

It, too, was empty.

"I don't believe it!" Chet gasped. "A vanishing patrol car!"

He looked up the dark, lonely road.

"Would they have gone up *there*? Why? Why would they have gone anywhere?"

He looked down the road. "I can't wait around *here*. I need to get wheels and go find those jokers!"

He started running south, as quickly as his out-of-condition legs could manage.

The moonlight shining through gaps in the forest cast eerie shadows around him as he ran—and then walked, caught his breath, and ran again—down the empty road.

After what seemed an eternity, he come to the Olsen driveway . . . ran along it to the high spot . . . took down the fence rails . . . ran across the grass . . . and staggered into the oak grove.

"I'd better first try up the road," Chet gasped. "They wouldn't have driven back to town. Unless they were pulled off . . . Oh, no—I don't want to think about *that*."

On reaching the Duchess, he jumped inside, dropped his ski mask and flashlight on the seat, pulled off his gloves, and threw them down. He started the engine and turned on the lights.

"Wherever they went," he said through clenched teeth, "They'd better be back by the time I get there!"

He yanked the gearshift into reverse, swung the car around, shifted into low gear, and accelerated.

The Duchess's rear tires spun crazily as she fishtailed through the slick, dry grass, then locked as Chet braked her for the opening in the fence. She skidded through the gap then jerked forward, plowing a small furrow in the dirt with her angled right front tire before it gained the center strip.

Steering her clear of the ruts, Chet coaxed her quickly and bumpily down the driveway to the entrance.

Over the neglected radio, as though urging car and driver onward, drummer Gene Krupa began his tom-tom pounding, seven-and-a-half-minute ride with the rest of the Benny Goodman band in "Sing, Sing, Sing."

With a roar from her engine and a squeal from her side-slipping tires, the Duchess gained the pavement and swung north.

"Patrol car, patrol car, patrol car," Chet repeated to himself, his eyes searching the road ahead. He laughed sarcastically. "Whoever would've thought that *I'd* be looking for a patrol car!"

Racing past the Polucca driveway, he glimpsed no sign of light or activity along it—and no sign of a police car.

Chet braked hard, steered the Duchess into the side road, and brought her to an abrupt stop.

There was no one there.

"Keep going, Morton! They must be up the road!"

The Duchess backed out fast, dust flying from beneath her furiously spinning rear tires. They chirped and slid as they reached the pavement.

Chet shifted into first, pressed the accelerator to the floor, and turned the wheel. The shriek of the tires nearly drowned out the thundering of the engine as the car fishtailed two curved stripes of burned rubber across the road, then sped north.

Her tires squealing from the pressure of centrifugal force, the Duchess tore to the left and then to the right around a shallow double curve.

As she came out of it, Chet slowed her to a stop.

For a long stretch ahead, the road lay straight and empty.

"This is crazy!" Chet shouted. "I can't run up and down North Shore all night! If these lunkheads want to play hard to get, I'll just go to town and fetch some more!"

He turned the Duchess around and pushed her gas pedal to the floor. The spinning tires screamed, then grabbed hold, and the car leaped forward.

The double curve . . . The lane . . . The driveway entrance . . . The double curve beyond it . . . The Olsen driveway . . . All went past in a blur.

"It must be true!" Chet shouted, his hands tightly gripping the steering wheel. "When you *want* them, you can't *find* them!"

The Duchess all but flew down the road to Bayport, the increased stability of her lowered center of gravity proving itself again and again as she tracked steadily through the many curves.

At a telephone booth on the outskirts of town, Chet braked her to a skidding stop. He jumped from the car, ran to the booth, lifted the receiver, and dialed for the operator.

"Bayport operator," answered a female voice.

"This is an emergency!" croaked Chet. "Get me the police!"

"I will connect you. One moment, please."

There was an interval of silence.

"Bayport Police Department," said a male voice at the other end of the line.

"Sergeant Riley—is that you?"

"And who else would it be, now?"

"I've just come from the Polucca place. Frank and Joe Hardy

are trapped there by a gang of smugglers—the same gang that's holding Mr. Hardy prisoner!"

"Is that you, Chet?"

"Yes, it is. You need to send all the men you've got, right away!"

"Good night, Chet," said the voice.

There was a *click,* and the connection was broken.

"Hello!" Chet shouted, jiggling the receiver cradle. *"Hello!"* He pounded his fist on the phone. *"You can't do this to me, Con Riley!"* He slammed the receiver down on the cradle. *"Idiot!"*

He stood still, breathing hard, glaring at the telephone. Then he looked at the Duchess and took a deep breath. "Pull yourself together, Morton. There must be another way to handle this."

Tony Prito, wearing pajamas and looking barely awake, leaned out of the open second-story rear window.

"If you're the sandman," he said to the dark-clothed figure below him on the lawn, "you'd better throw lighter sand. That stuff nearly broke the glass. And it's all over the floor."

The figure dropped a handful of gravel.

"It's me—Chet," he said softly.

"I've been out at the Polucca place, with Frank and Joe. This afternoon, they found a trapdoor in the garage leading to a tunnel that goes to the cave in the point. They told Chief Collig about it. But when he got there to see for himself, the garage floor was covered with dusty engine blocks and other heavy pieces of metal. So he thought they were just making up a story."

"Why didn't somebody *tell* me 'bout all this?"

"We've been pretty distracted. Mr. Hardy's missing, and—"

"Missing?"

"Since this morning. I guess I mean *yesterday* morning—Wednesday. I don't know what time it is."

"After midnight, I guess. Go on."

"Tonight, we—Frank, Joe, and I—found the memo book Mr. Hardy keeps in his car. The crooks had hidden it. The last entries show that he followed one of the gang to the Polucca house. Frank and Joe are pretty sure he's shut up in a storage room they saw in the tunnel, below the door that leads to the gang's secret living quarters."

"Secret living quarters?"

"A basement hideout, sounds like."

"The storage room's *below* it?"

"It's farther down the tunnel, which slopes down to the cave. The bottom part of the tunnel—the longest part—is steep, with a sort of mining car on rails. Are you getting all this?"

Tony squeezed his eyes shut, then opened them. "I *think* so."

"A few minutes ago, Frank and Joe broke into the Polucca house to see if they could find the entrance to a hidden stairway they think leads from the pantry or kitchen to the hideout, so they could tell the authorities how to get down there. But they got caught!"

Tony's head jerked up. "They got *caught?* How d'ya know?"

"I was watching from the trees."

Tony shook his head. "Oh, Mama, Mama!"

Chet talked on, faster and faster: "I ran to find the patrol car that Chief Collig posted by Polucca's driveway tonight, after the Hardys finally convinced him that Alex Polucca's a crook. But it was gone! Then I drove up and down the road looking for it—but I couldn't find it! So I phoned the police and told them what happened, but they didn't believe me!"

He held out his hand to Tony. "They'll believe *you!* I'll drive you to the police station. You can show them the memo book, and—"

"Take it easy. I'll be right down."

About half a minute later, the back door opened and Tony, in pajamas and slippers, stepped out onto the lawn.

"You need to get dressed so we can go to the station, quick!" insisted Chet.

"Not so fast," Tony replied.

He ran a hand through his hair. "If the cops surround that house, what'll happen ta Frank, Joe, and Mr. Hardy?"

"I hadn't thought about that," said Chet, coming to his senses.

"We'd *better* think about it."

"There's something else to think about: I forgot to mention that Mrs. Hardy phoned the FBI."

"Oh?"

"They have to put together a team from one out-of-state office or another, so it'll take them a while. But they'll be at the Polucca place sometime tonight."

"Uh-oh," said Tony. "The gunfire's on its way."

He started pacing.

"You said there's a garage entrance to the tunnel, but it's covered up."

"With a pile or two of heavy car parts."

"So the FBI can't go that way without moving a lotta metal and making a lotta noise."

"Right."

"And the hidden stairway, wherever it starts, goes to the hideout."

"Apparently. There might be a wall and a door between the stairs and the hideout, but we don't know."

"Even if there is, if the crooks hear the authorities breaking in and looking for the stairway, there'll be one big shootout—and the gang'll have the Hardys for hostages."

"That's why Frank and Joe wanted to find the hidden entrance—so the FBI team could get to the hideout fast, without making searching noises that would alert anyone. If the smugglers were caught by surprise, they wouldn't have time to haul Mr. Hardy out of the storage room and—"

"Storage room. You say it's downhill from the hideout?"

"That's what Frank and Joe told me."

"And they're pretty sure that's where their father is?"

"Yeah."

"So that's probably where the gang's gonna put *all* the Hardys."

"I suppose."

"Sounds like we could get to that from the other enda the tunnel, by taking *Napoli*."

"How?" asked Chet. "Chief Collig's got the police boat sitting out by the point."

Tony stopped and stared at him.

"And a Coast Guard cutter should be there, too, by now."

"Oh, yeah? You didn't mention *those* little details."

"I forgot. We thought we'd never get past the patrol boat. And with that cutter—"

Tony held up his hand. "Is there anyone else coming you haven't told me 'bout? Is the cavalry on its way? How 'bout the Marines?"

Chet shook his head.

"Just the FBI," said Tony. "And the Coast Guard. And the cops."

Chet nodded.

"Well, that oughta be enough," Tony remarked sarcastically. He resumed his pacing.

"So they've got the patrol boat and a cutter out there . . ." he said after a while. "How *big* a cutter?"

"I don't know."

"A small one could outmaneuver us . . . But they probably sent a middle-size one. Or a *buncha* little ones, but that's not their style. A medium-size cutter could chase us down in the open sea . . . But we won't give 'em the opportunity. The police boat's fast as greased lightning . . . But it's a bit too wide to follow us in through that entrance in the rocks."

"We didn't realize that. But still—how can we get around it?"

"By going 'round it, that's how. We'll go 'round whatever's there."

"But *how?*"

"Evasive tactics. We'll thinka something."

"Well, that *sounds* easy, but—"

"Then we could sneak up from the cave, check that storage room, set the Hardys loose if they're in there, and escape back down the tunnel."

"They said the part with the rail car's pretty steep."

"We'll hafta climb it."

"We need Biff. He should be able to manage that."

"Yeah, if anyone can."

Tony stopped pacing. "Did any of the crooks see you?"

Chet shook his head. "It was dark where I was hiding. I made sure nobody saw me running away. And they wouldn't have known what it meant when the Duchess raced up and down the road a few minutes later—if they heard her through the trees and stone walls and closed windows."

"They don't know we've found the cave," said Tony, "so they won't be expecting anyone at that end. They might be expecting the law at the other end, looking for Frank and Joe, but that shouldn't hurt us any."

"The police won't drop by," Chet replied, "because they have no idea that we went to Polucca's tonight. And Mrs. Hardy won't be calling them or the FBI about Frank or Joe, because I haven't told her they got caught. So things ought to be pretty quiet—until the FBI shows up."

"Get Biff," said Tony, "and meet me at the boathouse as soon as ya can. Tell 'im ta wear dark clothing."

"*Warm* dark clothing. Joe said the tunnel's like an icebox."

"I guess it would be."

"And I'll tell him to wear some old socks over his shoes, like what I've got on, so they won't make noise."

"Good idea. And have 'im bring a couple flashlights and a pocketknife."

"Okay. And I've got a flashlight in the car. What else'll we need?"

"I'll bring a flashlight and our glasses—and some tools to fix those speedboats so they can't come after us. I'll wear dark clothes—and I've got some black deck shoes. They're 'bout as quiet as you can get."

"Wait a minute—what if *we* get caught?"

"I'll leave a note for Pop, explaining what we're doing. He and I get up early for the produce run. If we're not back by the time he reads the note, he'll call the cops. Okay—let's *move!*"

A few minutes later, the Duchess, her lights and engine switched off, rolled to a stop by the Prito boathouse. Chet and Biff, the latter carrying a knapsack, stepped from the car, closed the doors quietly behind them, and hurried inside.

Having slid open the bay doors, Tony quickly cast off the lines, and the three boys climbed into the runabout.

Tony turned the key and pressed the starter. The engine came to life, the lights went on, and the *Napoli* sped out into the night.

Boss Man

"*I'll* ask the questions," snapped Alex Polucca.

He scowled at the three prisoners in the storage room.

Fenton Hardy was tied, by his hands only, to a chair to the left of the door. Diagonally to his left, Frank and Joe were bound hand and foot to chairs, their backs to a shelf-lined rock wall.

"You won't learn any more than you have already," said the detective wearily. "Which you'd have realized by now if you were as clever as you seem to think you are."

The short, stocky, square-faced young man standing next to Alex glanced uneasily at his boss.

"Clever?" Alex sneered. He looked down and picked a piece of lint off the sleeve of his pinstripe suit. "Compared to some, I suppose."

He looked up and focused his shifty attention on Fenton Hardy's face. "I'm clever enough to *not* walk into a dark garage and peep into an open trapdoor, only to be knocked down a flight of stairs! You're lucky it's only your *ankle* that's swollen, and not your *head!*"

He paused and smiled. "*It* was probably swollen to begin with."

He regarded the investigator's sons. "And I'm clever enough to *not* leave footprints in that garage to advertise to anyone with a working brain that I'd been inside it."

He glanced restlessly around the room, then looked at the

brothers again. "I'll tell you who's clever—your two flames. They had me neatly conned, until I came to my senses and checked their story. I wish they were in my organization—my family's organization. They'd do a lot better than some of the stale adventurers I've got working for me."

His henchman giggled nervously and shifted his weight from one foot to the other.

"You're the ghost!" Joe exclaimed, staring at him. "That *laugh!*"

Alex turned to the "ghost" and pointed his thumb at Joe.

The square-faced young man stepped forward, slapped Joe, then stepped back.

"It's *you* who's going to be a ghost," Alex declared grimly. "But you won't be haunting *this* house."

He adjusted the knot of his tie.

"As for *him*," he remarked, jerking his chin toward his subordinate, "he's a bucket-head. Instead of loosening the fuses to all the above-basement circuits but the one he needs for the signal light, he leaves the entire power on—which tells anyone who sneaks in and pushes a switch that the house isn't as deserted as it appears. He and his equally nowhere assistant carry the light and a transformer across the ground floor and up the main stairway, rather than use the hidden stairs to the second floor—because, they say, it's too tight in there. Thus making it necessary for another imbecile to sweep the stairway and two floors."

"He didn't sweep them very well," Frank remarked.

"He wouldn't have needed to sweep them *at all*," Alex rejoined hotly, "if the fools had simply fixed the front-door lock when it broke, instead of leaving it until *I* noticed it."

"We didn't know how," whined the ghost.

"You could've told *me*," Alex snarled. "I'd have had a locksmith here immediately."

"Whenever anyone came snooping around," the ghost returned with a simpering smile, "we just scared 'em away, same as always."

"You were a little late scaring *these* snoopers away."

"Well, someone accidentally turned the front-door intercom off."

"*What* intercom?" asked Joe. "We didn't see any intercom."

"You're not supposed to," the ghost replied curtly. "It's hidden above the light fixture."

"I'm surrounded by idiots," Alex commented with a shrug. "And *I'm* the idiot who didn't get out here often enough."

He gestured toward the prisoners. "But *you're* idiots, as well—which makes us even."

He put his hands in his pockets, smiled sardonically, and studied the faces before him. "Now it's my turn to play detective and deduce the facts of the situation."

He fixed his eyes on Fenton Hardy. "Apparently *you* only learned of our location by recognizing my disguised second-in-command and following him here. That means either that your sons told you nothing about what they'd seen, or that they did tell you something but you dismissed it. And the fact that no one has come for you—aside from your sons, if coming for you is what they were doing—indicates that you neither voiced any suspicions about this house nor told anyone you were coming here."

He turned his attention to the brothers. "Chief Collig and Officer Moscone paid me a friendly visit, which means that you told them something but they didn't know whether to believe it. Since they left, no police squad has shown up to search the premises or arrest me, which means that we effectively canceled out whatever you said to the official forces.

"The two of you are here, I deduce, because no one has taken seriously what you've said about your discoveries—if indeed you've said anything to anyone beyond the police. I anticipated that you might try to find an unobstructed passage to the tunnel and, as you've seen, arranged a reception. Since, according to my reception committee, you only discovered the location of our hidden stairway entrance tonight, you've told no one where it is. The chances are very good that either you've said nothing to anyone about suspecting the existence of a stairway, or no one has believed you. Certainly no one else has come looking for one.

"Nor has anyone come around yet looking for you, which is a pretty fair indication that nobody knows you're here or suspects you *might* be here. When I went back to my room to dress after our brief interview in the kitchen, I thought I heard a car making noise out on the road and for a moment entertained fancies of a police raid. But when I made myself presentable and went to investigate, there was nothing there."

Alex paused, as though contemplating the look of fear that had suddenly come into the brothers' eyes. Then he continued: "If no one shows up for you within the next couple of hours, I'll be quite sure that no one knows where you are. There's a chance that you left a note indicating where you were going, but it's only a chance. If it turns out that you did, I'll deal with that situation as I've dealt with the others so far—applying my unfailing friendliness, helpfulness, and charm."

He removed his hands from his pockets, pushed back his coat sleeve and shirt cuff, and looked at his large gold watch. Then he put his hands back in his pockets, regarded his captives, and smiled.

"In a little over two-and-a-half hours from now," he went on, "the three of you will leave here, transported in a comfortable Chrysler Crown Imperial to an accomodating out-of-state freighter that will take you on a long, entertaining ocean voyage. Her crew can keep you occupied for many, many months. Perhaps even longer. But one never knows . . . Life is so uncertain in these unsettled times . . . There is always the possibility that something *unpredictable* might happen to you at sea—something that no one, despite the best intentions, will be able to prevent."

Alex looked around the room, then concluded: "And now I'm going upstairs, to make the necessary arrangements and to keep a lookout for any visitors who might drop by."

He turned to his hired help. "I'll send someone to relieve you in a minute."

He removed his watch, bent down, and placed it on the floor, propping up its face with the expansion band so it could be seen by the prisoners.

"Aren't you afraid we'll steal it?" Joe asked.

Alex stood up and pointed ominously to the watch. "In precisely two-and-a-half hours, I'll return, with help, for a final interview—after which I'll send someone to bring around your

191

limousine. That will give the three of you time to recall all that you know of our activities and all that you've told others about them. That is the information I want. Keep this in mind as an incentive for communicating it to me: Your full cooperation might well save your lives. But anything less than that . . ."

He smiled, shook his head, and walked to the door.

Runabout

Tony pulled back on the throttle. The *Napoli*, which had been gradually decreasing speed, slowed to a crawl.

She was now southeast of the easternmost rocks off the end of Walton Point, her running lights off, her engine chugging softly.

Chet turned to Biff, who was seated on the port side. "See anything up there?"

"All dark," Biff replied, gazing around the edge of the windshield through the binoculars at what could be seen of the house.

"Okay," said Tony. "Let's take a look at the opposing team."

He pulled the throttle to neutral.

All three stood, leaned on the windshield, and studied the scene ahead on their left.

In the shadowy water off the end of the point lay a large white vessel with red and blue stripes. Her eastward-pointing prow was about even with the eastern end of the long rock landward of the maze entrance. No lights were visible on her.

"A hundred-footer," Tony commented. "So called. She's actually a bit longer than that."

"Long enough," Biff said grimly.

"Gimme the glasses."

Tony took the binoculars and lifted them to his eyes.

"I wonder why she's lying so close to the rocks," he mused aloud, peering at the cutter. "*Awful* close for a tub that size. No lights . . . Nobody on deck . . . Not on starboard, anyway."

He lowered the binoculars. "I'll bet the FBI told the CG they don't want the boys up the hill ta know that something's gonna happen till they pop up. 'Hide the cutter, please.'"

Chet laughed. "*Hide* it? It's about as inconspicuous as a whale in a fish tank!"

"They can't see 'er from the house, though. Chances are, they don't know she's there. Unless someone happened ta look out that window and see 'er sneaking in."

"Don't overlook the rest of the opposition," said Biff, pointing.

To the right of the entrance, her bow aimed toward the cutter, lay a large white runabout with a dark canvas cover. She, too, had no lights on.

Tony looked at her through the binoculars. "Yeah—there they are, the local law. No way ta know how many cops're in 'er."

Tony handed the binoculars to Chet, then opened the glove box and pulled out a chunky, large-barreled pistol. He pushed the release and flipped the barrel open, made sure that it was loaded, then closed it and put it on the seat. He reached into the glove box again, took out two short, red cylinders, put them in his pocket, and closed the door.

Having quickly studied the patrol boat and cutter, Chet gave the binoculars to Biff. Then he noticed what Tony was doing.

"What's that?" he asked.

"A Verys pistol," Tony answered. "Also known as a flare gun. The Fourth of July's night after next, so I thought I'd put on a little show."

Biff lowered the binoculars and turned to Tony. "You're going to fire a distress signal and draw them over here?"

Tony shook his head. "Not quite. I don't wanta send flares *up*. I wanta fire 'em off at eye level, to blind the boys in blue for a few seconds."

"And *then* what?"

Tony smiled. "Being cops, they'll come after us."

"That's *good*?"

"We've gotta draw 'em away from there. But not too fast. I wanta get as close to 'em as I can while they're still seeing stars."

"Why?"

"Their boat's fast as anything on the water, but her engine's so powerful that if she has ta turn 'round quick, her stern'll over-steer. So we'll make 'er turn 'round quick. We'll head for the entrance, fast as we can. When the coppers come up to us, we'll stop. When they stop, we'll run. They'll turn ta chase us, and that'll gain us a little time. The closer we are to the entrance when they stop and turn, the less far we'll hafta race 'em. If we try ta out-run that wave burner over a long distance, she'll catch us for sure. Got it?"

"Got it."

"You'd better sit down," Tony told the others, taking a seat.

As they sat, he pushed the throttle forward and turned the wheel.

The easternmost rocks pulled to starboard as the *Napoli* swung diagonally landward, her bow aimed at the entrance to the maze.

When she was about five hundred feet from the cutter, Tony stopped her.

"Everybody up," he said, standing.

Biff and Chet got to their feet.

"Okay, Chet," Tony said quickly. "Keep your eyes open so you can tell me where the flares explode."

"Roger."

"Biff, you and I'll hafta close our eyes when I fire. We can't nav-igate or do whatever else has ta be done if we watch the fireworks first."

"Gotcha."

Chet took the binoculars from the seat and focused them on the cutter.

Tony picked up the flare pistol, gripped it with both hands, and rested his elbows on the top of the windshield.

"One man on the cutter's deck," Chet announced. "Now another one's come out. They're watching us!"

"We'll give 'em something else to watch," Tony promised. "What about the patrol boat?"

Chet moved the binoculars down and to the right. "I can't see anybody stirring."

"This oughta take care of that," said Tony.

He aimed the muzzle between the two prows, then raised it

slightly. "The instructions say this thing'll shoot flares a hundred fifty yards straight up. According to my math, that's four hundred fifty feet—against gravity. I'm allowing another fifty feet or so for horizontal travel."

"Whatever you do," Biff cautioned, "don't hit the boats!"

"Protect your ears," said Tony, waiting for the *Napoli* to level off after a wave. "Okay, Biff—close your eyes!"

He slowly, smoothly pulled the trigger, then shut his eyes at the *bang*.

With a faint *whish*, the flare shot out in a low arc. It exploded with a *thud* a few feet above the water, just short of the cutter's bow, in a burst of brilliant white stars.

"Zowee!" shouted Chet. "What a show!" He lowered the binoculars and turned his head. "Aim just a bit to the right, next time."

Tony pulled a flare from his pocket, reloaded the pistol, waited a moment for the boat to hold steady, and aimed.

"Close 'em!" he yelled, then fired.

"Perfect!" Chet announced, as the darkness ahead exploded in light.

Tony opened his eyes, reloaded, waited a moment, then aimed.

"Close 'em!" he yelled again, and fired.

For the third time, a shower of stars lit up the vessels and rocks.

"Whoopee!" Chet cheered, waving the binoculars above his head. *"Happy nearly Fourth of July!"*

"Get down!" Tony shouted, sitting hard and dropping the pistol on the floor.

As Biff and Chet collapsed into the seat, he pushed the throttle full ahead. The *Napoli* slid eagerly forward.

The distance between her and the rocks quickly diminished to four hundred fifty feet . . . Four hundred . . .

In the dark water by the maze entrance, a powerful engine started up.

The patrol boat's running lights blinked on, as did a bright red light on her foredeck, which flashed slowly as she swung about.

Three hundred fifty feet . . .

Her engine roaring, the patrol boat shot toward the *Napoli*, leaving a wide wake of churned water behind.

196

Three hundred feet . . .

Running figures appeared on the cutter's deck. Two of them aimed searchlights at the *Napoli*. On the bridge, a microphone was switched on. A loud, amplified voice spoke out:

"Ahoy, runabout! You have entered a restricted area! Your improper display of visual distress signals is in direct violation of United States Coast Guard regulations! Heave alongside immediately! Repeat—heave alongside immediately!"

Two hundred feet . . .

With the approaching craft almost on her, the *Napoli* halted.

The patrol boat came to an abrupt stop along her starboard side, and the officer at the wheel leaned out, blinking.

"Tony Prito!" he shouted, as the boats rocked dizzily in the colliding wakes. "What the blue blazes—"

Tony grinned, waved, and slammed the throttle forward.

The *Napoli* rode over the waves of the larger boat's wake like a bucking horse, and headed on toward the rocks.

With a shout of anger, the pilot of the patrol boat accelerated and swung the wheel.

The rear deck slid around and kept sliding, throwing spray for yards. Then the stern pulled back in line, and the boat hurtled forward.

"Ahoy—runabout! You are ordered to heave alongside! You are ordered to heave alongside!"

The small rocks at the entrance, little more than a hundred feet from the *Napoli* now, grew steadily larger as she raced at her top speed toward them.

Behind the *Napoli*, the patrol boat grew steadily larger, as well, rapidly shrinking the gap between boats from one hundred feet to seventy-five . . . Fifty . . . Twenty-five . . . Ten . . .

Her spotlights switched on now and pointed straight ahead—but made unnecessary by the searchlights brightening the water around her—the *Napoli* tore past the cutter's prow, slowed at the last possible instant, corrected course, accelerated, and slipped between the rocks.

Behind the Veil

"I don't *believe* it!" Biff shouted, turning to look at the receding gap in the rocks—and, just beyond it, the flashing red light of the patrol boat. "We're still *alive!*"

Chet blinked his eyes. "Are you sure?" he asked.

He looked around at the huge stone shapes gliding swiftly by. "How do you know we haven't died and gone to heaven?"

He rose unsteadily to his feet, clutched the edge of the windshield, and surveyed the eerie labyrinth. "On second thought, it looks more like the other place."

The beam of a Coast Guard searchlight swung over the east end of the long rock and lit up the *Napoli.* As she hurried on, the rock rose higher and blocked the light.

Biff turned to Tony, a worried look on his face. "Can they get in here?"

"The police boat's too wide. But the cutter crew might launch their rescue boats and come after us. So when we get in ta the cave, we'll need ta shut 'em out."

He glanced back at the probing searchlight beams and groaned. "They're gonna lock me away for ninety-nine years! I can hear 'em now: '*Improper and reckless display of distress signals, harassment and evasion of a police vessel, refusal to respond to orders of the Coast Guard . . .* '"

"Don't get too wacked up about it," Biff advised him, leaning back in the seat. "When we rescue the Hardys, the authorities'll give you a medal."

"Yeah," Tony replied sarcastically, "they might even lemme outa jail for the ceremony."

He thought for a moment, then added: "*If* we rescue the Hardys."

On the foredeck, Tony regarded the stone-colored curtain just beyond the bow, as he stripped to his swimming trunks.

"The bottom of that thing's probably not far below the low-tide line," he told the others.

He handed his clothes over the windshield to Biff.

"Okay," he said to Chet, at the wheel. "As soon as you've got clearance, head in."

Chet stared uneasily ahead. "What if they're meeting a freighter tonight?"

Tony grinned. "I'll let you worry 'bout that while I'm worrying 'bout how ta open this door."

He eased himself over the bow, took a deep breath, and went under.

About three feet beneath the surface, he found the curtain's bulky, weighted bottom edge. Gripping it, he pulled himself under and past it.

He came up in an unevenly lit cavern. Some of it, by the appearance of its jagged, irregular ceiling, seemed to have been made by enlarging natural fissures in the rock.

Ahead of him, the water curved around to the left and divided into two channels, each perpendicular to the other.

The narrower left channel, which appeared to have been made for boats to head into to reverse direction, ended after about thirty feet, like the short arm of a check mark. The small amount of light leaking into it from around the corner revealed drilled and blasted walls and a comparatively low ceiling.

Along the far side of the longer, wider right channel was a floating dock connected by rope rings to long, vertical metal members resembling the sides of ships' ladders, which were bolted to the wall. The near end of the dock extended almost to the corner of the channel intersection.

Tied to the dock were three remarkably long black speedboats pointed toward the entrance, illuminated by a string of light bulbs running high along the wall behind them.

Above and beyond the dock's far end was a wide, cement-topped platform cut from the rock. Leading down from it was a long, rough-surfaced wooden ramp, its unattached lower end resting on the planking.

Above the platform was visible the upper part of a rusted metal door, lit by high-wattage bulbs in fixtures on either side of it—the only other source of light in the cave.

Attached by metal braces to the wall above the near end of the dock was a large winch, its electric motor encased in windings of what appeared to be waterproof fabric. A cable led up from it to a series of pulleys fastened to the ceiling, then dropped downward to connect to the middle of a length of chain, each end of which was attached to the top of a strange-looking contraption.

"Oh, *Mama!*" Tony exclaimed, treading water. "It's a monster-size *window shade!*"

Recessed partway into the smoothly surfaced rock along each side of the cavern entrance was a long, vertical, five-inch-diameter pipe with a full-length slot facing the opening, through which passed a side edge of the curtain. Fastened to the rock just above the top ends of the pipes, just over the entrance, was a long, horizontal, rubber-faced roller over which the back of the curtain passed. A foot or so above the roller, the sheet of heavy fabric ended, wrapped and stitched around a pipe, to the ends of which were attached the chain connected to the winch cable. Each side edge, visible at the top of the curtain, was sewn around a large-diameter rope, apparently to keep it from pulling out of the slots in the pipes.

An electrical conduit, Tony noticed, led from the winch motor to somewhere above the platform.

He swam to the dock, climbed the ramp, and pushed the highest of three buttons on a control panel by the door.

The winch slowly lifted the curtain.

As the *Napoli* pulled inside, Tony pushed the middle button, then the bottom one.

The curtain stopped, then slowly descended.

"Nylon," Tony said to himself, watching it thoughtfully. "I'll betcha."

After he tied the *Napoli* to cleats forward of the lead speedboat, Biff and Chet handed him his clothes and, from the rear seat, two large towels, a knapsack, and a toolbox—all of which he placed well in from the front edge of the unsteady dock. Then they climbed out.

Biff put his arms through the straps of the knapsack and lifted it onto his back.

"Dig this rug cutter," he said, walking over to the nearest speedboat.

The long, narrow craft sat high in the water. Behind her single, far-forward bench seat were double cargo-hatch doors running back almost to the engine hatch. Everything on her, down to the smallest fitting, was painted black.

"Custom built, I'd say," Tony commented, coming up beside Biff. "Like their crazy curtain."

He turned to Chet. "A real hot rod, huh?"

Chet nodded weakly.

"Hey—your face is green!" I thought you *liked* motion."

"Cars are one thing," Chet replied, trying to balance himself on the gently rocking platform. "Boats are another."

Tony smiled. "Dry land's coming up."

He pointed to the door beyond the platform. "Let's see what's in there."

"What *isn't* in here?" asked Biff, as they looked around the cement-floored stone chamber.

Most of the thirty-foot-square room was occupied by rows of stacked wooden crates and cardboard boxes. Light bulbs glowed from sockets on boards fastened to the nine-foot ceiling. Attached to one of the rough walls was a fuse box with electrical conduits running to and from it. A conduit passed through a hole above the metal door. Set into a much larger hole next to it was a spinning ventilation fan.

Across from the door was the room's second entrance, a crudely formed opening in the rock. Along the wall to the left of it were placed a battery charger, four truck batteries, a large toolbox, two pry bars, a stack of narrow boards, boxes of nails, a long crate containing pieces of conduit and water pipe, several balls of twine, three pairs of scissors, a pile of shop towels, some cans of oil and gasoline . . .

"There's a lot more here than drugs," Chet observed, looking at the labels on a stack of boxes. "And I'll bet a good deal of this stuff isn't going overseas. Some of it, at least, must've *come* from—"

"Later, Clyde," Biff said impatiently, heading toward the hole in the wall. "We need to get topside."

The others followed him along a short, cement-floored passage leading to the left.

All three groaned as they came to a halt at its end.

By the feeble light of a final overhead bulb, they saw, well below the edge of the floor on which they were standing, a few feet of ties and rails, running uphill in a narrow tunnel into darkness.

"Well . . ." began Tony, the first to speak. "I'm afraid that climbing that thing's gonna hafta be up to you two."

"What?" said Chet, swinging around. "Is it going to take you all night to sabotage those speedboats?"

Tony looked at him and shook his head. "No. But it's not that simple."

"Oh? Why not?"

"I've been doing a little thinking. If something happens ta this expedition, somebody's gonna hafta fetch help from the outside. The more ways the authorities have ta get ta the crooks, the better."

"Then why don't *I* stay here and fix the boats while you athletic types—"

"Tony's right," Biff interjected, gazing down at the rails. "He can find his way through those rocks to get help. You can't."

"After I discombobulate the boats," said Tony, "I'll smash the end light bulb or two, so that little side channel'll be nice'n dark.

Then I'll back *Napoli* into it, swim to the dock, dry off and get inta warm clothes, and wait here for developments."

"Why hide *Napoli*?" asked Chet.

"Just in case. Who knows what's gonna happen? Remember— we're here 'cause something went wrong with the previous plan. We need ta be prepared for something going wrong with *this* one."

"Come on," Biff said suddenly, turning around. "There're some things back there we can use!"

He hurried to the box room, with Tony and Chet close behind him.

"Here we are," he muttered, fishing around in the long crate against the wall. "Yeah, that'll do . . ."

He took out two short pieces of pipe. He tucked one under his belt and handed the other to Chet.

"What's this?"

"A weapon."

Biff fished through the pipes again, pulled out two four-foot sections, and laid them on the floor. "And these'll be our climbing sticks. Like what they use in mountaineering."

He reached over, grabbed a pair of scissors, and cut off a couple of two-foot pieces of twine. He gave one to Chet.

"Double one of those shop towels over," he said, "wrap it around the end of your stick, and tie it on with this. We need to be as quiet as we can."

Walking the Line

"Ow!" exclaimed Chet, as softly as he could, for the second time.

He paused to rub his temple. Then he continued climbing, with his right foot close to the inside of the left rail.

"You're too far over," said Biff, in a voice just above a whisper. "Why don't you move back toward the middle?"

He jabbed the towel-wrapped tip of his water-pipe climbing stick down against a tie and pushed off.

"I'm trying to go around the ends of the ties with my left foot," Chet explained, panting. "So at least one of my feet won't have to step on those stupid things."

"So you hit your head on the stupid rock."

"It'd help if I could see what's coming."

Chet shone his light up, onto the uneven wall. "Why'd they decide to save on their lighting bill *here?*"

Biff stopped. "We're both sweating like mad."

"Yeah," replied Chet, halting and wiping his forehead with his sleeve. "This tunnel isn't so cold after all."

Biff put down his flashlight and climbing stick, bracing them so they wouldn't roll. Then he removed his knapsack. "Let's get down to our undershirts."

They took off their shirts and tied them around their waists.

"What's in the knapsack?" Chet asked, still breathing hard.

"A canteen of water and a bag of nuts, for the Hardys. And a knife, a spare flashlight, and some batteries. I put in our gloves and ski masks, too, in case you wonder where they went."

"A bag of nuts, you say?"

Biff looked sharply at his companion. *"For the Hardys."*

He picked up his knapsack, flashlight, and stick and resumed climbing.

"How's Jeanie?" asked Chet, breathing with a little less difficulty on their second rest break, a few minutes later.

"Fine," answered Biff. He took a deep breath. "We went out to dinner Monday night."

"Just out of curiosity, what do you think of Cynthia Malloy?"

"She's attractive. No doubt about it." Biff gave an exaggerated sigh and shook his head. "If I were a younger man . . ."

"Younger? She's the same age we are!"

"Well, she's still younger."

Chet paused, thinking. "Do you suppose she'd ever go out with me?"

"She probably would if you were a hero."

"And how am I going to manage *that?"*

"Keep climbing."

When they stopped again a few minutes later, Chet put down his stick and flashlight, pulled his shirt from around his waist, and used it to mop his face and neck.

"I wish we could walk on the rails," he remarked, breathing deeply. "I tried it, but I slipped right off."

Biff ran the beam of his flashlight along the rail by Chet's foot.

"Yeah, they're too smooth for traction. Even with these rough socks on."

"The ties're driving me crazy. I step *over* them, I step *onto* them . . ."

"Wait a minute."

Biff stared at the slotted center rail. Then he knelt and ran the back of his flashlight hand along the perforated surface.

The edges of the holes were raised and sharp enough to scratch his skin.

He smiled and looked up at Chet. "Solid, Jackson!"

"It doesn't look solid to me," Chet said wearily, gazing down at the cog rail. "And my name's not Jackson."

Biff stepped onto the rail, put one foot ahead of the other, and started walking, jabbing his climbing stick down like a ski pole.

"That's more like it!" he declared.

Chet, holding both climbing sticks, looked anxiously up the tunnel as his partner peered under the storage-room door.

Close to his left, Biff glimpsed a brown shoe, sock, and pants' cuff, and the lower part of the right front leg of a chair. Beyond them to the left, he saw two pairs of sock-covered shoes, the rope-bound bottoms of two pairs of dark pants' legs, and the lower parts of the front legs of two chairs. Surveying the room from side to side, he could see no sign of anyone else's presence.

Biff got to his feet, looked at Chet, and put a finger to his lips.

He pulled the short pipe from his belt with his right hand, put his left hand on the small metal knob on the right side of the door, and slowly turned it. Then he cautiously pushed the door open a few inches . . . And froze.

A couple of feet to his right, slouched in a chair tilted back against the wall, was a tall man in work clothes, wearing a pistol in a shoulder holster. His eyes were closed. He was breathing deeply.

Biff motioned for Chet to wait. Then he eased the door open and stepped carefully inside.

He moved silently around until he faced the sleeping guard. Watching him warily, he returned the pipe to his belt. He bent down, gripped the protruding bottoms of the front chair legs, and jumped back, yanking the chair away.

The man's head hit the floor with a soft *thump* and went limp.

Chet peeked into the room, then stepped inside, put the climbing sticks down quietly, and gently closed the door. He came to attention and saluted the three smiling Hardys. Then he walked over and looked down at the face of the unconscious figure on the floor.

It was long and narrow, with a prominent forehead, deep-set eyes, and a mouth like a straight line.

Chet studied the puzzled expression on Biff's face.

"You look disappointed," he remarked.

"I didn't know it'd be that easy."

"By the way," said Chet, "I don't believe you two have been introduced. Biff Hooper, this is Ivan Slovacic. Ivan, this is Biff. No—don't get up."

"You haven't seen Ivan's photograph," Joe said to Biff, "but you may have noticed his footprints on Polucca's stairway three days ago. And Chet saw them tonight, in the dirt at Olsen's farm."

Biff and Chet looked at the soles of the man's shoes.

They were large, with lines across them.

"So that's the situation," Frank told the rescuers after the Hardys had been released, Ivan bound and gagged, and the nuts and water quickly consumed. "Dad's weak from being tied up and starved for hours, and his ankle's badly swollen."

"He had a tough time," said Joe, "just limping on and off that thing." He pointed to a hand truck in the corner. "That's what they used to wheel him up to the hideout for bathroom breaks."

"They let you use their bathroom?" asked Chet. "That was decent of them."

"Yes—they're such decent people," Joe replied sarcastically. "Who're going to haul us off to sea to be murdered if those FBI agents don't show up soon, or use us as hostages if they *do*."

"If you get on the hand truck, Mr. Hardy," said Biff, "I can push you down to the tunnel car, fast. We need to get going."

The detective shook his head. "As soon as that cog drive starts, the gang will hear it and know we're trying to escape."

"The car moves along at a nice pace," said Joe, "but it's no speedster. Or so they told me when I asked. They'll sprint down and grab us before we get very far."

"We could sneak up the hidden stairs," Chet suggested.

"They'd see us," Joe replied. "There's no wall between the stairway and the hideout, after all. Just a partition, to the left of the door as you go in."

"Oh."

"And Tony can't help us," Biff remarked with a frown. "He's at the bottom of the tunnel, sabotaging the speedboats and waiting for us to show up."

"How many are in the hideout?" Chet asked Frank.

"Four. Ivan made five."

"Do they all have guns?"

"They don't wear them. Ivan said he had to search to find that shoulder holster. But I'm sure they'll be armed when they come to get us. And their hideout's an arsenal."

"Your only chance to get away," Fenton Hardy said firmly, "is to leave me and run for it down the tunnel. *Now.* I'll hold them off. I can barricade the door and—"

"No dice," said Joe.

"And no time," Frank added, looking at Alex Polucca's watch on the floor. "They're coming for us in twenty-two minutes. It's a long, steep way down to the cave. We'd lose energy after a while. The car may not be quick, but it's steady—it'd catch up with us before we reached the bottom."

"I have a plan," said Chet.

"Aren't we in enough danger already?" Biff asked harshly.

"There's no time to discuss it," Chet countered. "Bring that hand truck over here. We need to move fast."

The End of the Tunnel

Joe ran up to the hideout door, put his ear to it, and listened. Then he noisily turned the knob, opened the door a few inches, and yelled in a rasping voice:

"*Hey! There's some funny noises up at the garage end a the tunnel! Check it out! Everybody! Everybody up there!*"

He closed the door and ran as fast as he could, around the corner and down the tunnel to the storage room.

From behind the hideout door came loud grumblings of protest:

"There's nothing up there!"

"Nothing but a ton of metal!"

"What's the matter, Ivan—getting bored?"

The door swung open and the small man with the chimpanzee-like face stepped out. He turned and called to the others: "Let's go, you slobs! Move it!"

"Aaah!"

"Take it easy!"

"You don't need *all* of us!"

"*Everybody outa there!*" shouted the small man. "*Now!*"

With Chimpanzee Face in the lead, the four men walked, with no discernible sign of interest, down the side passage and into the main tunnel.

"Hey!" shouted their leader, coming suddenly to a halt. His followers halted with him. He pointed up the tunnel.

The end of the tunnel was dark.

"The lights're out!"

"Two, looks like!"

"Maybe three!"

"Well, come on," said Chimpanzee Face, a bit nervously. "They just shorted out or something."

The men, noticeably wary now, walked onward.

Just before they reached the darkness, the noises began.

First came a distant thumping, like the sound of footsteps on the garage floor. There was some hurried scraping . . . It and the thumping grew louder . . .

There was a great *crash*, as though something heavy, made of metal, had fallen down the trapdoor steps.

Then came—so rapidly that it was hard for those standing in the light to comprehend it all—the fast tramping of feet descending the stairs, the noise of something dragging on wood, and the lively tread of footsteps reaching the cement, all echoing loudly from the floor, walls, and ceiling.

Three flashlights were suddenly switched on, sending out low shafts of light that wavered this way and that as they quickly advanced.

The beams rose up, jerkily outlining the figure of a man in a suit, standing straight and still at the head of the invading force, holding out what appeared to be an open credentials folder.

"*FBI!*" he bellowed. "*We've got every door and window up there covered! Our men'll be coming down that stairway from the kitchen at any moment! There's no escape! Give up now!*"

The smugglers stood as though petrified, dazed by the nerve-racking sights and sounds.

Then Chimpanzee Face yelled to his companions: "We've got one way out—the boats!"

The gang members turned and ran for their lives.

From behind them, inspiring them to greater effort, came the sounds of metallic banging and clanging, more footsteps, and deep-voiced shouts:

"Let's *get* 'em!"

"There're only four of 'em!"

"They won't get away from *us!*"

In the rear of the hard-running group, the stocky, square-faced "ghost" tripped and fell. He staggered up, tried to run before he was completely on his feet, and fell again.

In a state of total panic, he scrambled up and ran like a madman, screaming to the others: *"Hold the car! Don't let them catch me!"*

Behind the fleeing smugglers, the noises and voices of their pursuers—who had not yet emerged from the darkness—grew louder.

"There's no hurry—they're trapped!"

"Wait'll we slap our handcuffs on those cuckoos!"

"Save one for me!"

Soon the loud grating of the double cogwheel reverberated back up the tunnel.

Joe opened the door of the darkened storage room and looked cautiously down the tunnel to make sure the heads of the gang members had descended from view. Then he ran up to the "FBI" team as they—minus their chuckling, unmoving leader—staggered into the light, dropped their pieces of pipe, put down their flashlights, and collapsed in fits of laughter.

"Boy, did *you* three kick out!" Joe exclaimed. "And you, too, Dad!" he called to the end of the tunnel.

Frank stopped laughing.

"Keep it down," he cautioned his brother. "They probably can't hear us over that racket, but let's not take any chances."

Joe gave a subdued cry of victory and threw his arms around a very happy-looking Chet Morton.

Biff slapped his fellow tunnel climber on the back. "You really aced 'em, Slick!"

Frank, smiling broadly, shook hands with the long-maligned chief prankster of Bayport. "Thanks, Chet. I owe you a lot for that."

"My pleasure," Chet modestly replied.

Frank, still smiling, turned to Biff. "You'd better pick up what's left of the hand truck and—"

"I think I'll use another one, instead," Biff interjected with a grin.

"Wheel Dad into the hideout, so he can lie down on one of the beds. And get him some food."

"Food?" said Chet, interested.

"Joe and I'd better run down the tunnel to see if Tony manages to take the car up after the crooks abandon it."

"That's right," said Joe, turning serious. "Once they find out their boats don't work—"

"Come on."

Frank and Joe, breathing hard, halted under the last light bulb.

From far down the tunnel came the steadily diminishing noise of the cog drive.

After what seemed a long time, it stopped.

"Come on, Tony!" Joe exclaimed softly, clenching his fist. "Grab it and get up here!"

The seconds slowly passed.

"What's *that*?" asked Frank.

Faintly to their ears came the sound of speedboat engines. It grew louder, then faded, as if the boats were moving quickly off into the distance.

The brothers looked at each other.

"I thought Tony was going to fix those things," said Frank.

"Maybe something happened to him."

"Let's just hope they didn't catch him monkeying with their boats."

"Or coming to meet them, thinking they were us."

From the end of the tunnel came the sound of the cograil car.

"Oh, I fixed 'em, all right," replied Tony, grinning as he stepped off the car. "I cut their fuel lines quite a ways back and sealed the ends. I figured if the crooks went after us, that'd give 'em enough gas to get outa their fortress and meet the Coast Guard and the cops.

"After they tore away, I shut the door on 'em to make sure they wouldn't have an easy time getting back in, and hopped on the elevator."

He laughed. "That's some ride. Sorta like the Tunnel of Love. *The Tunnel of Claustrophobia.*"

As the three gangbusters walked away from the cog car, Tony clapped a hand on each brother's shoulder.

"Hee-hee—you shoulda *seen* 'em! They went ricocheting outa there like Ping-Pong balls!"

Frank, Joe, and Tony were catching their breath after their fast walk as they passed through the doorway in the foundation wall.

Just inside to their left were the narrow, thickly padded steps leading up to the kitchen.

Joe nudged Tony and pointed to a large, bulky light on a folded tripod leaning against the wall, next to a louvered metal box with a handle on top.

The light was faced with a thick, round, convex piece of glass deeply faceted by concentric circles.

"An aero-marine beacon," said Joe. "That's what they told us it's called. They said some fancy company made it for them. Its globe and lens give a super-bright, focused beam."

Tony laughed. "We can all testify to *that.*"

He shook his head admiringly. "A portable lighthouse. They're one clever family, those Poluccas."

Frank and Joe turned to each other.

"*Alex Polucca!*" they both exclaimed.

They took off up the steps at full speed.

"Come on!" Tony called to the others. "I think we're gonna need some help!"

He started up the stairway after them.

At the top of the stairs, the brothers rushed through the opening and past the pulled-away cupboard into the lighted kitchen.

Seeing no one there, they ran toward the far door on the right, with Frank in the lead.

They slammed through the swinging door into the lighted hallway and ran down it to the darkened living room and the lighted stairs.

There they paused, undecided, gazing up the steps, as Tony ran up to them.

Hearing the sound of a quiet-running auto engine, Joe turned toward the unlit entry hall.

The front door was open.

"Come on!" Joe shouted, running for all he was worth.

He raced through the hall and out the doorway, leaped from the stoop, and hit the ground running.

The Packard was swinging around, its headlights sweeping the trees. It straightened out, then accelerated, heading for the driveway.

Joe jumped onto the running board by the driver's wing window, pushed off against the side-mounted spare tire cover, and grabbed the near wiper arm at the top of the windshield. He pulled himself up and grabbed the other arm, blocking Alex's view.

Alex slammed on the brakes to throw him off. Joe's head smacked against the glass, but he held on.

As the car jerked to a stop, Frank jumped onto the running board, took hold of the driver's door handle with his left hand and the forward-mounted handle of the rear "suicide" door with his right, and pushed down. The driver's handle didn't budge, but the rear handle went down and Frank pulled the door open.

He fell inside as Alex accelerated, bouncing off the seat cushion onto a leather-covered suitcase on the floor.

The rear door slammed shut as Alex stamped down on the brake pedal, failing again to dislodge the obstruction from the windshield.

He accelerated hard, then braked again, as Frank tried in vain to get to his knees.

"Get off, you fool!" Alex yelled through the partly open window. "You'll wreck us!" He pushed down on the accelerator.

"You'll wreck yourself!" Joe yelled back. "If you don't stop!"

Frank dived over the back of the front seat as Alex switched on the windshield wipers, throwing Joe to the right and almost off the hood.

"Here," Frank gasped, as he wrenched Alex's foot off the gas pedal with both hands. "Let me help."

As the Packard lugged to a halt, killing the engine, Alex kicked free from Frank's grip, pushed the door open, and jumped out.

Seeing Biff and Tony racing toward him, he turned to run down the driveway. But he went nowhere.

Several dark-suited men had stepped from behind the trees and were fanning out before him, holding machine guns at the ready.

The man in the lead held out an open credentials folder with a gold shield.

"FBI!" he declared.

Five dark-colored, unmarked cars were waiting in the turnaround, pointed toward the house, their lights on, their engines running. All but one were unoccupied.

By that one, two FBI agents were standing, looking in a rear side window at a handcuffed, sullen-faced Alex Polucca.

An empty patrol car was sitting in the driveway, its engine rumbling, its headlights on, its roof light flashing.

The two policemen, seventeen federal agents, the Hardys, and Tony Prito were occupying the various floors of the brightly lit house.

Alex Polucca's Packard was parked by the front door. Its silver paint and chromium trim flashed in the glare of the headlights like the facets of a diamond as Biff Hooper and Chet Morton walked over to it.

"What a machine!" Biff said admiringly. "It looks like a jewel and goes like a rocket!"

"With a twelve-cylinder engine like the one it's got," Chet remarked wearily, "you could make anything go like a rocket."

"Jealous?"

"No. Just worn out."

Chet sat down on the running board, sighed with relief, and leaned back, closing his eyes against the headlights.

"What a night!" he marveled. "We'll never see another night like this one!"

He turned his head to the right, away from the glare, and opened his eyes. A faraway, thoughtful look came into them. His mouth lifted into a smirk.

He started giggling, stopped, nodded reflectively, then began again. The giggles dropped in pitch, turning to ripples of laughter. He started rocking, gleefully pounding his knees with his fists.

Biff leaned against the front fender and looked down at the suddenly revived jokester.

"What's so funny, Laughing Boy?"

Chet stopped rocking, looked up and replied: "I was just thinking."

"That's a novelty. What about?"

Chet squinted into the distance.

"I can hardly wait," he declared, "to see the look on Con Riley's face."

Aftermath

Although Bayport's heat wave had passed, the weather was warmer than usual for the early-evening dinner party taking place in the Hardys' backyard.

From an open upstairs window at the rear of the house came the sound of a radio playing:

I search for phrases
To sing your praises,
But there aren't any magic adjectives
To tell you all you are—

You're just too marvelous,
Too marvelous for words . . .

Fenton Hardy stood at the head of a banquet table formed from two picnic tables joined end-to-end on the lawn. Down one side sat Mrs. Hardy, Gertrude Hardy, Callie, Iola, and Chet. Coming back up the other side sat Biff, Joe, Frank, Tony, and—until now—Mr. Hardy.

"While all of you start in on your pie and ice cream," the latter began, "I'd like to say a few words."

He paused and cleared his throat. "First of all, I want to thank certain of you here—and we all know who you are—for getting me out of the mess you got me into by not telling me what was going on as soon as you found out about it."

"*Mmrmph,*" said Chet, his mouth full. "Sorry Murfder Hardy. We divint realize what *truvul* we'd be causing you."

The detective held up both hands. "There's no need for further apology. That's all been explained, many times over. But I hope that *in the future* you'll communicate any such important discoveries to me or the authorities, and save everyone a good deal of difficulty."

"Hear, hear!" exclaimed his wife, tapping her glass with a spoon.

Gertrude Hardy gave her nephews a look formidable enough to strike fear into the heart of any student at Bayport High.

"We won't, of course," she remarked caustically, "spoil the fun by saying anything about the matter of certain members of this household sneaking away at night to go on a dangerous, clandestine boat ride—after telling us they were going to bed early."

"Considering that we've gone over that already," said her sister-in-law compassionately.

"But if they ever do anything like that again—"

"Concerning blame for what happened," Mr. Hardy continued, "there's enough of it to go around. I followed a suspicious character into the Polucca garage unaided. Chief Collig disbelieved what four responsible teenagers told him—"

"And pretty thoroughly discounted the well-founded concerns of two adults," Aunt Gertrude interjected.

"When he finally did begin to believe that there was something to what all of you were saying," replied her brother, "he posted only one police car at the driveway entrance."

"Which the dispatcher," Evelyn Hardy pointed out, "pulled off guard duty to respond to Mrs. Adams's burglar call up North Shore."

"All of these," said Mr. Hardy, "were big mistakes. And they were made by adult professionals who ought to have known better."

He paused dramatically, then added: "But the actions of you young people made everything right."

"Lucky for us, huh?" remarked Tony, looking up from his dessert and smiling.

"And lucky for Mr. Hardy," remarked Callie, more seriously.

"Thanks to all of you," Fenton Hardy went on, "the authorities are demolishing a ring of thievery and smuggling that was far bigger than any of us had imagined. You're heroes in Bayport and across the nation. You've had your pictures in the papers. You've been interviewed on radio. And now you've been given a substantial reward."

"Reward?" Chet sputtered indignantly. "*What* reward? Nobody gave *me* any—"

"Down, boy," Biff commanded. "You're not fooling anyone."

"That's right," Joe agreed. "We saw you put it in your pocket."

"Oh. *That* reward."

"The acclaim given to your actions," Mr. Hardy imperturbably continued, "is a refreshing and encouraging change from the ordinary in a society that says very little, if anything, positive about teenagers, yet glamorizes gangsters on a daily basis in movies, radio shows, magazines, and books—and then complains about the nation's high level of criminal activity and the high taxes necessary to combat it.

"All of you working together in your investigative and rescue efforts have demonstrated to the nation the importance of *teamwork*—something that all of us would do well to keep in mind, for our success and our survival."

"Even if you didn't," remarked Aunt Gertrude, putting things in perspective, "demonstrate the importance of communicating one's suspicions in the very beginning to the police."

"Speaking of the police," said Fenton Hardy with a smile, "I ought to mention that something truly astounding has come out of all this: *The Bayport Police Department has developed respect for Chet Morton.*"

"They *love* him!" Iola declared, putting an arm around her brother. "Even Chief Collig!"

"I wouldn't go *that* far," Biff cautioned her. "Human nature has its limits."

"Well, the chief *tolerates* him now," Iola retorted. "And that's a *big* improvement!"

She turned to Chet. "Tell them what happened to you today."

"Oh, they wouldn't believe it," Chet replied, pushing his fork around his already-empty plate.

"Try us," Callie said encouragingly.

"All right . . . On my way out of Thayer's this afternoon, I bumped into Con Riley."

"Ahem!" said Aunt Gertrude.

"Sergeant Riley. And instead of him saying—well, what he always used to say whenever he'd see me—he shook my hand, as solemn as a judge, and told me, *'The next time you phone the station, Chet, I'll believe you.'"*

Forkfuls of food on their way to open mouths halted in midair. Chewing stopped. A hush descended upon the table.

"Chet!" exclaimed Evelyn Hardy. "Surely you wouldn't take advantage of—"

Chet held up a hand. "Don't worry, Mrs. Hardy. I know what you're thinking."

He shook his head. "From now on, I'm a changed man."

Forks continued on their journeys. Chewing hesitantly resumed.

"After all," said Chet, "if I'm going to be involved in any more crime-solving activities, I'll need to be on good terms with the police."

The speed of chewing increased.

"On the other hand," he added, after a moment of thought, "if there isn't any more of that to do around here, I might reconsider and have some—"

Swift kicks from three directions brought his remarks to a conclusion.

Much later in the evening—after the guests had left, the remains of the meal had been put away, and the dishes washed—Fenton Hardy sat between his sons on one of the picnic tables. The back-porch light behind them cast their shadows on the grass.

"So," Mr. Hardy said to Joe. "Not only has the Police Department developed respect for Chet Morton, Joe Hardy has devel-

oped respect for his sister. Amazing changes are taking place in Bayport!"

"Iola's all right," Joe replied thoughtfully. "She's smart, good-looking . . . Her personality just got in my way, that's all—until she broke down and stopped being sassy Iola for a while."

"Did that surprise you?"

"You bet. All of a sudden, I didn't know who she was. And then I began to wonder if that pushy personality was a . . ."

"Facade?"

"Well, it's *her*—but there's more to her than that. Maybe her Goofy Iola act is some sort of shield to keep the rest of her safe."

"Like her brother's clown act," Frank remarked quietly.

"She did her best to help us," Joe concluded, "and I admire her for that."

"Good for you!" Fenton Hardy exclaimed.

He gazed across the lawn and beyond it, as though regarding something a great distance away. "I've always encouraged the two of you to put forth your finest effort in whatever you do. Knowing that we've done our best is vital to our self-respect. But it's important for another reason.

"When it comes to whatever we most want to accomplish in life, we sons eventually have to in some way equal or surpass our fathers. If we don't, we can spend our adult lives feeling to some degree inferior or incomplete.

"As you know, my father died when I was younger than you are. I was the elder son; Gertrude was the eldest of four children. We had a family to take care of and something to prove. I was out to show that I could do as well as—or would *someday* do as well as—Lieutenant Hardy of the Boston Police Department.

"The medals and commendations awarded my father were for hardly more than the beginning of what should have been a long, illustrious career. So I'll never know if I could do better at solving crimes and apprehending criminals than he would have, had he lived. But I've been trying for most of my life to find out. And that, I believe, is why I tend to go it alone and to take risks that others in my profession don't take.

"Your mother's softened my attitude a good deal. She's helped me to be satisfied with what I've done. But the desire to prove myself is still there.

"So, while I don't mean to negate anything I've said about the importance of communicating with one's parents, I have to admit that, had I been in your position in this case, I would have done the same as you."

He paused, looked at Frank and then Joe, and smiled. "Well, you did it—you solved it without me. And I congratulate you."

He shook hands with his sons.

"Thanks, Dad," said Frank.

"Yeah," said Joe. "Thanks for telling us that."

"Before we turn in," Fenton Hardy remarked, "how about going for a little ride? There's something I'd like to show you."

In the garage, Frank, Joe, and their father climbed into the family car, a maroon 1940 Ford DeLuxe Fordor sedan.

Mr. Hardy started the engine, backed the car down the driveway, and into the street.

He turned right, drove to the corner, and turned right again, down Sycamore.

He followed Sycamore down the hill to the bay, then made a right at South Edgewater.

After a couple of blocks, he pulled into a driveway on the left.

He drove down it to the water's edge and stopped behind a narrow white building on pilings sticking out into the bay.

"What do you know!" Frank exclaimed. "Mr. Swenson's finally fixed up his run-down old boathouse!"

"Somebody's renting it," his father told him. "Let's take a look."

"Fresh paint," Joe observed, as they walked up the ramp to the door.

"The final coat was put on yesterday," said Fenton Hardy. "Or so I was told."

He took a key from his pocket and unlocked the door.

"Where'd you get the key?" asked Joe.

"Oh, from Mr. Swenson."

The detective walked in and turned on the lights.

"What do you think of *that?*" he asked.

Stepping onto the walkway, Frank and Joe saw—rocking gently on the water, her bow facing them—a mahogany runabout with twin bench seats, spotlights, and glistening trim.

"What a dream!" Joe exclaimed.

"Whose is it?" asked Frank.

"I'll tell you in a minute," his father replied. "But first I'll tell you whose it *was.* Or *almost* was."

"Some high-riding hepcat," Joe speculated, staring at the runabout, "with a lot of do-re-mi."

Mr. Hardy laughed. "Who's also, as you would say, a bad actor— a wrong number. A slippery operator who paid Simpson's one-third of the purchase price as a deposit shortly before he was arrested for thievery and smuggling."

Joe turned, grinning. "Someone we know?"

"You met him once. We all did."

"I think I remember him," said Frank, with a smile. "He drove a silver Packard."

"And," Joe recalled, "he wore a pinstripe suit."

"According to an attorney who was asked to look into the matter," Fenton Hardy continued, "the receipt for deposit did not transfer the title to said operator. That's why the authorities didn't confiscate the boat as one of his possessions.

"I happen to know about this because a friend of ours was the one who consulted the attorney. He then came to me with an idea of his, and asked what I thought of it. I approved of the idea, so he talked with Mr. Simpson, who agreed to mark the boat's price at cost. Then he went to the merchants of Bayport and asked them to contribute whatever they could to make up the difference between the deposit and the new purchase price."

Mr. Hardy paused, then added: "And that's how you got the boat."

His sons stared at him, speechless.

He smiled. "You two have a lot of friends in this town. Especially the one who made it possible"—he pointed to the runabout—"for you to have *that.*"

"Who?" Joe managed to croak.

"Chief Ezra Collig."

"I feel weak," said Frank, sitting down on the walkway.

"Me, too." His brother did the same.

"I, by the way, contributed the price of the renovation and rental of this boathouse."

"How can we ever thank you?" Frank asked. "All of you."

"Yeah—how?"

"I'm sure you'll think of some way to express your appreciation to the others. You can thank me by keeping the boat in top condition and by piloting her safely and responsibly. Do you think you can manage that?"

"Yes, sir!"

"You bet!"

"Insurance, maintenance, and repairs are to be your responsibilities. And we—your mother and I—expect you to handle them wisely, without exhausting your savings or your reward money."

"Agreed."

"Absolutely."

The boys hurried to their feet.

"I had Irv Wister paint a name on her," Fenton Hardy told them. "He can change it, if you want."

Walking quickly to the stern, the brothers saw, in gold letters on the transom: *Sleuth.*

Frank turned to his father. "It's perfect!" he declared.

Joe nodded. "Couldn't be better!"

"It seemed appropriate," his father remarked. "You two have earned the title."

"I don't suppose we'd better take her out tonight," Joe said longingly.

"I don't suppose you'd better," replied Fenton Hardy, smiling. "Wait until daylight. And take Tony with you as instructor. His father's going to give him the day off. But Tony doesn't know it yet. And he doesn't know about this, either. Chief Collig swore all the merchants—including Mike Prito—to secrecy."

"Boy, will Tony be surprised!"

"Oh—do me a favor, will you?"

"Sure, Dad," said Frank.

"What is it, Dad?" Joe asked.

"Stay away from those rocks off Walton Point."

The boys looked at each other. They looked at their father. Then they laughed.

Following are the main additions, listed in chronological order, that I made to the plot of *The House on the Cliff,** after reducing it to what I considered useful:

The point of land beneath the house; the cluster of rocks beyond it; the garage; the footprints and marks in the dust; the left-on electricity; the moved motorcycle, frisked jacket, and fingerprints; Fenton Hardy's stolen-pharmaceuticals investigation; his theory of the smuggling gang's method of operation; the Hardy boys' decision to keep their discoveries secret and their reason for doing so; Chet's telephone pranks; Frank's doubts about his discoveries; the imitation rock wall; the light from the window and the reply; the tire tracks in the Polucca driveway; the movers and their van; the Packard; the soda-fountain conference; Callie's and Iola's participation in the investigation; the abandoned farm; the tunnel and cogway; the tour of the house; the monogrammed hat on the back seat of the car; the side road and tire tracks; the engine parts and fuller's earth; the moving and inspection of Fenton Hardy's car; the search at the waterfront; the police and Coast Guard vigils; Mrs. Hardy's altercation with Chief Collig; the smugglers' auto and truck; Fenton Hardy's memo book; the mysterious car on North Shore Road; Joe's near discovery by the police; the break-in; the secret stairway in the wall; Chet's ride for help and

*All references herein to *The House on the Cliff* pertain to the original (1927) edition.

phone call to the police; the rescue of the Hardys by the three friends; Chet's "raid"; the gang leader's attempted flight; the FBI raid; the Police Department's new regard for Chet; Chief Collig's and Bayport's new appreciation of the Hardy boys; and the presentation of the *Sleuth* (loosely adapted from the subsequent story in the series).

In *The House on the Cliff*, the smugglers were sneaking opium into the United States. For *The House on the Point*, I changed their operation's commodities, scope, and direction.

Unlike Franklin W. Dixon, who set his stories in the present, I set this one (or it set itself) in what seemed an ideal time for the plot:

In 1947 World War II was over, and America had a spirit of youthful energy and optimism that would be gone by the 1970s, destroyed by political assassinations and the resulting national withdrawal into drug-taking, selfishness, cynicism, and increasingly conservative politics. Adolescents were a good deal older for their age in 1940s' society—which, for all its faults, at least encouraged young people to be positive, strong, responsible, and self-reliant—than they are in our present society, which encourages young people to be quite the opposite. Teenagers hadn't been given the automatic respect as consumers that they would be given a few years later, when Frank, Joe, and their friends would have had less incentive for proving themselves. The recent war had created large-scale opportunities for black-market smugglers. And the crime-solving process in fiction and fact had not yet been one-dimensionalized by America's monotonous obsession with technology and firepower.

My research for this story, which I enjoyed almost as much as the writing, enabled me to better understand a time that I had been born too late to experience—when the glorious, energetic "swing era" was giving way to the more sedate, family-centered "baby boom." In 1947, I was pleased to learn: There was as yet no sedentary, subnormal-intelligence television culture; the hot trends were still being created largely by youthful minds rather than by manipulative entertainment corporations; some big bands were still touring the nation; and my favorite vintage American automobile, the 1940 Ford, was practically everywhere.

As for the characters in general: I changed the original old man Polucca's first name from Felix to Leo, equipped him with creative abilities and cunning, and gave him a rock-blasting profession and a large extended family—both of which were necessary to build his tunnel (which was inspired by the work of my grandfather, a mining engineer). I replaced Ganny Snackley, rough-hewn leader of *The House on the Cliff*'s smuggling gang—who had likely turned to a life of crime in retaliation for remarks made about his name—with polished, quick-witted Alex Polucca, whose personality, behavior, and success at fooling the authorities were based on those of an individual I'd once investigated. I added Oscar Volchek, Ivan Slovavic, Lane Anderson, and other minor characters. I changed Chief Ezra Collig from an obstructionist imbecile to a conventional police chief with blind spots (*teenagers* being one of them). I promoted Con Riley to sergeant, which I'm sure he appreciated. I transformed Tony Prito's father from a wealthy native Italian building contractor into a hustle-for-the-money native New Yorker produce store owner.

Regarding the members of the Hardy family: I added two years to the ages of the Hardy boys and their friends (as eventually did Franklin W. Dixon). I gave Mrs. Hardy some personality and pluck, and changed her almost-never-mentioned first name from Laura (and, later in the series, Mildred) to the one she chose in my imagination. I changed Fenton Hardy's past territory from New York to Boston, gave him a family background, and provided him—as I did his sons—with some investigative methods and intelligence. I transplanted Gertrude Hardy from later books in the series, changed her from a visiting relative to a permanent member of the household, gave her a job as an English teacher, and had her explain herself a bit. And had her brother give an explanation of his own.

When Aunt Gertrude first appeared in The Hardy Boys Mystery Stories, she was described as a hefty, domineering demander. Later she was depicted as a tall, angular worrier. She appeared in my mind as a thin, nervous, and abrupt busybody who isn't as formidable as she likes people to think she is.

I moved the family from Elm Street, where later in the series they were said to reside, to a different-appearing house on South Bayview Street, near its intersection with Sycamore Street (on the hill, sunny location, wonderful view). I thought they'd like it better there.

I gave the Hardys more rescue spirit than did Franklin W. Dixon, who had Mrs. Hardy respond to her husband's disappearance by worrying and doing nothing and had Frank and Joe respond by waiting to look for him until the following week, when school vacation began. (The original story took place earlier in June.)

I tried to endow the Hardys and other characters with some emotional life—an element lacking in the Hardy Boys series and in mystery stories in general. (To this reader, the mystery genre's proclaimed trend toward "realism" in storytelling is merely an escalation of grisly and smutty details, foul language, and negativity, rather than a progression toward more believable characters and plots. It seems to me that if detective stories were to include some emotional content, they could be more truly realistic—as distinguished from *cynical* and *sensational*—and the genre could move out of its well-worn "hard-boiled" rut. A further suggestion: If the genre were to outgrow its depressing death fixation and deal with such subjects as fraud—America's number-one crime, currently costing the nation's businesses $400 billion a year—it could attract a great many more readers and help create an informed, alert, hard-to-fool public.)

Unlike the Hardy Boys series' generic, take-charge leader of Bayport's youth, the Frank Hardy who appeared in my imagination was a rather introspective lone thinker, a sort of unsullen James Dean—a leader because his self-driven personality attracted people to him. In *The House on the Cliff,* Frank's all-mastering heroism left little for anyone else to do. In *The House on the Point,* I spread the heroics around.

Joe Hardy was described in the original stories as more impulsive than his brother, with light, curly hair. That's about all that readers were told about him. The Joe Hardy I saw in my mind was a take-it-as-is-comes, action-oriented counterbalance to his more patient and reflective older brother. His counterbalancing went beyond action versus reflection. When Frank was sure of something, Joe had doubts. When Frank hesitated, Joe cheered him onward. When Frank forged ahead, Joe urged caution. This Joe, in other words, behaved like a brother.

My favorite Franklin W. Dixon character in childhood was Chet Morton, a one-dimensional clown in the Hardy Boys series who changed himself in my young imagination into a more complex individual. From the beginning of my acquaintance with him, the Chet I saw in my mind was smarter than most of the people around him (the funny ones usually are), including the steady, practical souls of the Bayport Police Department. He was so practiced at hiding his intelligence and sensitivity behind a jokester facade that no one, not even he himself, knew they were there. What he needed, I thought from the start, was an opportunity to win some self-respect and respect from others. I'm glad he finally got one.

In the original stories, Chet drove a yellow jalopy, the Queen. In this one, I saw him driving something else.

By the way: Despite the Hollywood-fueled myth that hot rodding began in California in the 1950s, the first significantly souped-up cars were vehicles made and then modified by Ford and Marmon in the early 1900s—in Michigan and Indiana, respectively—and raced to promote sales. By the 1920s, a small industry of aftermarket hop-up parts for racers had sprung up around the factories and tracks. In the early 1930s, articles and advertisements in the new auto racing publications began the circulation of professional engine-modification methods and equipment to backyard enthusiasts in the East and Midwest and—a bit later—on the West Coast. The many resulting on-the-street speed shops kept the hop-up movement growing. In 1941, *Throttle*, the first national automotive magazine devoted exclusively to "soup jobs" or "hot irons," appeared—published, like many similar magazines to follow, in Los Angeles. During the Second World War, a large number of GI mechanics learned from necessity and from speed publications to coax additional horsepower from army vehicles, a practice that many of them continued with their own cars when they returned home. By the end of the war, hot rodding—including use of the newly coined term, "hot rod"—had become popular from coast to coast. The July 1947 issue of *Road and Track* (later *Road & Track*) featured hot rods. Six months later, the first issue of *Hot Rod* magazine was released.

Beyond Frank, Joe, and Chet, the boys in the original series were barely delineated character types, the literary equivalent of cardboard cutouts. As scenes from *The House on the Point* ran through my mind, Tony, Biff, Phil, and Jerry took on appearances, personalities, and tendencies different from those sketched out in the original stories: A more naturalized Tony Prito dealt with difficult situations and a difficult father; now-outdoorsmen Phil Cohen and Jerry Gilroy dealt with new knowledge, outlooks, and identities; and a slangier, faster-minded Biff Hooper dealt with his new pal and patsy, Chet Morton. I was sorry to write Phil and Jerry out of the way, but there were too many people for the plot.

The original Callie Shaw and Iola Morton—the brothers' *almost* girl friends, who would make one or two brief appearances in each story—were the series' paper dolls. They had next to nothing in the manner of personalities, interests, or abilities. They didn't even have consistency. Callie was a brunette for several books, then became a blonde. Iola was plump, then slender. Her hair color turned from brown to blond to black. Not being particularly fond of vagueness and inconsistency, I told each of them to become someone definite, then sat back and imagined.

Two strong characters appeared—the sophisticated Callie Shaw and the saucy Iola Morton. The first was sensitive on the outside but tough on the inside; the second was pretty much the opposite. I liked them as individuals. I liked them as a team. I liked Iola so much that—rather to my surprise—she quickly became my favorite character in the story.

A final word about the characters: In working out plot details, I often put the characters into situations to see what they would do about them. I soon learned to have faith in these people, who became so real to me that I stopped thinking of them as fictitious. When they solved a problem, I was happy for them. When they were in danger, I worried about them. I knew they would get out of whatever unpleasant situation they were in; I just didn't know *how.* But they did.

One night, for example, I went to sleep wondering how the tension I'd created between Joe and Iola was going to be resolved and how Tony was going to get past the boats guarding the maze entrance. At about two o'clock in the morning, I awoke and in my imagination saw Iola sitting on a sofa, sobbing, and Joe staring at her. Then I saw Tony in the *Napoli*, pulling a flare pistol from the glove box. I congratulated Tony and Iola and went back to sleep.

Although I wrote *The House on the Point* as a movie on paper, which is a new way to write a book, I tried to remain true to the spirit of America in 1947 as I've come to understand it. I did my best to avoid doing what American authors often do, and what American movie makers always do, when they create a story set in the past: dress people in clothes of the period but have them think, converse, and behave as they would at present. I attempted to follow the more historically faithful approach I've seen taken by English authors and screenwriters, which could be summed up as: Respect the past, research it thoroughly, empathize with the people who lived it, and shape the characters, setting, and plot accordingly.

In *The House on the Cliff*, Franklin W. Dixon named practically nothing in or around Bayport. The shore road, for instance, is referred to by everyone as "the shore road." So if a place, street, or store in *The House on the Point* has a name—with the exceptions of Bayport and Barmet Bay—it's because I decided it needed one.

Whittier Head, for example, I named in honor of John Greenleaf Whittier, who unintentionally summarized in writing what for me is the appeal of Frank and Joe Hardy and friends:

> *Of all sad words of tongue and pen*
> *The saddest are these, "It might have been."*

Young people solving crimes and other mysteries . . . Maybe that never happened—but maybe it could. I thought so as a child. I thought so as a teenager. I think so today.

One late-spring day when I was in the fourth grade, some biology-oriented friends and I marked off a two-foot-by-two-foot area on the playing field of our school in Sylvan, Oregon, with a fence made of pencils stuck in the ground, connected with string. We challenged each other to find as many life-forms as were there. For a few days, between baseball games and other activities, we studied our miniature world through magnifying glasses.

Other students would pass by, stop, watch us, and laugh. "What's the matter?" they would ask. "Haven't you seen *grass* before?" "If you've seen it," we would reply, "tell us what it looks like." They would attempt to describe what was all around them, and it would be our turn to laugh. We would hand them a magnifying glass or two—one above the other worked better than one by itself—and ask them to take a look.

Examining a blade of grass, they would see that it was made of parallel lines of material joined together, like those in the fabric of their blue jeans—which they hadn't noticed, either, until we made the comparison—with a larger, stiffer, riblike line running down the center. Some blades had fuzzy hairs and soft, rippled edges; others were smooth and sharp-edged.

"What are these little crawling things?" the newcomers might ask, peering through the lenses. "We don't know yet," we might answer. "They just showed up today." "What do they do?" "Watch

235

and find out." Within a few minutes, the ridiculers would become investigators of a world they hadn't seen before.

Beyond the boundaries of string and the hours of the school day were other worlds to explore. At the edge of the playing field was a swampy stream. Beyond it, the woods began. All of that, and the rest of what was then a semirural neighborhood, made up a learner's paradise, a firsthand science classroom.

If only what I was taught in the school's secondhand science classrooms had been half as enlightening as what nature taught me outside of them, I would have better appreciated my early education.

One morning, after two or three years of winning gold and silver ribbons in grammar school district science fairs, I watched as my science teacher wrote statements from our textbook on the blackboard. Suddenly I became aware that something about them bothered me. I read them again. The statements, it appeared, were presenting certain theories and hypotheses as though they were principles to believe in. And they were ignoring or dismissing other possibilities. And I wondered why.

After thinking for a few days about my sudden misgivings—which, I came to realize, had been in the back of my mind for some time—I arrived at the disturbing conclusion that science wasn't necessarily scientific. It didn't consistently play by its own rules. Too often for my liking, it saw what it chose to see and overlooked what it chose to overlook—for example, when it rejected one thing or another as unscientific without first open-mindedly examining it, or when it assessed non-human intelligence on the basis of biased and idealized concepts of human intelligence.

As a result of these growing reservations, I began paying more attention to the other discipline of observation—art.

My parents were artists. My father was chief of graphics at Bonneville Power Administration. My mother had taught drawing and painting and had been director of children's classes at the Portland Art Museum (the building for which had been designed by her friend, the now-renowned architect Pietro Belluschi). Over the years, my parents had developed certain observational skills

236

and habits. Through them and their friends, I learned that success in any endeavor is first and foremost a matter of *accurate seeing*. In order to solve a problem, for example, one has to see precisely what the problem is. Then one has to see alternatives in one's imagination. With your eyes you see what isn't working; with your mind you see it working; then you figure out what makes the difference.

Today I would call that practice "whole-brain reasoning." It combines nuts-and-bolts observational analysis from the left side of the brain with free-association image building from the right side. In contrast, the reasoning I was taught in science class was mostly *left* brain—linear-sequential, technical, exclusionary. It was shaped—out of necessity, my teachers assured me—by science's habitually imposed restrictions. Its view was limited by its narrow viewpoint—a viewpoint that, I found, interfered with both my ability to observe and my ability to imagine.

Thomas Huxley, the eminent self-taught biologist and creative thinker who freed Victorian biology from the constricting dogmas of religion, wrote a brief piece of advice that impressed me greatly:

Sit down before fact as a little child, be prepared to give up every preconceived notion, follow humbly wherever and to whatsoever abysses Nature leads.

It seemed to me as a child, as it does to me now, that the tutor of science ought to be nature, not the confining precepts of standardized scientific thought. In the field of art, nature has always been, and presumably will always be, the tutor—despite the comparatively recent influence of the abstractionists and other reality-ignoring stylists.

In many ways and in many areas, science is going ever further from the wisdom of nature—and, therefore, from the wisdom of art, the creative reasoning of which scientific seekers could utilize, as did Leonardo da Vinci, to form a whole that is greater than the sum of its components.

It could be said that our science is growing increasingly distant from the wisdom of nature and the wisdom of art primarily because our system of education is itself growing ever distant from them. It could further be said that our system of education has had very little contact with either form of wisdom since its beginning.

The shortcomings of the science education I received in my grammar school were insignificant compared to the shortcomings of what little *art* education I received there—an education that could be summed up as: *Treat art as self-expression.*

"Express yourself," my teachers would say, from the first to the last of my meager grammar school art interludes. "Use the colors to express your feelings." "When you draw a tree, make it *your* tree." And that is about all I remember being told in grammar school about how to create art.

In the many years in which I received non–public-school training in the visual arts—from the early-childhood Easter egg painting sessions and hunts for well-camouflaged eggs organized by my parents to the two college-age years I spent in art school—I don't believe I heard the professional artists around me say much of anything about "self-expression." Instead, I heard them talk about line, texture, shading, depiction of volume, color charts, composition, and so on. Mostly I heard about observation. "Notice the light and shadow on that arm," an art-school teacher might say. "Observe the edge defined by the thin line of light." And the point of it all was: *Use your eyes.*

Self-expression in that training process was pretty much taken for granted. No two artists communicate what they've seen in the same manner. But before one draws or paints, one must learn *how.* And that involves learning how to see accurately, how to visually communicate what has been seen, and how to think clearly in order to do both.

Throughout my public school education, however, I was told in one way or another that observation and reasoning are the skills of science, not of art; art is merely mindless, ego-centered fun. Such was the attitude of educators then.

In the majority of schools, apparently, it still is.

Whereas science is today more highly than ever respected,

238

funded, and emphasized in American education, art in schools is being steadily eliminated. The judgment is being made, by many people raised on American school "art" and on the incomplete thinking promoted in most of our public and private schools, that the world of art has little if anything of importance to offer young people, who, they say, need to forgo the "frills" of an art-balanced education and concentrate on "practical" (left-brain) skills, in order to compete for a good life in a world of rapidly changing technology.

In response to that judgment, I offer this essay.

Before proceeding further, I would like to define terms. For reasons of brevity and practicality, the general terms "American educational system" and "American education" in the following mean "the vast majority of this nation's public and private schools." In other words, they signify the educational rule, not the exceptions to it. They are not meant here to include those courageous, creative, and imaginative teachers who work their magic against great odds and despite the increasingly constrictive structure around them, or those exceptional schools that blaze their own trails to excellence. I'm tempted to herein distinguish between public and private schools in the quality of education each provides; but I'll resist the temptation. The difference, it seems to me, is more one of degree than one of kind. There are a few first-rate public schools; there are many no-better-than-yesterday's-average private schools. In theory, private schools ought to provide a higher-quality education, if only because they have more money with which to hire talent. But America has an unfortunate tendency to believe that more money spent means better education provided. And, from what I've seen, most American public *and* private schools are presently spending their money more on technology than on talent—thereby taking the same road that our healthcare system started down years ago, a road that leads to mediocrity and economic disaster.

The question of precisely what is wrong with American education and the accompanying question of what can be done to make it substantially better constitute what might be called a long-unsolved mystery. In presenting what I believe are some over-looked clues to that mystery's solution, I would like to first bring up for consideration a largely forgotten influence on the methods by which mysteries today are solved—that of certain pioneering authors in the field of detective fiction, beginning with the most influential of them all, Sir Arthur Conan Doyle, the creator of Sherlock Holmes.

Although relatively few of his readers have known it, Sir Arthur was himself a solver of crimes, disappearances, and other puzzling occurrences. His innovations in the field of detection include the use of plaster of Paris to preserve footprints, the analysis of substances found at the scene of the crime, and the close observation of crime-scene details. The methods and philosophy he passed along in his not completely fictional Sherlock Holmes stories greatly modernized and systematized the investigative practices of London's Criminal Investigation Department (Scotland Yard) and France's Sûreté, and shaped from the beginning those of America's Federal Bureau of Investigation.

So what was the family background of this father of modern crime detection?

Michael Edward Conan, Sir Arthur's great-uncle and godfather, was an artist and, in turn: a foreign correspondent for the London *Morning Herald*; the literary, music, and dramatic critic for that newspaper; and the Paris correspondent for *The Art Journal*.

John Doyle, Sir Arthur's grandfather, was an artist who had studied under the Italian landscape painter Gaspare Gabrielli and the Irish miniaturist John Comerford. One of the most influential political caricaturists in London, he developed his own gentle style of satire based on close observation of faces and clothing. Like someone in a mystery novel, he hid his identity behind the initials "HB" and had his drawings conveyed to the printer in a closed carriage, delivered by a confidential intermediary, and printed in secrecy.

John Doyle's son Richard was a painter and graphic artist, illustrator to John Ruskin, Charles Dickens, and William Makepeace Thackeray. He created the cover design of the humor magazine *Punch*, which was retained for 107 years. An astute observer of the life around him, he eased his occasional moods of sadness by playing his violin, often while watching the scene outside his window.

A second son, Henry—another painter—became director of the National Gallery of Ireland.

A third son, James, was an accomplished portrait artist and caricaturist, as well as author of *The Chronicle of England.*

A fourth son, Francis, was a skilled painter of miniatures when he died at fifteen.

A fifth son, Charles, was an architect, designer, and builder who sketched criminal trials for various magazines, and illustrated children's books. He is best known, however, for being the father of Arthur Conan Doyle.

Educated as a physician, young Arthur Conan Doyle set up practice as (appropriately for someone of his acute vision) an eye specialist. Unable to attract patients, he began to write for publication stories featuring Sherlock Holmes, a character based on family members, himself, and his favorite teacher at Edinburgh University, Dr. Joseph Bell—a surgeon, criminal psychology expert, and shrewd observer of humanity.

Considering Sir Arthur's heritage, it should hardly seem surprising that he made Sherlock Holmes the descendant (from Holmes's grandmother) of a well-known family of painters—thereby giving a clue, as Sir Arthur was fond of doing with his "fictional" characters, to the great detective's primary real-life original. In "The Greek Interpreter," Holmes briefly describes his lineage to his friend Dr. John H. Watson, remarking that "Art in the blood is liable to take the strangest forms."

Dr. Watson, who resembles his creator in appearance, medical training, and scarcity of patients, is very unlike him in three other ways: He is not a man of art, he has little imagination, and—as Sherlock Holmes frequently points out to him—he does not *observe.*

In *The Sign of the Four,* Dr. Watson—in friendly retaliation for Holmes's scolding—smugly attempts to put the detective's theories of observation and imaginative reasoning to a practical test:

"I have heard you say it is difficult for a man to have any object in daily use without leaving the impress of his individuality upon it in

241

such a way that a trained observer might read it. Now, I have here a watch [that] has recently come into my possession. Would you have the kindness to let me have an opinion upon the character or habits of the late owner?"

I handed him over the watch with some slight feeling of amusement in my heart, for the test was, as I thought, an impossible one, and I intended it as a lesson against the somewhat dogmatic tone [that] he occasionally assumed. He balanced the watch in his hand, gazed hard at the dial, opened the back, and examined the works, first with his naked eyes and then with a powerful convex lens. I could hardly keep from smiling at his crestfallen face when he finally snapped the case to and handed it back.

"There are hardly any data," he remarked. "The watch has been recently cleaned, which robs me of my most suggestive facts."

"You are right," I answered. "It was cleaned before being sent to me."

In my heart I accused my companion of putting forward a most lame and impotent excuse to cover his failure. What data could he expect from an uncleaned watch?

"Though unsatisfactory, my research has not been entirely barren," he observed, staring up at the ceiling with dreamy, lack-lustre eyes. "Subject to your correction, I should judge that the watch belonged to your elder brother, who inherited it from your father."

"That, you gather, no doubt, from the H.W. upon the back?"

"Quite so. The W. suggests your own name. The date of the watch is nearly fifty years back, and the initials are as old as the watch; so it was made for the last generation. Jewellry usually descends to the eldest son, and he is most likely to have the same name as the father. Your father has, if I remember right, been dead many years. It has, therefore, been in the hands of your eldest brother."

"Right, so far," said I. "Anything else?"

"He was a man of untidy habits—very untidy and careless. He was left with good prospects, but he threw away his chances, lived for some time in poverty with occasional short intervals of prosperity, and finally, taking to drink, he died. That is all I can gather."

I sprang from my chair and limped impatiently about the room with considerable bitterness in my heart.

"This is unworthy of you, Holmes," I said. "I could not have

242

believed that you would have descended to this. You have made inquiries into the history of my unhappy brother, and you now pretend to deduce this knowledge in some fanciful way. You cannot expect me to believe that you have read all this from his old watch! It is unkind and, to speak plainly, has a touch of charlatanism in it."

"My dear doctor," said he kindly, "pray accept my apologies. Viewing the matter as an abstract problem, I had forgotten how personal and painful a thing it might be to you. I assure you, however, that I never even knew that you had a brother until you handed me the watch."

"Then how in the name of all that is wonderful did you get these facts? They are absolutely correct in every particular."

"Ah, that is good luck. I could only say what was the balance of probability. I did not at all expect to be so accurate."

"But it was not mere guesswork?"

"No, no: I never guess. It is a shocking habit—destructive to the logical faculty. What seems strange to you is only so because you do not follow my train of thought or observe the small facts upon which large inferences may depend. For example, I began by stating that your brother was careless. When you observe the lower part of that watch-case you notice that it is not only dinted in two places but it is cut and marked all over from the habit of keeping other hard objects, such as coins or keys, in the same pocket. Surely it is no great feat to assume that a man who treats a fifty-guinea watch so cavalierly must be a careless man. Neither is it a very far-fetched inference that a man who inherits one article of such value is pretty well provided for in other respects."

I nodded to show that I followed his reasoning.

"It is very customary for pawnbrokers in England, when they take a watch, to scratch the numbers of the ticket with a pin-point upon the inside of the case. It is more handy than a label as there is no risk of the number being lost or transposed. There are no [fewer] than four such numbers visible to my lens on the inside of this case. Inference—that your brother was often at low water. Secondary inference—that he had occasional bursts of prosperity, or he could not have redeemed the pledge. Finally, I ask you to look at the inner plate, which contains the keyhole. Look at the thousands of scratches all

round the hole—marks where the key has slipped. What sober man's
key could have scored those grooves? But you will never see a drunk-
ard's watch without them. He winds it at night, and he leaves these
traces of his unsteady hand. Where is the mystery in all this?"

The connection between art and detection in the adventures of Sherlock Holmes is hardly unique in the field of early mystery fiction. Perhaps a more obvious connection can be seen in the character of E. C. Bentley's jovial crime solver, Philip Trent—a painter "whose training had taught him to live in his eyes." A training he makes use of, for example, in "The Inoffensive Captain," in which he and Inspector Charles Muirhead go to visit a second-floor flat in which a stolen jewel may be hidden:

"I thought it better," said the inspector, pausing on a stair, "to go up
unannounced. He can't say he won't see us if we just walk in and
make ourselves pleasant."

As the two men reached the first landing they heard the sound of a
door closed gently on the one above and of light-stepping feet. A tall
girl, in neat and obviously expensive tailor-made clothes, appeared at
the head of the short stairway and, apparently not seeing them, stood
for a moment adjusting her hat and veil. Mr. Muirhead uttered a
growling cough from below, at the noise of which the young lady
started slightly and hurried down the stairs. In the half-light on the
landing, they received, as she passed them, an impression of shining
dark hair and barely perceptible perfume. Trent looked after her med-
itatively as she went swiftly along the ground floor passage and let
herself out.

"Smart woman," observed the inspector appreciatively, as the
front door slammed.

"A fine example of healthy modern girlhood," Trent agreed. "Did
you see the stride and swing as she went to the door? From the cut of
her clothes I should say she was American."

There was a note in his voice [that] made the other look at him
sharply.

"And," pursued Trent, returning his gaze with an innocent eye,

"I suppose you noticed her feet and ankles as she stood up there and as she came downstairs."

"I did not," returned Mr. Muirhead gruffly. "What was there to notice?"

"Only the size," said Trent. "The size—and the fact that she was wearing a man's shoes."

For an instant the inspector glared at him wild-eyed, then turned and plunged without a word down the stairway. He reached the door and tore at the handle.

"It is useful, sometimes, you see," Trent remarks to a villain in "The Clever Cockatoo," "to have a mind that notices trifles."

In *Trent's Last Case*—recognized upon its publication as a groundbreaker in the field of mystery writing, and acclaimed today as the first novel of detective fiction's "Golden Age"—journalist and humorist E. C. (Edmund Clerihew) Bentley shows readers an investigative artist at work:

Trent, seated on the bed, quickly sketched in his notebook a plan of the room and its neighbour. . . . [He] stared at the pillows; then he lay down with deliberation on the bed and looked through the open door into the adjoining room. . . .

[He] opened two tall cupboards in the wall on either side of the bed. They contained clothing, a large choice of which had evidently been one of the very few conditions of comfort for the man who had slept there. . . .

Suddenly his eyes narrowed themselves over a pair of patent-leather shoes on the upper shelf. . . . They were a well-worn pair, he saw at once; he saw, too, that they had been very recently polished. Something about the uppers of these shoes had seized his attention. He bent lower and frowned over them, comparing what he saw with the appearance of the neighbouring shoes. Then he took them up and examined the line of junction of the uppers with the soles.

As he did this, Trent began unconsciously to whistle faintly. . . .

He turned the shoes over, made some measurements with a marked tape, and looked minutely at the bottoms. On each, in the angle between the heel and the instep, he detected a faint trace of red gravel. Trent placed the shoes on the floor, and walked with his hands behind him to the window, out of which, still faintly whistling, he gazed. . . .

The active relationship between the whole-brain skills of art and the investigative skills of crime detection was not long confined to stories in magazines and books. It soon went beyond the world of fiction to the world of fact.

To a large extent, the principles and practices of modern crime detection were brought into existence during the formative years of the mid-1800s to early 1900s through the influence of mystery stories on the public—who, impressed by the new fictional detectives, pressured the police forces to adopt their methods and philosophies.

Probably the three most influential authors of detective fiction during that period were: Wilkie Collins (1824–1889), author of several short mystery stories (the exact number depends on how strictly one defines *mystery*) and two immensely popular and much-imitated mystery novels, *The Woman in White* (1860) and *The Moonstone* (1868); Sir Arthur Conan Doyle (1859–1930), author of four novels and five short-story collections featuring Sherlock Holmes, published between 1887 and 1927; and E. C. Bentley (1875–1956), author of *Trent's Last Case* (1913), *Trent's Own Case* (1936), and a collection of short detective stories (some of which had been published in magazines and anthologies many years before), *Trent Intervenes* (1938).

These authors, who were as different from each other as any three people are likely to be, had one element, at least, in common: art.

Sir Arthur, as previously noted, grew up in a family of professional artists and created a detective descended from such a family. Although E. C. Bentley revealed few details of his personal life—in *Those Days,* his collection of reminiscences, for example, he mentions that he married someone, but doesn't even tell readers her name—three of his connections with the world of art can be given. First, his closest friend for most of his life was author, former art student, and occasional illustrator G. K. Chesterton, who was for some time, as the latter wrote, "almost wholly taken up with the idea of drawing pictures." (G. K. Chesterton, to whom *Trent's Last Case* is dedicated, was the creator of one of the most popular amateur detectives in mystery fiction, Father Brown, and was in all probability the primary model for Philip Trent.) Second, E. C. Bentley's son, Nicolas, became an accomplished illustrator. Third, Bentley's detective, as already noted, is an artist. Wilkie Collins (William Wilkie Collins), though educated in the law, drew and painted skillfully enough that a picture of his was exhibited at the Royal Academy of Arts. He was encouraged by his father, the distinguished landscape artist William Collins, R.A., to study the designs of nature. He was the godson of the painter Sir David Wilkie, the friend of acclaimed painters Sir John Millais, William Holden Hunt, and Dante Gabriel Rossetti, and the brother of painter Charles Allston Collins. The hero of his most famous mystery novel is an artist.

Before Wilkie Collins, popular mystery stories were of the Gothic horror-and-romance sort originated by Horace Walpole in *The Castle of Otranto* (1764) and developed further by a succession of writers such as Ann Radcliffe, author of *The Mysteries of Udolpho* (1794) and other bestselling novels—mysteries, one might say, for the feeble-minded. Typically featuring a heroine trapped by a sinister character in an isolated, faraway castle filled with black dungeons, secret chambers, and hidden passages, these morbid fantasies had nothing to do with the application of any sort of reasoning, but were mysteries only by their perpetual atmosphere of "Whatever in the world is going to happen *next?*"

The first substantial advance in the development of the modern detective story was the publication of three short mysteries by Edgar Allen Poe—"The Murders in the Rue Morgue" (1841), "The Mystery of Marie Rogêt" (1842), and "The Purloined Letter" (1845)—in which appear not only the procedures and character types of the future observation-and-deduction crime story, but even the future Holmes-and-Watson pairing of sleuth and companion/narrator. The public showed little appreciation for these tales, however, which are primarily monologues by the narrator or the investigator—lectures, not adventures. Like the mystery stories before them, they take place in a setting of gloom and decay far removed from the daily experience of most readers:

> *I was permitted to be at the expense of renting, and furnishing in a style [that] suited the rather fantastic gloom of our common temper, a time-eaten and grotesque mansion, long deserted through superstitions into which we did not inquire, and tottering to its fall in a retired and desolate portion of the Faubourg St. Germain.*

And then along came Wilkie Collins. "To Mr. Collins," wrote novelist Henry James, "belongs the credit of having introduced into fiction those most mysterious of mysteries, the mysteries . . . at our own doors."

In *The Woman in White,* Wilkie Collins demonstrated to the reading public that an Englishwoman needn't be held captive in a castle in the Apennines in order to experience terror; she could find herself imprisoned at home in England—like the story's Laura Fairlie, who, after marrying the handsome and charming Sir Percival Glyde, is shut away in a manor house and then in a private asylum by her scheming, abusive, inheritance-hunting husband. Fortunately for Lady Glyde, her drawing instructor, Walter Hartright—based largely on both William and Wilkie Collins—investigates her situation and her husband's character and past.

From its prebook serial publication in *All the Year Round,* Charles Dickens's new magazine, *The Woman in White* was an overwhelming success. On press day, enthusiastic readers lined up at the magazine's office to get the first copies of the latest installment. "Woman in White" costume parties were held all over London. Dances and songs were named after the story's main characters. A staggering variety of "Woman in White" products appeared. Because of its vast acceptance—which, like that later accorded the detective fiction of many an English author, was repeated on the other side of the Atlantic—the novel brought widespread attention to the vulnerability of married women under laws that gave them no control of their own money and afforded them little protection against unwarranted imprisonment in asylums.

In addition to its masterly, fact-based plot of almost relentless suspense, *The Woman in White* presented readers with two unforgettable characters: Count Fosco, mystery fiction's most chilling personification of evil, and Marian Halcombe, its most revered heroine. (Miss Halcombe's phenomenal popularity—men would send marriage proposals to her in care of the book's publisher—foreshadowed that achieved years later by Sherlock Holmes.)

In his next mystery novel, *The Moonstone*, Wilkie Collins gave fiction a new kind of police detective, the observant and introspective Sergeant Cuff—a lean, elderly man with a face "as sharp as a hatchet."

Sergeant Cuff is asked to the home of Lady Julia Verinder and her daughter, Rachel, to investigate the theft of a famous diamond. The house-steward (the narrator) accompanies him on a walk through the grounds, then takes him upstairs to the room containing the cabinet in which the jewel had been placed:

> *In due time his course brought him to the door [opening into Rachel's bedroom], and put him face to face with the [recently dried] decorative painting [on it]. He laid one lean inquiring finger on the small smear, just under the lock.*
>
> *"That's a pity," says Sergeant Cuff. "How did it happen?"*
>
> *He put the question to me. I answered that the women-servants had crowded into the room on the previous morning and that some of their petticoats had done the mischief. "Superintendent Seegrave ordered them out, sir," I added, "before they did any more harm."*
>
> *"Right!" says Mr. Superintendent, in his military way. "I ordered them out. The petticoats did it, Sergeant—the petticoats did it."*
>
> *"Did you notice which petticoat did it?" asked Sergeant Cuff, still addressing himself, not to his brother-officer, but to me.*
>
> *"No, sir."*
>
> *He turned to Superintendent Seegrave upon that, and said, "You noticed it, I suppose?"*
>
> *Mr. Superintendent looked a little taken aback; but he made the best of it. "I can't charge my memory, Sergeant," he said, "a mere trifle—a mere trifle."*

Sergeant Cuff looked at Mr. Seegrave as he had looked at the gravel-walks in the rosery. . . .

"I made a private inquiry last week, Mr. Superintendent," he said. "At one end of the inquiry there was a murder, and at the other end there was a spot of ink on a table-cloth that nobody could account for. In all my experience along the dirtiest ways of this dirty little world I have never met with such a thing as a trifle yet. Before we go a step further in this business we must see the petticoat that made the smear, and we must know for certain when that paint was wet."

After questioning the maid and the man who had painted the door:

The Sergeant's next proceeding was to question me about any large dogs in the house who might have got into the room, and done the mischief with a whisk of their tails. Hearing that this was impossible, he next sent for a magnifying-glass, and tried how the smear looked, seen that way. No skin-mark, as of a human hand, printed off on the paint. All the signs . . . told that the paint had been smeared by some loose article of somebody's dress touching it in going by. That somebody, putting together Penelope's evidence and Mr. Franklin's evidence, must have been in the room and done the mischief between midnight and three o'clock . . .

"This trifle of yours, Mr. Superintendent," says the Sergeant, pointing to the place on the door, "has grown a little in importance since you noticed it last. At the present stage of the inquiry there are, as I take it, three discoveries to make, starting from that smear. Find out, first, whether there is any article of dress in this house with the smear of the paint on it. Find out, second, who that dress belongs to. Find out, third, how the person can account for having been in this room, and smeared the paint, between midnight and three in the morning. If the person can't satisfy you, you haven't got far to look for the hand that has got the Diamond."

The detective stories of Wilkie Collins, Sir Arthur Conan Doyle, and E. C. Bentley demonstrate today, as they did to the public and the police forces of the past, that the creative reasoning of art can be applied to the solving of problems beyond the supposed boundaries of art.

The process of whole-brain seeing is simple: One first observes something in the world of physical reality; then one observes it in one's imagination—looking at it from various points of view, shifting elements around to form a more harmonious pattern, and eliminating the unnecessary.

This procedure is followed by an artist studying a landscape and composing a painting of it, or a detective examining a crime scene and puzzling through what took place there. It can be followed as well by anyone wanting to learn a new activity, improve existing skills, or achieve greater life awareness and understanding.

Even the most ordinary object has a story to tell to someone who sees both with his eyes and his imagination, as poet Ted Kooser reveals in his "Abandoned Farmhouse":

He was a big man, says the size of his shoes
on a pile of broken dishes by the house;
a tall man too, says the length of the bed
in an upstairs room; and a good, God-fearing man,
says the Bible with a broken back
on the floor below the window, dusty with sun;
but not a man for farming, say the fields
cluttered with boulders and the leaky barn.

A woman lived with him, says the bedroom wall
papered with lilacs and the kitchen shelves
covered with oilcloth, and they had a child
says the sandbox made from a tractor tire.
Money was scarce, say the jars of plum preserves
and canned tomatoes sealed in the cellar-hole,
and the winters cold, say the rags in the window frames.
It was lonely here, says the narrow gravel road.

Something went wrong, says the empty house
in the weed-choked yard. Stones in the fields
say he was not a farmer; the still-sealed jars

in the cellar say she left in a nervous haste.
And the child? Its toys are strewn in the yard
like branches after a storm—a rubber cow,
a rusty tractor with a broken plow,
a doll in overalls. Something went wrong, they say.

In our society, the word *mystery* has come to signify *book*, or *movie*, or *television show*—and then, in most cases, to signify *murderer identification puzzle*. Our outlook on *mystery*, it would seem, has become quite narrow. In reality, most crime mysteries concern activities such as robbery or fraud, rather than murder. And, in reality, most mysteries in this world are not about crime, they're about the everyday life around us. How many of us are prepared to solve them?

The art of seeing—the foundation for the solving of life's mysteries—is rarely taught in classrooms. What counts in the typical American school is the production, or reproduction, of answers. From the first day of our first class, we are bombarded with them. Do they necessarily help us see or understand? An answer given to us by a teacher, book, or machine is someone else's answer, not our own. As far as we know, it could be wrong. All too often, it is. "The sun revolves around the earth." "Earthworms are produced by spontaneous generation." "Man is the only animal that uses tools." These were correct answers, once.

In whole-brain learning, the answer is of less practical value than the question. *Question* comes from the same root as *quest*—the Latin *quaerere*, "to seek." A teaching question—one that requires more than a push-button answer—impels seekers on a journey to find the truth. Mastery of a subject comes only to those who follow the journey of each of its questions to the end. It does not come to those who peek ahead to the solutions. Without the exercise of the quest, an answer can be incomplete, meaningless, useless, or even dangerous. In all likelihood, it will not be applied in any arena of life beyond the testing room, and it will soon be forgotten.

Through solving one after another of life's mysteries, the growing mind builds knowledge, intelligence, and self-reliance—and, whether or not it has guidance from other minds along the way, it builds them firsthand, as nature designed it to from infancy. When this natural process of making sense of the world through direct experience is sabotaged by forces working against it, a comprehensive education cannot take place.

For years now, in attempting to show the public that it can adequately instruct its students and prepare them for the trials of life beyond the classroom—despite steadily mounting evidence that it is failing dismally to do so—the American educational system has been resorting to acts of desperation: extending school hours; increasing the homework load; "dumbing down" textbooks and tests so its growing number of incompetent charges can go on to the next level or graduate; spending millions of dollars per school district on machines to provide instant (but unreliable) answers; and eliminating classes in anything creative or imaginative, in order to fill students' minds and time with more and more left-brain information processing.

But none of this has solved the problems. Our educational system remains, reportedly, the worst in the industrialized world—and the most expensive.

Like the baffled, conservative-minded police inspector in many a detective story, American education is not changing its flawed approach; it is only trying harder and harder to make that approach work. How can it help its students learn if it cannot, or will not, help them question, observe, reason, or imagine? And how can it help them gain a useful education if the very subjects of study it eliminates as unnecessary help build whole-brain intelligence?

Music classes, for example, have never been considered vital in American schools, have never been well funded or respected, and have been removed completely from schools across the nation. Yet one of the many advantages of a musically broadened education is that the learning of music skills facilitates the development of spatial intelligence, a vital element in the art of whole-brain seeing.

Spatial intelligence enables one to mentally form three-dimensional images of objects, alter them, and move them around—and move around *them*—in space. It is applied in activities as diverse as the solving of higher mathematical equations, the designing of

253

buildings, the planning of chess, sports, business, and military strategies, and the writing of novels and screenplays.

The connection between music and spatial intelligence has been attested to by the renowned physicist and accomplished amateur violinist Albert Einstein—who devised his theory of relativity while imagining he was riding on a light beam traveling through space—and by various other problem solvers (including this author, who has studied and practiced music since childhood and who always visualizes story structure, plot flow, characters, and events to music).

The effect of musical training on spatial intelligence has been measured in tests conducted by Dr. Frances Rauscher, a research psychologist at the Center for the Neurobiology of Learning and Memory at the University of California, Irvine, and Dr. Gordon Shaw, Professor Emeritus of Physics, a neuroscientist and member of the CNLM. Doctors Rauscher and Shaw are best known by the public for their much-reported 1993 study in which college students who listened to ten minutes of Mozart's Sonata for Two Pianos in D Major before taking a spatial IQ test achieved significantly higher scores than did students who sat in silence before the test or listened to taped self-hypnosis instructions.

An example of their work is "Study 2—Early Music Training Enhances Spatial Task Performance," in their 1994 report, "Music and Spatial Task Performance: A Causal Relationship." It compared the spatial IQ scores of fifteen children in two Los Angeles County preschools with those of twenty-two children in the same programs who had, in addition, been given weekly piano instruction and daily singing lessons during the eight months of the study. The non-music group achieved a 6 percent improvement in spatial reasoning performance. The music group achieved a 46 percent improvement.

Testimony to the importance of music in education includes the following, paraphrased and condensed here in the interest of brevity:

Music participants received more academic honors and awards than did non-music students, and the percentage of music participants receiving As and Bs was higher than the percentage of non-participants receiving those grades. (NELS [National Education Longitudinal Study]: 88, First Follow-up, National Center for Education Statistics, 1990)

In a study of 811 high school students, 7 percent of minority students identified athletics instructors as their primary role models; 11 percent credited elementary-school teachers; 28 percent credited English teachers; and 36 percent credited music teachers. ("Music Teachers as Role Models for African-American Students," Journal of Research in Music Education, 41, 1993)

According to a study of the undergraduate majors of medical school applicants conducted by physician and biologist Lewis Thomas, 66 percent of music-major applicants were admitted to medical school—the highest percentage of any group in the study. In contrast, 44 percent of biochemistry majors were admitted. ("The Case for Music in the Schools," Phi Delta Kappan, February 1994)

Music and visual arts education emphasizing sequenced skill development (referred to in the study as "test arts") was given to first-grade students who had underperformed in kindergarten. By the end of the first year of the study, they had surpassed their non-underperforming, non–"test arts" classmates by 22 percent in measures of mathematics competency. The study was continued for another year, with these results: "The percentage of students at or above grade level in second-grade maths was highest in those with two years of test arts, less in those with only one year, and lowest in those with no test arts." ("Learning Improved by Arts Training," Nature, May 23, 1996)

In a 1993–1995 study of three groups of preschoolers, the first group, which was given no special lessons, improved their spatial-temporal IQ by .50 points as measured on the Wechsler Preschool and Primary Scale of Intelligence-Revised. The second group, which was given computer lessons, improved by .35 points. The third group, which was given piano lessons, improved by 3.62 points. ("Music Training Causes Long-term Enhancement of Preschool Children's Spatial-Temporal Reasoning," Neurological Research, February 1997)

Students with experience in music performance scored 53 points *higher on the verbal portion of the Scholastic Aptitude Test and 39 points higher on the math portion than did students with no music performance experience. Students with coursework in music appreciation scored 61 points higher on the verbal portion and 42 points higher on the math portion than did students with no coursework in music appreciation.* (1999 College-Bound Seniors National Report: Profile of SAT Program Test Takers, *The College Entrance Examination Board*)

In 1988 the International Association for the Evaluation of Educational Achievement tested the science proficiency of fourteen-year-olds in seventeen nations. The United States—which was spending twenty-nine times more on school math and science programs than any other nation—came in fourteenth. Schools of the top three nations—Hungary, Japan, and the Netherlands, respectively—provide extensive art and music training from kindergarten through high school. In Hungary, music is the foundation for education, and is believed to help children think logically and critically. The Japanese school music system is based on the Hungarian. ("A Dynamic Movement: Music's Power to Educate," Good Music, Brighter Children, *by Sharlene Habermeyer, Prima Publishing, 1999*)

In the prestigious Third International Mathematics and Science Study, held during the 1994–1995 school year, high school seniors in the Netherlands—which has one of the strongest school art and music programs in the world—came in first in general mathematics and second in general science. ("U.S. Students Fare Poorly in Comparison," Los Angeles Times, *February 25, 1998)*

Even if America's educational system were in existence to teach only the sciences (as it increasingly appears to believe it is), it would improve the quality of its education by incorporating into it instruction in the arts and by emphasizing the art of seeing. For it could be said that the greatest discoveries in science have been made by those who have gone beyond the limitations of traditional scientific reasoning and operated, if only briefly, in the state of whole-brain vision more common to the arts.

An example is the work of Friedrich August Kekulé, a former

architecture student and renowned chemistry professor and lecturer. Kekulé's ability to imagine structure was crucial to the evolution of organic chemistry and brought about one of the most brilliant series of insights in the history of science.

Like many other scientists of the mid-1800s, Kekulé wanted to ascertain the structure of organic (carbon-containing) compounds. It was believed that if it could be determined how the carbon atoms were arranged in benzene, the simplest aromatic hydrocarbon (C_6H_6), that knowledge could be used to help deduce the structure of other compounds. Kekulé spent years experimenting, analyzing, and theorizing. And he practiced seeing in his imagination what could not otherwise be seen. In 1858 he proposed that carbon atoms can link together and combine with other atoms to form chains. He later described the origin of his proposition:

One fine summer evening, I was returning by the last omnibus, "outside" as usual, through the deserted streets of the metropolis . . . I fell into a reverie, and lo! the atoms were gambolling before my eyes. Whenever, hitherto, these diminutive beings had appeared to me, they had always been in motion; but up to that time, I had never been able to discern the nature of that motion. Now, however, I saw how, frequently, two smaller atoms united to form a pair; how a larger one embraced two smaller ones; how still larger ones kept hold of three or even four of the smaller; whilst the whole kept whirling in a giddy dance. I saw how the larger ones formed a chain, dragging the smaller ones after them. . . .

One night in 1865, he visualized the structure of the key compound, benzene:

I turned my chair to the fire and dozed. Again the atoms were gambolling before my eyes. This time the smaller groups kept modestly in the background. My mental eye, rendered more acute by repeated visions of this kind, could now distinguish larger structures, of manifold conformation; long rows, sometimes more closely fitted together; all twining and twisting in snakelike motion. But look! What was that? One of the snakes had seized hold of its own tail, and the form whirled mockingly before my eyes. [The core structure of benzene is a ring of six carbon atoms.] As if by a flash of lightning, I awoke.

Like Kekulé, geniuses in every field of endeavor see more clearly and imagine more freely than other people. They are the natural teachers of humanity. A forward-thinking educational system would honor them not merely by describing their achievements but by studying and teaching the ways in which their minds work. Ours does nothing of the sort.

In its perpetual disregard for the development of observational powers and creative problem-solving skills, our educational system stunts and weakens the minds of students, lessening their chances of survival in the world of man, in which there are more dangers than ever before to watch out for, and the world of nature, in which—due to shortsighted human tampering—all life is now in peril.

An expert in the skills of observation and imagination, Sir Arthur Conan Doyle had his fictional detective solve mysteries by utilizing a principle long employed by portrait painters and advocated in print before him in the largely ignored detective fiction of Edgar Allan Poe: *Put yourself in your subject's place.* As Sherlock Holmes described it in "The Musgrave Ritual":

> *"You know my methods in such cases, Watson. I put myself in the man's place, and, having first gauged his intelligence, I try to imagine how I should myself have proceeded under the same circumstances."*

Through emphasizing this practice in his stories, as well as in his own investigations, Sir Arthur gave the world's detective forces a principle that would forever change their approach to the solving of crime: *Put yourself in the position of the criminal.* To find out how and why the criminal committed the crime (and, therefore, who he likely is), don't only look at what he did from the outside, from *your* point of view; look out from the inside, as clearly as you can imagine it, of someone who would do such a deed in such a way. Mentally become the criminal in order to solve—or, in some cases, *prevent*—the crime.

Following this practice, one develops empathy—defined by *The American Heritage Dictionary* as "Identification with and understanding of another's situation, feelings, and motives."

In its principle of "Put yourself in your subject's place," art—whether that of the portrait painter, the novelist, or the actor—teaches empathy. Science, for the most part, does not. Science traditionally rejects empathy as a distorter of reason, a destroyer of objectivity. Like the police detective of 1850, the scientific reasoner is trained to look in at phenomena from the outside, at a mental and emotional distance, and to dismiss any other approach as unprofessional. Science therefore does not empathize with the beings it manipulates and experiments on or the network of life it tampers with. If it did, the condition of the earth would be quite different from what it is.

The enormous damage science inflicts on nature clearly indicates that much of its self-proclaimed "objectivity" and "unbiased vision" is in fact habitual insensitivity—a form of blindness. What is not so obvious is that any such insensitivity increases that of the society that supports it.

As a society's ability to empathize deteriorates, respect for others declines while selfishness, law-breaking activities, violent behavior, and ecological damage increase. Can anyone in a position of power who has never experienced poverty even begin to address the problems it causes without understanding through empathy what it means to be poor? Or address the problems of wildlife habitat destruction without knowing through empathy what it's like to have no home? Without empathy, how complete can our knowledge of the world possibly be?

We have available to us ever-increasing quantities of second-hand information and an ever-growing number of push-button answers. Our education conditions us to believe that information is knowledge (which is rarely true), that knowledge is power (which is often true), and that, therefore, if we can gain enough information, we will have the knowledge and the power to solve our problems and make the world a better place. Anyone who takes a clear look at that belief will see that it is incorrect, and its reasoning is flawed.

Might it not, therefore, be beneficial to shift educational and societal goals from the collecting of secondhand information and push-button answers to the mastery of the art of seeing with a whole mind? Which is better prepared to survive and prosper in this precarious, ever-changing world—the mind that has been told the answer, or the mind that has been trained to question, observe, reason, and imagine?

POSTSCRIPT

The following quotations are from letters and telephone calls responding to the manuscript for this book during the nearly three-year search for an agent, and then a publisher, willing to take it on:

> The House on the Point *rests on the most insubstantial of mysteries. . . . [The story] consists of too many characters and the dialogue doesn't help differentiate them. . . . As a mystery, I feel this book might be lacking that special something that Franklin W. Dixon made seem so easy to create. . . . There's not enough suspense. . . . The story is dated—it reads like a book from the 1940s. . . . The writing's not good enough for a hardcover, and the story's not mass-market enough for a paperback. . . . The book contains no lessons to be learned, no wisdom. . . . Adults who may be interested in a rein-terpretation [of* The House on the Cliff*] would not find enough here to sustain them. . . . It has no crossover potential. . . . It's just another Hardy Boys story.*

For more than twenty years, I have attempted to create books that go beyond the long-standard literary categories, styles, and view-points, only to see the majority of my proposals rejected by increasingly corporate, conservative-minded publishing houses. Just when it appeared that *The House on the Point* would suffer the fate of previous manuscripts, it was enthusiastically accepted by Minotaur, the "Rolls-Royce" of mystery publishers.

I feel deeply grateful to Minotaur's Michael Denneny, Senior Editor, and John Cunningham, Associate Publisher, for responding warmly and immediately to the manuscript, and for their guidance and support.

I feel equally grateful to Natasha Kern, my literary agent, for believing in this project, for persevering despite almost unanimous negative reactions to it, and for connecting *The House on the Point*'s nearly doomed manuscript, and author, to the right people.

—B. H.

Benjamin Hoff has been attracted to various kinds of mysteries since his childhood. The descendant of two family lines of creative problem solvers—artists, inventors, engineers, and explorers—he has been professionally a writer, an investigative photojournalist, a recording musician and singer, a songwriter, and a tree pruner. Among other subjects, he has studied architecture, music, fine arts, graphic design, Asian culture, martial arts, and Japanese and Chinese fine-pruning methods. He graduated (finally) with a B.A. degree in Asian Art. He enjoys playing classical guitar (he owns two custom-built instruments—a six-string and a ten-string), composing music, photographing nature, and "improving things." He is the author of the international bestsellers *The Tao of Pooh* and *The Te of Piglet,* both of which utilize the A. A. Milne Pooh characters to explain the Chinese philosophy of Taoism, and the American Book Award–winning biography of 1920s naturalist and bestselling author Opal Whiteley, *The Singing Creek Where the Willows Grow.*